CALL ME AL

CALL METAL

THE HERO'S HA-HA JOURNEY

SHEHERYAR B. SHEIKH

HarperCollins *Publishers* India

First published in India by
HarperCollins *Publishers* in 2019

Building 10, Tower A, 4th Floor, DLF Cyber City, Phase II,
Gurugram Haryana – 122002, India
www.harpercollins.co.in

2 4 6 8 10 9 7 5 3 1

P-ISBN: 978-93-5357-147-4
E-ISBN: 978-93-5357-148-1

Typeset in 10.5/13.7 Adobe Caslon Pro at
Manipal Digital Systems, Manipal

Printed and bound at
Microprints India, New Delhi

Unsung heroes are everywhere. This work is for two of them: the late great Sheikh Ghulam Mohiuddin, my Yaya, and the later, greater Zakia Mohiuddin, my Nani.

Contents

I Ordinary World

'The hero of yesterday becomes the tyrant of tomorrow, unless he crucifies himself today.'

– Joseph Campbell, *The Hero With a Thousand Faces*

1

Call to Adventure

You know you're in political exile from Pakistan when you've figured out a three-tier mnemonic device to recall fifteen-to-nineteen-figure alphasymbolonumeric access codes to Panama, Cayman, and Swiss Bank accounts that have no names attached to them, even as you constantly doubt the order of the 7 and 3 in the five-digit phone number of your childhood home in Karachi.

I. George Gary Gregory Jaffar

When I meet him at the pub on Edgware Road, the first thing Al tells me is something he says he figured out early in life: most people live up their own arses. He asks me if I am like most people. I say, 'I hope not.' He smiles like my grandfather, which doesn't make Al clean. It makes my grandfather greasy. I surprise myself by reaching for his hand before he reaches for mine, and he has me proper surprised by his firm and solid handshake. With men as round and thick as him, a vigorous handshake is a dangerous thing. It adds menace to the weight.

The younger Al, the one who could cross one leg over the other without encumbering rolls of thigh and belly fat, peeks out from behind his tinted spectacles and hawkish eyes. I hold his stare just to hold his stare. *You are fat like Jabba the Hutt; you are enormous and hideous*, I keep muttering in my head. My eyes are saying, like sweet nothings, *You bastard*, to him.

Will I drink something? He asks. 'What are you having?' I ask back, willing to buy a round for him and his three bodyguards sitting at the other table. It's the least I can do in exchange for this exclusive interview. Maybe I can get the office to cover a couple of rounds, as long as I keep it under fifty-five quid and as long as the bartender is willing to make a receipt.

'I'm a true Muslim,' Al says, without a hint of irony. I could strangle him. In the centre of the table is a toothpick holder; I could take a couple of toothpicks and nonchalantly play with them for a few seconds before lunging across the table and puncturing his jugular. There are table knives too. I could grab one and smash it through the eyeshield of his spectacles, and lodge the negligible serrations a couple of centimetres into the jelly of his left eye. Maybe even reach brain matter. Only one of the bodyguards is perked enough to be looking at my hands.

'You don't drink?' I ask. Al doesn't answer my question. He is going to be one of those people who doesn't answer questions. I'm prepared. I have seen countless videos of him breaking into Broadway-style songs midway through interviews and political speeches; it is a madman's way of dodging intellectual bullets.

'It's a beautiful day,' Al says. 'Perfect weather.' He doesn't look out the window as he says these words. By saying them in the way he does, he is telling me to turn my face towards the window, be the first one to look away, and also, to agree with him. I don't look out the window. I smile.

You murderer. You bastard. I have to keep that thought contained in my head and not let it slip through the blood red lines of my staring eyes. I feel like a wolf trying to hide in a sheepskin coat; like a serpent trying to come across as a dove. Then I remember the assignment, the interview, my job, my family, and the nature of the man who sits across from me. I change my mind. I look out the window and say, 'Yeah, the weather is great.' My wolfskin slides, and into the open appear tufts of wool.

I take my sweet time watching the goings-on out the window, savouring the clean sights. The blood of the innocent is not pouring out of the heavens. The earth has not cracked apart to spit out its secrets. The sky is grey and soft. Twenty-four degrees Celsius was the temperature forecasted for this afternoon, and twenty-four degrees Celsius it is. Typical London summer masquerading as spring. Buses and cars and pedestrians still seem to be operating fine, getting along with each other. No honks, no shouts. Just blokes and gals, and bikes and buses, and machines being machines.

When I turn my gaze back to the room, I don't face him just yet. Inside the pub, the few people scattered about the room seem to be part of the fixings. Regulars. Even the three bodyguards, who aren't as uninterested in me as I thought they were a few moments ago, seem at home here. The job of Al's protection has been split between them; they are looking at different areas of the pub. The front door, the back area with its access to the kitchen and the washroom, the chatters on the stools. All of that must be covered. I am not the only man or thing that could wish Al harm.

I turn again to my subject. My smile is expansive. It is fake; Al can probably tell that. But I can't turn it off. 'Where would you like to start?' I ask. *Your show, mate. You lead.*

I know there are going to be dances and flirtations with the truth in the stories that Al will tell me about himself. He has no reason to make confessions.

But there's one thing I know for certain. I can listen the pants off any person in the world. I can listen like a black hole can suck.

II. Altamaash

The first lesson I remember learning while observing my grandfather, the Pir of Bhopal, in one of his extensive gatherings of people dying to ask for his blessings, was: People live within deep recesses of themselves. Grandpa Pir's fluttering eyelids, his chanting lips, the cocoon of peace he always seemed to be enveloped in – all contributed to that lesson. I watched with unblinking eyes, my mouth agape, the dribble of spit and bubbles playing at his lips as he muttered something with his eyelids hovering just above completely shut.

'Mummmbblleesummbleesummbblesummblleemummbll emummmmblle,' he warbled. The people took *this* seriously? They apparently did.

Upon encountering someone new, like this reporter from the *Guardian* – someone whose airs I have taken a liking to, someone with a presence that seems to teeter on the cusp of stations in life that are of mythic referents and proportions – I begin introductions unflatteringly with this fact: Most people live up their own arses. It disarms the listener and produces the opposite of charm. Because, of course, words are not meant to be minced.

To dredge up my whole story every few months for the reporters that come calling, hardly taxes me. Of course, I could consider being honest about the recall, if it interested me. But there's life to be lived, the future to be storied into existence; and what the laws of luck, causation and the force of unbending will have brought into existence cannot be rendered understandable in the myopic scope offered by a four-page news-magazine biography. It takes reams to play a single thought out to its full unfurlment. The exponential occurrence of thoughts – to put any coherent stream to page – now, wouldn't that be an endeavour? Damn. What a thought.

But … life must be lived.

Serving choice liquor since Allah knows when, *Chaplain & Rabbi* has become a regular escape from the domestic entrapments of my exile. No wife or wifely things here. The decor is fastidiously mahogany, the religiously regular relics, a reassurance. Who would have thought a pub would suit teetotaler Al? Not Al.

Ned's failing so far. His counting is off.

And this sad puppy of a reporter, what to do? Must I always provide the entertainment? Must I always break into an operatic enactment of myself? Would that they could leave my hours to my own modes of creation. But then, I am the one who called him over. More suffering to me. The poor, poor red-eyed reporter. His name is Greg or Jaffar. Something G-J based. Half a brownie. I see the white and the Indo–Pak strains like two rivers flowing separately inside him.

Youth. What a tragic time it is. A string of hopes leading a fool strapped to a barrel of fears.

O'Toole is off his stool at the bar, staggering for the toilets. His limp disappears when he drinks. Numbed knees for the old man. Reason enough to drink, at his age – soon to be my age, and, within one more blink, to be Greg-Gary-Jaffar Something's age. GGJ. That's his first initial.

Ned, daft Ned, is still missing a person. Five men went into the toilet, one by one, and only four came out. Five minus four leaves someone still unaccounted for – Ned won't do as anybody's bodyguard. Not mine, for sure. Phil and Jordan are giving me the thumbs down with their backs and shoulders. These many years of knowing what they mean with their gruff bodies and rough gestures. They're on the same page. No security goof-ups are impossible if you forget the basic tenet of counting people entering and leaving the room in which you are sitting.

The reporter, Jarrod or Jaffar or Greg or Jermaine, desires to be the strong silent type.

But his loud eyes reek of the noise inside him. Probably freaks his women friends out with this intense need of his. Looking for approval, looking for daddy's warm gaze and pats on the back.

Grandpa Pir could cure this need in one mummblesummble. But – wrong audience. That would only work in the India of long ago. Today's London – today's grey Edgware Road – this is no place to let a faith healer touch your coat with his contagious delusion. The reporter must rely on Al. Al must provide.

Greg, isn't it? I must name him something. G for Guardian. G for Greg. That settles it.

How embarrassing not to remember his name, though. I've talked to him twice on the phone already. Maybe it's an off-day.

No. No off-days for runaways. No off-days for us, or for our protectors. If I let myself off, then by do unto others I must let Ned off as well, for his crucial miscount. Guardian Greg. Maybe that's a sign. Maybe that's *the* sign. But, why settle? He is my malleable GGJ; mine to chisel into shape.

'It's a beautiful day,' I say. 'Perfect weather.' This is my gift to Guardian Greg. Take a look outside, breathe in the view, and, while you sit ensconced in a leather-upholstered booth, soak in the glory of being near hundreds of different alcoholic derivations. Not one to receive gifts easily, is Guardian Greg – though more Guardian than Ned he is.

Guardian Gary Greg Jeremy sinks his gaze deep into mine, one fathomless depth to another. But I can fathom yours, young GGJ. I can see the bottom of your soullessness.

This long a stare with Al, he dares. *We could be falling for each other*, the heart within my heart chuckles. There. He looks away and sees the world that Al has allowed him to share. My Edgware Road. God's, then mine, and then the Queen of England's. The dregs of Old Kent Road and the rest of the pitiful city can go to the masses.

That stare. Grandpa Pir would never allow such insolence. The two generations between his unbenevolent self and Al the Entertainer are witness to what time lays to waste. Grandeur, the elegance of being detached from care, a grace not granted any more to the mortals. All the saints, all the real Pirs, they are dead. Buried.

Ned is making me dead. The son of a colossal mistake of a bitch!

The question is shifting rapidly from whether to slash a knife across only any one of their jugulars, to whether both Guardian Gary or Nincompoop Ned deserve a joint *Exuent Stage Left* cue for an afterlife curtain call. From 'either/or' to an 'and'.

There's commonalities between them. Both require a helping hand of a different kind: Ned, a hand to count up to five; Guardian Gary Greg, a different bedtime story every night.

GGJ looks back from the vista offered by the wide window, and cuts a look across my gaze and my musings to take in the bar. It could be one of the last panoramas he inhales, and so I let him. Soon enough, he will require more things to be said and I will have to lead him like the fatherless child he is.

Must everyone be so basic as their halted spiritual growth?

I see it now; there's really no avoiding it. Grandpa Pir had it figured out: most people need something to believe in, and God is too lofty a something. Be less lofty, but no less mysterious; be a Pir. If not a Pir, be more violent. And there it is.

Nothing gathers the underdogs like a death; nothing grants more attention than the ability to take life. To rally my people, outsiders must die. And so, the emotional logic of my next calling in life: before I can go home, to the country that I love like I love milk-and-honey and spending-millions-at-Harrods, I must kill. It will be different from all the hits carried out by my people. This one will not be like pressing ENTER on a keyboard or punching a code into the phone and seeing a virtual effect. This will be skin against skin, the pressure of removing the heartbeat and breath from a mass that fathoms not the subversive, adverse motivation of ceasing to respire and pulsate.

Grandpa Pir had it easy: fool people to feed their spirit.

I have fooled myself too long that entertaining people to death was murder enough. The time has come to put in some of the hard work that I demand of my people. Plus, it'll be good for the muscles.

And why must men die, all of them? Because life demands sacrifice. Only from sowing blood into the ground does new flesh appear above the surface of dirt. And renewal and rebirthing must always be encouraged.

And must *I*, Al, also dig the earth and plant seeds? Can't I hire a gardener, like old times?

Yes, of course, I could. But I too, must do some planting. I too, must touch the soil. Despite the placidity in weather and mood.

Because active vision requires clarity, the lenses in my eyes must be washed. Tears, therefore, must be shed.

Gary Greg J looks at me. There, in his eyes, I see that he's okay with it. He's ready to give up. How much will I take from him? He doesn't know that just yet, but his look says he's ready to raise his hand and be the volunteer from the audience. Ned is just as worthy though.

Guardian GGJ asks me where I would like to start.

I take a moment to smile.

III. Edwin 'Ned' Steinberg

It's so easy. Al seems like a good guy; nothing like the papers say he is. Of course, it's the first day, so while I sit here looking back and forth from the bathroom to Al, mentally spending the three hundred I will earn from this trial day on a small pack of energy bars and have the good feeling about the incoming net gain of two hundred and ninety freshly earned pounds in my wallet, I have no worries that anything here can up my cortisol level.

Only six days before meeting Al, I was bouncing in the middle of the city, standing all night outside that swanky unnamed club off Tinworth Street. Never would have thought that one day I would work for a brown guy who was so friendly. But the bouncer gig has been getting old for a while. Years of sleeping during the day has rejigged my circadian rhythm into a nocturnal cycle, and constant insomnia has almost killed my libido – hence no girlfriends of late – and started to eat into me.

So here I am, getting hooked up with a master stroke of an offer: a politically charged job, Phil had said over phone. I would have to audition, he had mentioned. And at the *Chaplain & Rabbi* I'm doing just that. I'm auditioning: meaning, I sit menacingly in a chair while sipping water, eating chips, keeping an eye on especially the toilet and kitchen entrance. After this, I'll head home, definitely richer and likely re-employed.

Meanwhile, a few other things are happening. Al is here, of course. He looks sharp for an over-fifty, out-of-shape brownie in a pub. He looks happy, like he's celebrating something. This young chap from a newspaper has arrived to interview Al, though it doesn't seem much like an interview. They aren't talking much. Al's smiling a lot and he keeps looking at me like he's approving my work.

I get that a lot from the owners: I'm tough, built to last. Bouncing requires muscle and I have plenty of it. And it's all hardening up once more since I'm getting less stressed about being able to sleep at night again.

Al is going to be a good employer, I think. That's what counts. Whatever they accuse him of in the news, that's their business. My job is to protect him – take a bullet if he needs me to. But it won't come to that, surely not.

Yes, it's only the day of auditioning. But I haven't really had a chance to know the details of the job other than the fact that I have to be alert a lot. I do think I'm going to like this gig, though. Al's a smiling kind of guy. There's so many clips on YouTube of him doing the strangest, balmiest things. I've been watching those one after another since Phil called and told me about the job. What a funny guy, I've been thinking. It will be so much fun working with him. Although brown on the outside, he's all gold inside.

Once the audition is over, I take my cash from Phil and leave the pub feeling good. Find myself whistling an old Paul Simon song. I know I clinched it. All I have to do is look the part, and the size of my muscles does the rest. It's not bragging. I put in a lot of hard work at the gym to be able to play the part of the hired muscle. Every day, two to four hours, minimum. I eat healthy, do my cardio, put in extra effort on legs days, eat my greens, focus on proteins, take my supplements, and choose clothes that have the right cut and shape to suit my size. All that care to groom my intimidating looks – it's finally paying off.

The view of the world from the streets was never this good. Ringside is always where I wanted to be – right next to the grand act, but not too deep inside it. Here's my chance. 'If you be my bodyguard, ... mmm hmmm mmmm, You can call me Al,' I hum all the way home, like I've robbed a bank and got off scot-free.

2

Spiritually Guided

You know you're in political exile from Pakistan when you need to start the import process and Customs registration on Karachi Student Biryani (the old, authentic one in Jacob Lines, not that Clifton photocopy) five days ahead of the panic attack caused by not having it around the corner from your house any more.

I. George Gary Gregory Jaffar

I lie down on the bed for a while. Then I get up and pace my small, brown-carpeted room. Without papers in my hand, there is an urge to crack my knuckles again and again. I manage to squeeze a pop or two out of every joint. But then I can't breathe fully enough, my lungs already full of rage.

The walls of my bedroom don't have wallpaper and the room is without accent furniture. Not a single piece of wood except for the bed, the bedside table, a lamp, a desk covered with piles of papers and books, and an armchair on which I can never sit for more than five minutes without feeling anxious about work. I've lived in this apartment for over a year without making a home of it.

Only one of the walls has any decoration, a single piece of artwork: a scaled-down print of Picasso's *Guernica.* I've spent hours looking at the cubist work, trying to decipher its visible dimensions and the symbolic meaning, intended and otherwise, of the objects, human parts, the animal anatomy. The meditation has always calmed my nerves – especially close to deadlines. But today, now, pausing before Picasso's visionary artwork doesn't bring the same lull to my hyperactive brain; my shortness of breath is not eased. The flailing, dismembered faces, hands and feet annoy me with their insistence that I account for them; that I take revenge for them. *Do be serious*, I want to shout. *I'm only a fucking newspaper reporter.* The limbs lie severed and the faces lie screaming. I read somewhere that Picasso was inspired by an explosive event in Spain's history, a very specific incident I've looked up and read about, but it escapes recall; and yet this painting, a replica of the original, evokes the entire gamut of human effort to destroy the whole of human endeavour. For me it stands for the distillation of the worst, most disintegrative, part of humanity. To top it all, cherry-like, in the middle of the print stands the joke by the maestro: the horse with its arse turned to the viewer. I stand there watching that rump and the horse's mid-neigh grimace of tortuous pain. It feels as though there is amusement to be found here; but the humour is entirely at my expense. This is Al's joke on me. A cosmically planned joke, in which the universe and Al have conspired with Picasso, so there can emerge from spiritus mundi a painting with a horse's arsehole pointed straight at my face.

I move away from it, grab a few sheets of the article from the desk, and begin to walk up and down the length of the room, and around the foot of my bed, clenching and unclenching the hand that does not hold any papers. Now and then, as I pace and read, I watch the *Guernica* print out of the corner of my eye.

Here's what the introduction reads like, mostly in rhetorical flourishes meant to capture the mood and atmosphere of Altamaash's rise to power in Karachi. (Details follow later in the article, once the narrative hook is in place.)

> Karachi is a cesspit of crime. Everyone knows who is responsible, but the man isn't there. He was never really there. Let's start with the early days, before he was the syndicate man, and well before he ran the syndicate.
>
> Altamaash is lost to the cause, kept baseless and powerless in the one place he calls home: Karachi. Big, bold, hazard of a city. The pulse of it brings him to heart attack. It is the anxiety, the impatience, the hot blood of indignation coursing through his veins.
>
> Insults are easy to brush aside and mock. Al's tongue is Karachi sharp. The metropolis's streets have made him a keen observer of the Morse code of human traffic. People want something. But what? It's being figured out for him by that massive brain he carries about. He is too afraid, though.
>
> His grandfather, his hero, never gave Al much thought. Al was first the toddler who grabbed at his legs, then the precocious and quiet kid in the corner observing the processes of divine intervention, and after that he was the thing that returned sweat-laced from school. In the end, he was the angel in the hospital who brought food and prayers, and stood in the corner while his grandfather phlegmed his way through conversations with the man who was Al's father, but may as well have been one of the dolts sitting with a blank stare outside the hospital, chewing grass.
>
> His grandfather is all bones. Even Al's father is thin and top-heavy throughout his life. But Al knows about himself

that he will never stop growing. The love of food is one thing, a given. Salt and sugar lay him to waste. But it's the other things: the inability to sleep in peace, the propensity to worry himself into a storm over his own and other people's problems; his sensitivity to the cause. It's going to destroy him by ruining first his mind, then his body, until there is nothing left to keep him thinking of himself as a human being. The mind and body will become an esoteric set of things. Mysterious. Soupy.

He cannot go back to being his father's son. That is out of the question once he is grown up.

Karachi wars have escalated. Turf is precious, and plenty of men are jobless and desperate enough to need a violent outlet. Gangs form. Al can't yet handle gangs. The guns and the knives, and the drugs in the alleyways with their threat of darkness and sickness. What is to stop one man from stabbing another just on impulse? Just to see power take effect and the spectacle of blood spill out. A stream of thick red sherbet. That's how Al imagines his insides. A gush of red under his dark brown hirsute hide.

The cause is what calls to him. He's swallowed whole by it. He looks back at his childhood to find the answer, and finds one that doesn't address the question of his life's true purpose, but will do. The old days, when, one by one the people visiting his grandfather began bringing problems of race and ethnic discrimination. The word 'Immigrant' had to be looked up, and then the words 'Independence' and 'Partition'. Over months, parts of the picture formed a coherent image. Once Pakistan was carved out of the Indian landscape on 14 August 1947, the Pakistanis descended from Indian stock, the ones who had migrated across the border, would never be accepted as true Pakistanis by those who labelled themselves the custodians of Pakistani-ness. For such Immigrants and their offspring, there were:

No jobs.

No marriage proposals.

No quotas in government, either local, provincial, or federal.

It was an effective ostracism of a people who were informally labelled 'second-class citizens'.

Many of the Immigrants complained to his grandfather about a combination of struggles.

At first, the problems were too overwhelming, lasting years. Altamaash lived the life of a traumatized seedling. An introvert, they might have labelled him, if they'd heeded him at all. When he went to collect his national ID card at the government office, he was mocked for his sharp, accented, 'Indian' Urdu. It was just another straw amidst the infinite straws being put together to load him down like the spring that the bullies, the 'true Pakistanis' who had never needed to cross borders to stay alive, hoped would never recoil. But recoil is built into the Newtonian laws; and laws aren't theories. They come with force.

The incipient paragraphs run like this for a couple of more pages before the scant interview interrupts the flow, after which follows ambiguous doublespeak about Al's unethical practices. The rest of the pages lie scattered on my desk, but I don't feel like rereading the whole thing for the seventy-fifth time. It comes together, the long article, in a back-and-forth fashion, layering criss-crossly a whole life. It makes the right excuses for why Altamaash became the violent and results-oriented champion of the mass of immigrants, who lugged every bit of their lives they could carry from India to Pakistan in August of 1947.

The tone my editor wants is one of wryness and non-judgmental irony. I've achieved that, I feel, and without too much effort, succeeded in shaping the tenor into something different from my natural inclination on how to write the piece. It, therefore, looks as though I am amenable to the man and his past. Apparently, I don't blame Al for doing what he did. And the edited version of this article-interview-profile will reflect that. A job is a job, and I will do it. I will be dispassionate and not call him the bastard that he became. Nobody is born a bastard. Well. Not *his* kind; and not that bastardly a bastard.

I stop pacing and stand in front of the *Guernica* again. The explosion contained in it is making some sort of sense. A whole is coming together as well as apart.

As I have explained in the article, going back to Al's initiation to the dark side is as simple as pressing rewind on a VCR tape. The alleged murders and bribes by his henchmen are played out in reverse. But all of that would have to be played in forward slow-motion in court to make sense of all the crimes he's committed. Unfortunately, those trials will never come to pass. Not in this life.

I stare at the printouts in my hand, but don't really see them. They appear disjointed, like out-of-place segments of a large mosaic. In that instant, my vision reaches a depth so I don't just see things as merely themselves, but also as symbols of how everything is connected to the past, the future, and the power structures – the whole interconnected web of symbols and meanings that surround us. In my mind's eye, I see Al, in a General's uniform – or more like a militia get-up with a Saddam Hussein beret – standing over dead bodies in a ditch that his men are filling up with more corpses. There's rain falling from grey skies, and the landscape that surrounds him mimics the Welsh countryside, with gentle slopes and hardly any canopy. He appears, a cigar in mouth, against the mass grave, in lightning-flash-revelatory glimpses, as both the nearly obese creature of our interview at the pub as well as the sleek young man who made that early moral decision: killing is acceptable, it is regular politics. As he said at the pub, 'By any means necessary' became his life's refrain to get rights in Pakistan for the immigrants.

Of course, there were never any witnesses to corroborate the evidence of his crimes; and when there were witnesses, there was never any evidence to corroborate their testimonies. So, the article cannot explicitly state what everyone knows to be true: Al got people killed – political rivals; wives, parents, uncles, and kids of the big fish; dogs of the VIPs – all for extortion money or compliance. He didn't believe in the modus operandi of other gangs: kidnapping – too high a cost of infrastructure to be incurred and too many logistical responsibilities to be shouldered: place to keep the victim, food to enable survival until ransom was extracted, not to mention the bathroom trips that would have to be supervised. No, thank you. Plus, ransom collection meant leaving a trail; there was also the burden of route-planning via the highways of escape. Nope, too complicated and unnecessary. And so, people showed up dead in large gunnysacks outside some housing colony or factory, sometimes with the names and addresses written on paper (each sheet marked with thousands of fingerprints per inch) stapled on the insides of the jute bags.

The narrative portion of the article continues after the interview, explaining how Al fled Pakistan and sought asylum in the United Kingdom. It ends in questions that seem rhetorical and will likely never be published once the desk editors chop up the piece; but I have to ask them in my draft: Why doesn't someone do something about Al? That's on the thirteenth page.

I ask that of the officials in Pakistan, and of the British government as well, after he exiled himself to the mansion in St. Johns Wood. Why has Al been allowed to live here with all the rights and 'freedoms' that England offers? What secret deals with the people in charge of Her Majesty's leftover empire allow him such unfettered yet cozy access to asylum and citizenship in my country? And what backdoor channels of financial flow have allowed him to amass the millions of pounds laundered after his minions collect them from victims of extortion in Pakistan?

Feeling the weight of those questions again, a chant begins in my head: *I'm only a reporter. I'm only a reporter.* But the mantra is hollow. It is as empty of meaning as saying the *Guernica* is just another painting. Because even here, in the presence of a replica of the work of art, I feel the disillusioning force of the original. There is *presence* in it. It alludes to the distorted visions in my head of all that is wrong in life and the universe. It speaks idealistically. And I feel as though neither this facsimile of the painting nor the original – not even the painter Picasso – are my companions. But something *other*, from the conceptual dimension of art's very soul.

The room feels thoroughly paced and treaded, and my legs are weary with the miles. My thoughts are full of vows no journalist should make. My head has boiled over; everything except one conviction has evaporated: the next time I meet Al, it will not be a pleasant occasion. This I swear: If I end a human life, anywhere and at any time, it will be Altamaash's. I am convinced of it.

However, I am mature enough to know that this decision, too, will evaporate and my life will resume along its current trajectory, with the thought having remained a possible potential of a distant past. I will forget this adamant oath just as I have forgotten hundreds of make-the-world-better resolutions before it. This sense of self-awareness hovering at the peripheries of my certitude, makes me feel weaker.

What is absolutely certain, though, is that my work here is done. The article has been written. I have sat at the desk the night and day after the interview, sleeping and writing in fits and starts, all the while going through the news archives and video fragments of Al and his people on the Internet. Recalling his smug mug face and his cronies' flat gazes, the absence of guilt in their eyes – has left me numb with anger and I find myself hypothesizing – once again – how I am going to murder him if I were to get into the same room with him another time: ice-pick into the jelly of his eye? Saw the sharp and jagged edges of a bread knife past the film of sweat on his neck, cutting the thick leather of his skin, into the jugular vein, to sprout a black red blood fountain? Shove a sharpened pencil with full force up his nose and slam his head repeatedly into a wall again and again?

There is another fantasy built in slow-mo. That of Al's car bursting into flames and his fat head sizzling all the way to its innermost fluids.

Yes, I am convinced in this moment that I am going to kill him if our paths ever cross again. The method is the only thing that remains to be figured out.

And yet, of course, I am willing to let it go at that, submit the article by email, forget all about it, about Altamaash, and feel the fury dissipate hour by hour, day by day, until it is a distant memory. I am truly ready for such an unhurried catharsis.

That's when my phone buzzes and I read the message that can only be from him, look up from the phone, and find myself staring, yet again, at the arsehole of a horse. That's when, in my head, I run through the list of people I know can procure for me an untraceable handgun.

II. Altamaash

Time for a samosa break at the house and the ladies are fussing over preparations. I sit down at the head of the dining table and spoon some chutney on my plate in anticipation. Either three or four medium-sized ones should hit the spot. I'm in a mood to contemplate. Whole life flashing – total recall – that sort of thing.

Looking back to the beginning, as I often do these days, I recall taking hold of spiritual life in one instant lunge. Like a chameleon's tongue flicking out, laser-quick, sticking to its prey, then snapping back into its mouth to digest the catch.

God bless Grandpa Pir. His devil's eyes, his villainous cough; his slimy smirk, his lecherous stare; his oil-cold hands, his vein-rivered arms; the filth in his bladder; the belch of his voice; the grease on his temples; the stale snot on his moustache; the fetid reek of feet in his aura; the putrid stench of puke in his breath; and the trickling slowness of his shuffling walk.

The lesson: it all adds up yin-yangly. The many combinations of the hideous and the beautiful – they are the best kind. I love it when it is corroborated in the most ordinary occurrences, such as, when walking down my street, I see the most striking woman accompanied by an ogre. The incongruity works wonders for my blood pressure.

Isn't ugliness a beautiful concept? The most un-bland thing. And how it fits so marvellously in the gaps left by things other than all that is beautiful and all that is blah.

That's what Grandpa Pir possessed. The necessary ugliness from which only something better than itself can be borne.

His qualities cannot be undermined or underestimated. He was the Patron Saint of Unappealing Gastronomy; he was also the Armored Guru-knight of Conniving Whispers and the Guardian on Earth of the Guttersnipes.

For that's who came to him: the lowest creatures. I wouldn't have believed that human beings could be so utterly base. I wouldn't believe it still, if my memory weren't photographic. The geoid head swirls dervish-like at the thought.

'Pass the chutney, Altamaash.'

What? Oh.

'Right,' I say, passing the chutney down the table.

Here I am, years later, in London, England, sitting at the dining table of my home in the most comfortable corner of St. Johns Wood Road, scarfing samosas with chutney and slurping tea for a late afternoon snack-break with my mother, my wife and my daughter, while Phil and Jordan stand on guard duty just inside the front and kitchen doors, and my mind is with the man I wanted always to mirror. Well, that's achieved. I am just as low a creature. But I only have grease on my hands, and no blood. I have never slaughtered a chicken and I have never slit the throat of a goat for the annual Abrahamic ritual. All I ever did was touch the knife to bless the sacrifice.

Euphemisms galore there. The mind boggles.

And yes, all this time, my Grandpa-facing mind is also able to process, and smile at, my daughter's excitement for her new dress and toys bought by my wife. I do so all the while contemplating the extent to which I do not feel an iota of love for the women gobbling samosas at the table, individually, although there is no lack of devotion to the collective of the family that they make up for me. I wonder, too, what sullying force has kept Grandpa Pir lodged there in the centre of my head. It couldn't be anything other than the lash of his mumbles coming forward in time, and West in space, to hiss in my ears that 'Sonny, mummblesummble, mummblesummble, you're no killer. You don't have the fucking guts.' And the mumbling is pitched as though it is a scream of the most graceless, ungrateful beast from hell.

Imagine the Antichrist – enfleshed, emblooded, full of sound and fury – living in your head. And, given that things always carry the opposite of themselves with them, what must coexist with that is the Anti-Antichrist, and that – *that* – even if it isn't Christ, the Messiah, it must be something beautiful. Even if it slouches, and is the most slothful of beings, the most unhelpful of creatures in situations wherein the Devil's spawn rides your head, saying things like 'Murder ssummble someone and you'll be the man that people mmummble think you are.' And until then, until I have fulfilled who I am conceived to be, I am nothing. That is what the foulest being of the world insinuates.

The ugliest man in the world, my Grandpa Pir, with his congregation of the most disgusting people in that city by the sea. I despair at the thought of my ancestor and my grip on the chutney spoon loosens. But it's when I start recalling that other set of voices belonging to perfectly shaped men with regular heads, and stunning women with pearl necklaces, their heads temporarily covered for preserving their modesty – that I lose all hope in the human project. Their voices said things like 'please give me a prayer to have my husband killed in an accident' and 'please send my neighbours back to the hellhole they came from' and 'can you please pray that my mother changes her will and gives everything to me, nothing to my sister' and 'please find a way for me to fuck my boss's wife'. Grandpa Pir would bat not an eyelash at these requests. He would utter his mutterings and please these people.

Did I hear them wrong? I was young, in awe of the adult world. The stories could have stumbled upon the lack of understanding in the child-brain I had back then. And it's possible I didn't recognize some of the words, and so am making up the memories of my childhood in hindsight. But I am also a grown man now, and I know grown men and women, and what they want.

It strikes home. I once loved a woman; but for my failures she judged me harshly and did not give me the solace I sought. I gave up on her and she on me. Now I can love no woman that innocently, for I see through the facade of make-up-induced divinity and the false-bottom softness women bring to everything, under which they are rigid and unyielding. I feel an indifferent attachment to my wife, and an obligatory, resentful reverence for my mother, who is not nearly close enough to death for me to feel free from familial claustrophobia. And I fear for the woman that my daughter will become. Will she be called Pinky into her thirties – and beyond?

Also, my role is unambiguously bland in this brood. One cannot always entertain one's own family. Their demands are different – domesticity and dullness go hand in hand, to keep someone grounded, charging their batteries for the shows they must perform outside the house.

Speaking of which – at last, enough time has passed and I am ready. Six samosas have been eaten from my plate somehow and I am sitting alone at the dining table. The ladies have shifted to the TV lounge. They'll watch several hours of Indian and Pakistani soap operas until just past midnight. The evening light is fading fast.

There are the very few who still have faith in me and the many who think I am someone I am not.

It's time to give the people what they have always wanted: something and someone to believe in.

I remain seated in the kitchen until it's a little darker, close to dinner time. I will miss the last meal. But it's better not to leave any note.

Slipping out of the house to evade my wife and daughter is quite difficult. Not mentally, no. One can imagine and actualize true solitude in the midst of crowds. It is the oppression of their domesticating forcefield that is the hardest to avoid while manoeuvring myself out the back door. Too bad, that nobody in the media or politics ever reconciles the picture of me fulfilling familial obligations with my public image of a political goon in exile. The house is my cage, and the toys and make-up kits and kitchen gadgets and potted plants are the accoutrements of my imprisonment. Why, despite how they pour into every hour I spend awake, can't I be known for the domestic duties I perform as a trinity of demigods?

Absent-minded yet present-souled father: check. Conjugal bliss-inducing mass of husbandly false authority: check. Obedient but prevaricating son: check.

Out of the dining area, into the kitchen, keys in my pocket, I lock the door from outside, walk down the tiled steps in the back garden, latch up, latch down, and once out through the garden gate, slip around the change in Phil's night guard duty with Jordan's, and shuffle down the sidewalk while avoiding a clump of dog shit. I quickly hail a cab at the corner and get into its back seat. And, now, I breathe easy. Ned's address in Ladbroke Grove is the eventual destination, but I'll get off a mile or so from it and linger in a restaurant for twenty minutes. Now I have plenty of opportunity to ruminate. It's time to send that text to Guardian-Gary-Jericho though. I tap the phone's screen and watch the surreal glow from it light up the taxi's interior. I'm sure my face is lit in black gold, like the face of a dark ghost. Well, so be it. Light is not the only force.

I type out: 'Stop living up your own arse. Come meet me @11. Let's talk.' And I type out for the sullen newspaperman the address to which I'm headed. One more text to send, and then I can leave this phone and the other one at Ned's apartment after the deed is done. I look out the taxi's window, but see nothing out there that can improve on what's in my head. With the radio turned off, the taxi driver has decided to leave this night unsoundtracked. In the cab's rear-view mirror, his droopy eyes reflect my deepest fear of hell: a flatlined electrocardiogram, ennui, eternal boredom. All right then. I'll conjure my own symphony and it'll begin with a distant, resounding hum.

There it is. Rising just as much as will the smell of sweat, spit and blood in the days and weeks to come; a deep-throated groan of a tuba to begin the festivities of this opera.

III. Edwin 'Ned' Steinberg

The fifth and final beer is in my hand, and reruns of *The Office* are running on the telly. The phone hasn't been on silent mode or vibrate, and I haven't heard back from Al even though he said he would call. He said he'd call from a new number every time. But there are no strange numbers in the call log or in the texts. No contact from anyone in over a day. That's how unpopular I am.

Must have done something wrong.

No. Can't think like that. Al smiled the whole time at the pub, especially whenever he looked at me.

I miss a joke on the show, but hear the punch-line: 'That's what she said.' I laugh anyway, because the setup must have been funny. It's always funny when Michael Scott says that line on the show. Am I drunk, though? Laughing like that, without hearing the joke?

I really need to stop after the fifth bottle and I'm glad it's the last one in the house. Not used to drinking more than one a night since I took up bouncing.

Maybe Al has been auditioning more people, just to be sure I'm the one who fits the bill. I check my phone again and again and miss joke after joke on the show. I've blown through nearly all of seasons five and six in two days, thinking that an offbeat comedy about not working in an office would put me at ease about switching up work while I wait for Al's call.

But I need Al's gig for serious reasons. Not because I need money. That too, but not only that. There's more. My head's buzzing from it.

Bling-bling goes the phone. I open the text. It's an unlisted number with the message: 'I'm coming to save you from yourself.' Funny guy. There it is! That must be Al. He said he would always text from a new number. This was a new number, so it must be him. My head is swimming. I'm so excited from the beer and the text. I would have kissed Al's hand if he was in front of me right here and now. Save me from myself, he says.

Huh. That's funny. It almost seems as though Al knows what's going on in my head.

How does he know?

I've been trying to think of the dilemma, but I can't really fit the idea in my head long enough, or in the right order as a question to figure out its answer. It seems like an easy problem and I am sure discussing it with Al will help. He will know how I should think and what I should do.

Here's how I see it, four-and-a-half beers down. No, forget that. I chug the rest of the fifth bottle and put the telly on mute. I need to tidy up before he comes.

So yeah, five beers down, while fluffing up the sofa cushions, my dilemma, as I see it, is this: What to consider worth living for. It's related to the dilemma of not knowing who's worth dying for. And here's what I've got so far: Romantic ideas have become disgusting to me after suffering the constant shrieks of the short skirts and shitty behaviour of the club's clientele. After years of bouncing five to six nights a week, I'm completely turned off by surface layers of beauty. No matter how golden the woman's skin, under all that make-up is the same old product. If you're good-looking and you come to the club, it's to validate your looks by catching the eye of someone above you on the scale you see yourself trying to climb. So, yeah, the gig of ogling at the female clientele passed long ago. It's got to the point that all I see beyond the first person across the rope is a line of bodies waiting to get their fix of alcohol so they can thrash around and release their weekly dose of dopamine and serotonin.

I can't walk around in a farmer's market without mentally replacing even the homeliest and the downright minging with dressed up dolls in shimmering frocks, picturing them sweating and grinding against other men and women at the grocery store and on the sidewalks. I give them no chance. Even the cute teacher types with big spectacles – I put them at the back of the club, in the darkest corners, thrusting at strangers, with their pelvises leading the manic attacks.

I've waited for two days for the text from Al, and now I'll have to wait for something like half an hour for him to ring the doorbell. Funny, how these minutes seemed longer than days. Because the question riding my head is not being expressed as a question. It's coming as an answer, a solution for which I'm not ready.

'Awesome. See you soon, champ.' That's what I type out on my phone while clearing away the beer bottles, among other things. Maybe 'champ' is a bit disrespectful, but what the hell. I'm giddy. And it sets a friendly tone for the boss-employee dynamics right from the start. I send that as a reply to Al's text and go upstairs to put on my professional attire.

I get back to thinking my earlier thoughts. The job is simple: You need to know two things about being a bodyguard:

One, it's a full-time job. It's not like bouncing for a club. A club may shut down during the day and become a brunch joint, or a lounge, if it is a multipurpose venue, so off-time is built into the bouncer's job description; but a person who needs protection must still be protected while he sleeps. Bodyguarding is, therefore, a round-the-clock job. So, personal life for a bodyguard goes out the window.

Two, you need to be able to take a bullet for the person paying you for protecting him or her. It's that simple: A bullet will be fired from a gun aimed at your boss, and you must come between the bullet and your boss without any hesitation. The employer pays for your clothes, your transportation, your housing and your food. And usually the people requiring bodyguards have an awful, blingy taste in all such things – high carb snacks and flashy cars – but they also have plenty of money to give out salaries that match the risks. Sure, an economically inclined person may be able to weigh the plusses and minuses, and negotiate the right amount of money to bring take-a-bullet into agreeable territory. I'm sure my buddy Phil is one of those people. He was in the Prince of Wales's retinue of bodyguards back in the day, so he's as professional as they get.

But I can't put a figure on my life. That's too solid a thing to do with something abstract. It's like putting a dollar amount on happiness. I can't say 'one million' without it seeming low, or 'fifty thousand quid plus medical' without it seeming high.

The reason I can think this way, as I step out of my lounging shirt, and give a quick flex to my right bicep to check it in the mirror and contort my torso to let myself inspect and admire the engorged roundness of my deltoids, is that I don't know what I would sell my life for. Once, long ago, I believed I would love a woman enough, and be able to lay down my life for her should her happiness depend on it. First kidneys, then liver, eventually the eyes, even the heart – organ by organ – I would be part of her, become her. Childish, I know, and a literal representation of my back-then superhero saviour complex. That changed, however, once I grew older and lonelier, and I thought I would probably die in my sleep and nobody would find my body for days. After all, I had nobody who loved me enough to come around and check up on me, and call the police once they found my body.

After that, for years I thought I would be the victim of a drive-by shooting at the club, or get pushed down a flight of stairs by a mob of sweaty dancers, and become paralysed from the neck down, and have to live in a care home for twenty years like a sack of potatoes, slowly losing muscle mass, turning into a pudgy vegetable, dying in agony. And with that kind of imagination, there was no time to put a numerical value on my life.

Now, this. Al is coming over. He is going to solve it.

I am dressed in a button-down white shirt and black suit to meet my new boss tonight at my house; I wore clothes of the same combination at the pub. This uniform-like apparel, ironed and creased to perfection, is to demonstrate to him how serious I am about the job. And all the while, I'm thinking that I will be able and willing to step between a shooting gun and Al. It's a certainty in my gut. I can do it. I will put his life before my own. This is not to say that I will let myself be killed before I let him be shot. No; rather, I will absorb a bullet in my arm or leg, or even my shoulder or back – somewhere non-lethal – before I let him get shot.

There. I've solved it. 'Yes' is the answer to 'would you take a bullet for Al?' But then, what's Al going to help with? I'm buzzed, clear-headed yet fuzzy, suddenly uncertain about what he was talking about in the text. I look at my phone again: 'I'm coming to save you from yourself,' says Al's text. My boredom? Is that what he is going to save me from? Possibly. Maybe he realized I was wasting away without a job.

Anyway, I'm all set for the meeting. I sit down in front of the mute telly again, but more upright this time, so as not to wrinkle the suit. The buzz of the beer is still in my head. I've opened a window to let some of the crisp night breeze come in and refresh the place. Michael Whatsisname is doing his sour-puss face in *The Office*, because his employees won't let him interrupt their professional phone calls. He's hilarious. I know this episode and can almost recall the next few lines. I consider it, but don't turn the volume up. I don't want to miss Al ringing the doorbell. He could be here any minute. The remote is in my line of sight, so I can shut the machine off as soon as the bell rings.

Any minute now. Any second, even.

3

The First Threshold

You know you're in political exile from Pakistan if you dare to test yourself with spice level 6 (out of 6) of the roti canai at Mandalay, Edgware Road's Burmese restaurant, chowing down anonymously, without either being spat on or accosted for awkward selfies.

I. George Gary Gregory Jaffar

Like the dark knight swooping down from above – that's how I fly down the stairs of the underground station. I'll use the Northern Line, get to Bank, then switch over to the Central Line to go all the way to Marble Arch, and then walk from there. Enough left on my Oyster card for travel through Zones 1 and 2 for a couple of months. Wonder who will get to use it once the dust settles. Someone will just grab it from the evidence box, I suppose. Once it's processed, they'll give it to a schoolkid or a needy immigrant, I hope. Can't let a good Oyster go to waste. Not with the cost of travel as exorbitant as it is now.

There are five other people in my box on the Northern Line. They're subdued. It's a cold weekday night and the Tube will shut down in a couple of hours; so not many people riding the longer distances. There's my stop already. Bank. Time flies when you're funning it up. And here's me moving without knowing I would. Walking out the open doors and into the station, dreamlike, moving from tunnel to tunnel to switch trains on the underground.

There's a panhandling singer-songwriter-beggar-thief-vagabond with his guitar resting against the wall. He's scarfing down a burger and milkshake, taking a breather from the singing. His white fedora looks fantastic on him. But he's all muscle, and I'm all wire, so a fedora on me is not as fitting. And his dreadlocks – that's a look I can't pull off. I wonder what his music sounds like. If I had more time, I would stick around and listen to a song or two. Maybe on the way back. Acoustics are perfect here. Echo. Timbre. Walking a few steps behind me, the two other guys who got off the Northern Line are talking just above whisper level and the hall is reverberating their prattle about a concert or gig to make it seem more significant than it is.

There's a camera. Not too hidden, but out of the way up there in the corner. *Hi.*

Cheeeese. They'll see this clip and all the others from various time-stamping cameras, and me looking directly at them. Let's make it easy for them. Identify from this side. Check. Then turn my other cheek, and you've got me in 3D. Good? Let's move on.

Two more cameras on the way, and there's one here too, at the platform for the next ride on the Central Line. More people here. I give the camera a wink.

What am I doing? What *the fuck* am I doing?

Oystering my way around London, no specific destination really. Dithering. Or pretending to dither. Quite decided, I am, mostly. It's got to be done. I've got the address from Al's text message mapped out in my head. It's not the St. Johns Wood home of his that I know about, so we're probably meeting up in one of his safe-houses. Good. Safety first. Safety catch. Catch as catch can.

I should have done more push-ups in life. My forearms and shoulders would have been stronger. I'll need strength if his goons find the gun on me and try to hold me back. Sure, they didn't check me at the pub, but this is more private. This is where he hides. Or one of his minions does. I thought for some reason that Al never strayed far from his mansion off St. Johns Wood Road. So, this must be some other place. A place to conduct business, maybe. Keep it away from the family.

Al trusts me to be benign enough not to have me patted down at the entrance of our meeting place tonight – in this, I place pivotal hope.

My ride is coming into the station. The carriage grinding its brakes, still moving at considerable speed. Time for Cinderella – it's nearly time. I pump my calves and stand up tall on my toes, wondering if I'll jump in front of the moving train. But I don't. Somehow, I don't. The nose of the train whips past the point where I stand on the platform. They'll see this on the screen when they play it all back: me on my toes, leaning forward, teetering on the platform. And they'll know that I at least thought about it. Well, yes. I did. I do. I *am* thinking about it. After all, if they'll arrest me afterwards, life as I know it will be over – so why not just end it now? Here's me, giving the camera a big smile, with a twinkle in my eye. But I won't do it. Not just yet.

Too many cameras have my sequence mapped out now; there's no turning back. I've laid out the movements in the video footage that will be played out from several consecutive feeds. Once captured, I'll wait for the playback, maybe even get to see it when I'm negotiating the price of my confession.

I *want* to get caught afterwards. To become a symbol. This act I'm carrying out is the equivalent of self-immolation at the doorstep of the parliament.

But what right do I have?

The doors part and space opens up and I step into a busy carriage on the Central Line. Hard workers returning home from their sloshy stopovers at pubs by their workplaces. I judge not that indulgence, but am aware of it. There's enough room to sit between the couples and groups scattered about inside, but I stand and hold on to a metal bar over their heads. I'm a dead man riding.

But, really, what right do I have to do this?

Here's the right: By doing it I earn the right to do it. I rid the world of filth. Sure, the ancient argument comes out of the shadows, whispering the nagging concern: *removing scum does not remove the idea of scum*. But really, does it not? I see the matter differently. I see the removal of *any* scum as practical engagement with the idea of scum-removal. And one must be, above all, practical. If nothing else, that is.

One of the ads staring at my face is a poem about daffodils. London Transit Authority's idea of art to pretty up the sullen subsurface trains. This poet loves hills and fields and keeps on wishing flowers could grow beneath the ground too, and then looks around at fellow passengers to realize that different kinds of flowers bloom down here.

Pathetic. Like most of what they call poetry these days. People are not flowers. They don't bloom; they blast.

And, really, what right does anyone have? Suicide bombers – do they have a right to do their fucking explosion thing among the oblivious at cafes, trains and bazaars? And I'm not even going after an innocent crowd to make my statement, am I? It's a targeted assassination. He's made a misery of thousands of lives. He's claimed them as nonchalantly as one would have plucked daffodils. But the murders don't show on his face at all. His eyes don't murk up with death. He probably sleeps like a dog curled up next to the fire. Sure, chasms haven't opened up in the earth just yet, and we're not being led to any apocalyptic rapture, but maybe that should be brought about already. Maybe his darker and filthier blood needs to be pumped out of his hideously large body to flood London's streets. Like an unleashed plague.

But it's true: I don't have the right. Because *I* don't have the privilege of calling myself one of his victims. He did not send goons to point a gun at my head to get money out of my wallet at a traffic light; and he did not orchestrate the murder of anyone I know. He didn't do anything to me. But he did shitloads of shit to people *like me*.

The stop coming up next: Marble Arch. I'll walk from there and find more cameras along the way.

Another fact: I don't even know Pakistan. Every few years, we go visit Baba's family in Quetta. Ma doesn't go even then. She's got no connection to that part of Baba. But Baba enjoys the trips. Big, strong men, and shy, completely draped women. Tribal segregation laws. Tea breaks and swims at the four-star Serena Hotel. I get bored with the life there, with nothing to do other than the day-long hikes in the dry hills with a servant or four coming up the tracks with me. Never went to the big city, Karachi. Don't know much about the culture of Lahore. The capital, Islamabad – its hiking trails and the marble floors of its Faisal Mosque are a vague and distant memory from when I was twelve; and the rest of the country is not even a memory. Baba doesn't worry himself about Pakistan like most immigrants from that country, who keep looking over their shoulder like Lot's wife at the disintegration of a once-homeland. He seldom tunes in to watch Pakistani news channels. He doesn't even like most Pakistani foods. He's less brown than I am.

Only one of my Quetta cousins was ever robbed in Karachi, and we don't know whose people stopped him at gunpoint at a traffic light to grab his mobile phone. That's all the personal grudge I can muster. So, what right do *I* have to avenge anything done to that country or its people?

I'm already walking out of the station, already above ground. And it doesn't seem like something I am doing out of volition. A force beyond me is propelling me forward. No bystander or walking pedestrian is seeking me out for conversation in this crowd. I'm a man on a mission. Like I always wanted to be.

That's something else they'll backtrack into my psychology. The lone gunman theory will be plugged into the assassin's personality matrix. It'll shake up the news channels.

That's why I have to broadcast something over the Internet before they capture me and take away my story. Maybe Facebook Live. A video that streams the aftermath as well as my reasons. Let's go over them again. I'm doing this for at least two reasons.

One: Because the only recourse left to the ordinary man is to assassinate the symbols of evil that the most heinous politicians become. Can't *not* do anything. In *V for Vendetta*, V had at least one G for Grudge, and I've got none of that, personally. But G is the first letter in God's own name. G begins that which is all-encompassing. But Al is how Allah begins – G for God versus Al for Allah – it's divinity against Himself. Seriously, though, I wish that V had never had that personal angle for the motivation to kill corrupt and evil people. I wish he'd done it just to remove scum. And that's my other job – to go about correcting that narrative.

Two: I'm an idea man myself. To live fully – *meaning*-fully – is to bring together all of one's ideas into a place of objective meditation, where no arguments remain against the action one is ready to perform. And the idea starts now not with 'why', but with 'why not'? Why *not* remove his existence from the planet? And there's literally no answer to that.

Ladbroke Grove's here already. Here I am, ambling down the quiet and dark street.

It's that door on the left. 412. From four doors away, I spy no bodyguards at the doorsteps. Odd, that; neglectful, even. Exaggerating the swing of my arms, I brush the back of my hand against the bump at the small of my back to make sure the gun is still there, under my shirt and jacket, with its safety switched on. Yes. There's its solid grip and its concentrated bulk and heft. And flicking the front pocket with my thumb, I feel the metallic rectangle of my phone, which I made sure to charge fully. A live video feed after the act is imperative. If I am checked, I might have to surrender the gun. I know that much. The kitchen will have knives though. So, I'm ready to hand over the gun. But the hulky bodyguards are nowhere in sight.

Al texted to knock three times, then pause and knock four more times, and then enter even if nobody answered. He said the door would likely be open. Maybe the guards are just inside.

There have been cameras all along and I may not have been looking at all of them, but they have gathered all the video sequences they needed. If I see any on the way back, I'll throw victory signs to the audience. That should start the final revolution. Ha.

Indeed, ha!

Feel like having a last cigarette before the act. But why *last*? They have those in lock-up and I'll get at least a few for the interrogation room in exchange for confessing. So, no cigarette needed right now. I'm unnecessarily protracting this interlude. Let's do this. Here goes. I'm walking up the steps.

The door and my knuckles make contact. I'm a lens outside my body, watching as if through a peephole. That's the camera angle afforded me from the disembodied perspective I've suddenly developed. I'm not breathing like I usually do. Slower somehow; somehow faster. But I *am* knocking on the door.

Inhale, *knock knock knock*. Pause. Exhale, *knock knock knock knock*. That's three knocks and then four more after a pause. I wait still, and there's a 'Come in', from inside, which I probably half imagine, given my sucked-in sense of everything at the moment. But I twist the knob and it turns quite smoothly, as if freshly oiled. The door is heavy, but I push with my body's weight and I'm in the gap of the doorway.

Portals to other dimensions must feel more real than this empty rectangular space.

A few yards down the hallway inside the house, on a rug lit by a tall lamp on a dark wooden console, is standing one of the big bodyguards with his back to me and his head tilted up.

'Hello there, I'm here to see Altamaash,' I say. He does not answer, nor does he turn around. Will I have to kill him as well?

Is that nausea I'm feeling? As if I've overeaten a greasy pizza. My mouth oiled.

'Hello?' I say, stepping into the house as I close the door behind me.

I see Al's face extending sideways around the bodyguard's bulk. He's grinning. I smile back without any gladness. But it's good to see him. Despite everything, it's a joy to behold his face popping out around his bodyguard's waist. But why doesn't Al simply sidestep the guard to see me? Why bend like this at his considerable mid-section?

'Hey, Al,' I say.

'Stay right there,' says Al. I do, holding a pose and smiling as if for a photograph. The door clicks shut behind me. I should take my gun out pretty soon.

Then there is a loud *bark!* and something pinches the skin of my forehead. The squeezing sensation is very painful. It's more than just a pinch for sure. It feels like a needle has passed through my third eye.

And it hits me: I've been shot. Wow. This is what being shot feels like. It's getting more painful. I can't think of anything except that I've been shot. But it feels like a minor affliction. Like a stubbed toe.

Shot in the forehead. Feels as if all my life was leading up to this point. The rest was preparation. *This* is it.

The bodyguard's huge body slumps to the ground and there's a bloody hole in the back of his head. My torso is in the process of slumping as well. I'm going to die.

It began with nonsense gurgling sounds and now my life is ending with the same kind of gleeps and gloops coming from my throat. It makes sense, somehow, all of it. It connects. I was never supposed to come here and kill Al. I was always going to get caught by the bodyguards, or not get caught but be reminded of Baba and Ma and all my cousins, and lose my nerve. Or I was going to keep the weapon tucked away in the hollow of the small of my back, sitting less than twenty feet from Al for a couple of hours, discussing his life and my article about his rise to power, his thrust into exile, and it would end with my getting to know him beyond those words over nibbles and chatter, and then I would leave and dispose of the gun and bullets in separate trash cans along the way back after rubbing them clean of fingerprints. I would then somehow fall asleep at night in my cold bed.

Then again, I could have left the meeting with Al, gone to a pub and run into the love of my life – a meeting with a leggy blonde I would have likely squandered in a one-night-stand without understanding the need to place love and respect on a higher footing than a seizure of lust.

Those were some of the other lives I could have led and frittered away. Instead, I chose to walk down this one road, somehow knowing what would happen.

And here's my playbook: I die. There's Al, standing above one dead and one dying body. He's stepped over the other slumped form and is walking over to me. He is standing above me, looking into my face, scanning the hole the bullet has left in my forehead. He goes down on one knee, and then the other, kneeling. He sits down and looks into my eyes. Am I dead already? I don't feel pain any more. No pain; no feeling at all.

'You're better off this way,' says Al. And our eyes are locked. I can't speak, but all I want to ask him is: How'd you do it?

II. Altamaash

The symphony segues from the first movement to the next. A fresh set of scales is being employed in the piece I am composer of, and also conductor. It is only in my ears that it plays.

Here's the pit-stop. I ready myself to get out after paying the sullen cabbie a moderate tip. He's a handsome fella, the cabbie. One of the regular, angular-headed, blue-collar English blokes. What's he got to be sad about with a face like that? Bless him for providing such stark contrast. I'm the pumpkin in the carriage. An ugly, self-satisfied brownie out 'n' about, carousing around town in jolly ol' London. Safely whallumped out of the cab, bearing the full weight of the universe on my knees and feet. Nando's here now. That's where I'll cover the fifteen minutes left before walking to Ned's hovel. The cabbie trundles a U-turn in his black cab contraption and I walk across the pavement to the doorway of the chicken-fest establishment. Mustn't linger here. Mustn't order the thighs-n-rice with garlic bread combo for two and ensconce myself in a booth. The earlier samosas were enough fuel for the act. One must live *on* fuel, not *for* it.

But the samosas are long gone, and the garlicky hot-sauce fumes that seep out of this den of grilled hens are plucking my stomach-strings. Oh, the gastronomic delight that a chicken thigh or five could deliver! Oh. *Oh.* Why did it have to be so hard right here, at the start?

No; stick to the plan, Al. Hold yourself together. Nothing's hard. You can always come back here after the deed. You can eat here or anywhere. And *any*thing. The coppers will never venture this far to solve their mystery. You, Al, you can eat all the things you ever wanted to eat. You're free. And after tonight, you will be even free-er and have the kind of power Grandpa Pir could only dream of possessing.

Still. The samosas weren't enough. I can smell dough and flesh and cheese and heat.

My life drools away in spittle.

Shut up, stomach. Shut up, heart.

I linger in the doorway, waiting for the desire to be numbed. Presently, it is simpering with indignation. The crust and masala and potato filling of the samosas was enough fuel. *Enough.* I open the door.

There, in the front of the restaurant, next to a waiting area's benches, is the podium set up for the host of this fine establishment. The woman behind it stands erect, oozing confidence. As if within the folded menus and the register of reservations she holds classified government documents that reveal every customer's peeves and peccadillos. As if she controls the fortunes of relegating whoever she wants to a waiting status from her position behind the lectern. From my last visit here, months ago, I remember this blondie and her quickie sentences, but I give her a once-over anyway. Her badge says Lou. Pert. Pretty. A niche strain of the beauty-beast case studies says she should be a nasty one inside. The clipped sentences, said with the haste of a scorpion scurrying across scorching sand, begin: 'Welcome to Nando's. How're you? How many in your party? Would you mind waiting? We've got a fifteen-minute wait.' I give her the short name: 'Al.' Could be Albert. Could be Alfredo. 'Party of 3,' I tell her. I don't let on that the party will be elsewhere. It's in the game. Will the sirens come this far when they search for clues? Let's give them a shot.

I linger inconspicuously, not making conversation. The crowd and noise coming from the heart of the restaurant is thickening just now, swelling with hope of warmth in meal and company. Both will be devoured, and sated appetites and companionship will shift out of here in under two hours. I stay on my feet next to the bench at the front, refusing the hostess's offer to seat me at the bar or a four-seater table. I wave her off gallantly, continuing my solitary vigil at the entrance. There is no fiddling with a phone to pass the twelve minutes remaining until the next stage of the plans. I stand in place, gathering my thoughts.

It must be done. The subjects and objects of my sentencing have come together at last.

Time does not slow down, nor does it accelerate. My breath is not the choppy, resistant mess I thought it would be. The act is manifest in each moment that has passed from my birth until now. What remains is to use the fuel of the samosas and reserves in my blubber to put it into play. As if I have been given a role that will brook no negotiation, and the swollen body I have received to perform this role is only an encasement, a costume. The spirit that inhabits this drapery of tissues and organs and brittle bones and viscous fluids is as light and lethal as vapours of mercury.

I am standing here in the foyer. Fourteen of the fifteen minutes allocated for this pit-stop have passed away according to the digital clock on the wall, and I know not how much I have thought through the implications extraneous to the ones for which I am aiming. Raskolnikov, the hero of Dostoevsky's *Crime and Punishment*, did flit in and out of my thoughts at intervals. That nervous wreck. Killed an old woman to have a hold on her money so he could do good things with it. Bah! He was deficient – D set him up to fail, giving him a plague of purpose-driven thoughts. Purpose is for parasites.

Mine? My own interpretation of the act? I choose to view it as an aesthetic. And if the performance also delivers the by-product of a desired outcome – well, so be it.

Raskolnikov could have chosen this mood, were he real – but he was the stuff of novels. And novels like that one ruin the most peaceful actor by driving purpose into their acts.

I step up to the hostess. 'Sorry, gotta go. Mates not coming after all. Cancel the hold on a table, please. Been a pleasure. Nice night to you.' Unloaded my clip of sentences right back at her. I wheel about on my heels, ashamed. A red, swollen face, like a brown balloon gone crimson with warm air and hot blood filling it up from the inside, mirrors back at me from the tastefully reflecting decor. Why did I need to take revenge on blondie Lou with my mimicry of her welcome speech? Must be the lust for extra spicy meat, I excuse myself. But I know there's a more dangerous game afoot, and the flippant and facetious clown inside me is leaving too many clues for the constables. Isn't there anything I won't turn into entertainment? I despair at the thought as much as some part of me revels at the symphony's next movement.

This musical soundtrack holds back nothing. Such melodrama. Such tiresome accompaniment of action with interpretive note, pitch and timbre.

Now for a brisk walk to Ned's address without thinking about the well-oiled mechanism of two-birds-one-stone that's been put in play. The quickest, least painful route is *through* the shin splints. March on, lieutenant! The troops will follow! An ensemble of instruments keeps up with my up-paced conduction.

412 Ladbroke Grove is a two-storey building.

Cessation of music while I ring the bell, and then, in quick succession, knock once, then twice, then three times; Ned opens the door shortly afterwards, says hello and welcome, and other trite things, and we walk through, after dulling pleasantries rather than flamboyant and game-changing exclamations, to his living room. A few more minutes of banter is called for. Gregory Guardian Jaffar must already be en route. That's the leading edge of today's concert – he's got his own rhythms and melodies to bring over and add to Ned and my duet. Meanwhile, we sit, Ned and I, holding glasses full of water. The music is slow and soft; it's cueing an intermission.

Ned is big. He fills up all three dimensions. His voice booms out into the room. And it occurs to me that he isn't really dumb, just simple. Straight. Like a spring stretched linearly to its limit, thereby having lost its tricks of recoil and lunge. Does human mettle even come ready-made so? Of course, of course. I have Ned's kin to thank for my other experiences of such phenomenon: purpose-driven bodyguards like my own Phil and Jordan – especially Jordan, because Phil's still got some spark of misdirection left in him. Some artifice that's close to artistic.

'What's it like living alone?' I ask Ned. Even my jowls-bolstered voice is meek compared to his. We sit at diagonal ends to the room, on large and supportive sofas, for variant reasons of bulk. It's Muscles vs Fat, the Ultimate Showdown of Tissue. Here's the catch: The brain is nearly a hundred per cent fat. Thereby, my body is an extension of the cerebral cavity, while his striated, fibroid muscles lunk about a tiny mass of grey matter that is alien to their nature.

'Ohhh, living alone, sir? Ohhh, it's all right, sir,' Ned says. I let him say the 'sir' bit without interrupting by letting him know it's okay to call me Al. The 'sir' is like therapy to him. He wants a place in the hierarchy right at the bottom, a position which carries with it the responsibility of repelling away from the monument those unlucky masses who are displaced out of the pyramid. 'Can't complain,' he says.

'Do you think the love of your life has already come and gone, and you missed your opportunity?' I ask. It's been less than two minutes in the lamplit living room, counting the comfortable gaps in silence, and I've laid down a heavy card. Early, yes. But in Ned's matte-glazed look I have read something without meaning to read too deeply just yet.

He's a little inebriated which means that he is open to being led. A good kind of tipsy, too, because he isn't past the tipping point. How perfect this all is. Scripted, even.

'Well,' he begins to answer. A lonely *well* it is. No matter. I let the silence hang. Ned lowers his gaze to his glass, in which he is nursing his last drink of this life: water. Good. It'll baptize his gullet and purify his exit from material to void. 'I did love someone, sir,' he says, and goes wistful in a booming kind of way. Like Zeus pining. A libation of hydrated oxygen or oxidized hydrogen swirling gently in the glass in his hand.

'Was she beautiful?' I ask. A simple question, like a crumb thrown to the simpler being in the room. And crumb by crumb I'll lead him on until the ultimate act of his life. His sacrifice.

'Yes,' he says, 'quite beautiful.'

He's full-on nostalgic, waiting for me to ask the story he's been hiding away from public scrutiny. But little does he know that there is a bigger story around him. I inhale deeply, taking a gander around the room, trying to sum up Ned's life within the objects he keeps himself surrounded with: African art on the walls, including a dark wooden mask of some garish sort; an elephant-tusk lamp; two dark giraffes with their necks nuzzled against each other; abstract landscape paintings of savanna-lands; and the like. Ned was an outdoorsman, standing guard against the wilderness – never letting it enter the house. He never knew what he wanted to do in life. He was never brave enough to go and do what he loved. Needing to become an adventurer, he became a bulked-up doorstop. This much I can glean from just the surface of artifacts. Ned may just be all surface. The pathos of all this – the tragedy – it reeks of a dank failure.

'You were in love. But it's over,' I say. He looks up, startled. As if I've just now, in this sudden instant of uttering those words, given him the closure he's sought for years. I nod and gulp some water. Another large gulp and the water is gone.

'Yes, it's over,' he says. He's smiling awkwardly. No longer pining to tell me what happened. It's trivial, after all. It's a story within *the* story. An unnecessary digression.

I put my empty glass on a side-table. It sticks wetly to the coaster. I'll wipe it; or maybe I won't. Standing up, I ask him, 'Do you want to know what will get you the job, Ned?'

There is no music now.

'I do,' he says, also standing, the glass half empty in his hand. I walk over to him and reach for his glass of water. He gives it to me. I place it carefully on a flat surface. We stand in front of each other. He is a head taller.

'Will you take a bullet for me?' I ask him.

Ned smiles with pleasure, like he's been waiting for me to ask just this question. All his life is centred on this one abstract thought – the worth of his existence. And I'm going to make him sell it short.

The smile turns into a hideous grin that stretches out his lips. He nods slowly. 'Yes, sir. I will,' he says.

'Do you have a gun?' I ask.

He reaches with one hand and pulls a 38 or 45 from a holster behind his back. Poetic grace in his movements. Perfect coordination of muscle and bone and black suit draping it all. The flow continues: he presses a button on the gun, pulls out the magazine and shows me the clip is brimming with bullets; he reinserts the magazine, clicks the switch that turns the gun's safety off, and pulls back the mechanism that propels the first bullet into the weapon's active chamber. He points the barrel at his own chest and hands me his gun, handle first. Still smiling, like it's a chronic condition.

He's playing his part like a champion. I take the gun and feel its heft. The heavy metal and carbon thing full of pins and levers and oiled cylinders and adjusted triggers is its own orchestra of mechanisms. I feel the physical weight of its potentials. Oh, it'll do.

'You can have the job, Ned,' I say. 'But you'll have to prove that you can take a bullet.' He nods. I nod with him. That's us in the living room, sealing our agreement with signature movements of our heads. 'I will shoot you,' I say, once we stop nodding, 'to make sure.' I smile, and he smiles back.

'You've handled guns before?' he asks. His words deflect mine, swatting them aside. He asks a technicality. Of course, he doesn't believe I will shoot him. His mind does not process that sentence as a real threat.

'In a way,' I say. 'I have handled people who have handled guns.' What imbecile doesn't know how to pull a trigger? 'The safety's off, right?'

'Yes, sir,' he says. Oh, Ned. I'm going to miss all this sir-ing. Brother Al sure is going to miss minion Ned for that little contribution if for nothing else.

'Okay,' I say. 'Let's not make a mess on this carpet.' I walk us out to the entrance hallway. Ned follows calmly. I position myself and beckon him with the gun to stand with his back to the front door, but well away from it. I put the gun to my own temple, my finger on the trigger. 'This is tempting too,' I say. For a flicker, I see him worried, his smile faltering. He can probably take the gun away from me plenty of milliseconds before I squeeze the trigger to the point at which the pin collides with the bullet. He can save me from my proclivities for causing self-harm, can sweet Ned. But for now, he stands there, remaining a potential of it all, smiling uneasily. Will I do this? Squeeze the trigger at my temple? For an audience of *one*? Never!

'Don't,' he says, 'that's very dangerous.' I'm eased away from the parapet, no longer – nor was I ever – willing to plummet.

'Okay,' I say, pointing the gun first away from my own head, then directing its aim at his forehead. 'Your turn.'

A sense of comfort returns to Ned's smile. It's an infectious smile. I join him in the disease.

'Don't pull it at once. You have to squeeze slowly,' he says.

'I know,' I say, 'but not just yet.' I step closer and closer to him. His eyes are at the length of a head above mine, and I have to raise my gun-hand higher as the distance between us diminishes. His mouth is at about the level of my forehead and that's where I bring the gun.

Ned's smile flickers. It's about to blow out, but it doesn't. It stays like a stubborn ember, as a much more minute version of itself. Enflaming the pucker of his lips. Instinct, I guess. He knows where I'm going to bring the open hole of the gun.

'Open your mouth, Ned,' I say. He dare not refuse. I have a gun to his head. Even his O-shaped mouth seems to be full of mirth. I bring the gun closer. His eyes widen. His lips and those of the gun make a kissing couple. Then I shove further, the barrel is inside his mouth, with my finger hanging loose just above the trigger.

'Mmmff,' he says. Any person not watching would detect a hint of pleasure in that sound. Here, in Ned's case, I know there is surprise, fear, submission, resignation, hope, and faith that this is not how he will die. Poor thing.

'I'll make it easy for you, Ned,' I begin. 'I won't dole out my message in puffery. I won't even cloak it in oceanic layers of waves upon waves of excuses disguised as reasons. There will be no subtextual undercurrents in what I fling from my larynx to your eardrums. You hear that, Ned? I'll be direct.' I shift my feet. He follows my lead, arms on his side. We both get comfortable where we are. I start again, trying harder to be direct, creases on my temple. 'Someone has to be sacrificed, Ned. And it could be me, of course. I've considered that. Taking power as a symbol, with its potential to be an abstract ideal, rather than as a living being, with all of life's flaws, does sound appealing. I've seen it being done. You know, in the movie theatre, with drama, action and epic-scale music. The spectacle makes you think ol' Braveheart's sacrifice is akin to Christ's. Tears. La dee da. The whole thing. But there's got to be a way of becoming a symbol without crossing over, right? That's rhetorical, so you don't have to nod. I know you understand what I'm talking about. It's pretty simple.'

Ned drools from one side of his mouth and 'mmmfffs' in response.

'But then why you, Ned? Why did I pick you?' He's right not to nod, because this bit is also rhetorical. 'You're just right for it, Ned. You fit the scheme like seeds belong in the ground. You're the start of it all, Ned. I know, I know. You won't get to see the whole thing. Even I won't get to see the *whole* spectacle. None of us were meant to. But some of us do get the principle of it all. It's not difficult, when you put your mind to it. It's about what we want as human beings. That's not complex at all, Ned. That's not too indecipherable. We want lights, camera, action, symposium.'

My raised arm has numbed a little. To be expected. The man is moaning, questioning, but not panicking. I know he has not flown off the handle because he is amenable through alcohol, and I have lulled him further with my voice. He has not attempted to swat away the gun. It's too late for that. When the gun was aimed at me, he could have saved my life. But he can't save himself if he panics. I'll fire. He knows it now.

'Mmmfffmmm,' he mumbles. Not bad. Spiritually different, for sure, but not too far off the high standards that Grandpa Pir established for indecipherable utterances.

'Are you ready to become part of the spectacle, Ned?' I ask. Unfortunately, this too is rhetorical. The gun's barrel is coated on its open end with thick saliva. I sincerely hope the trickle doesn't gravitate down the barrel onto my hand before the right moment comes. 'I would ask you to kneel and be tested. And after that, I would ask you to rise and be welcomed to a new life. But it will be more difficult for me to do this if you're kneeling, Ned.'

That shuffling sound outside the front door. It must be our awaited guest. But, oh no.

This could have been better. I could have actually explained everything to Ned, to give him a worthy ending. *Knock, knock, knock*, on the door. Not too tentative, is Guardian Greg. Not too ready, am I. Could have used a few more minutes with Ned here. The bouncing hulk and I stare at each other with our deepest fears bared. I don't think it's the gun that he fears, or the bullet, to be more precise. We do not move.

Knock, knock, knock, knock. The full three and four equals seven. It's him. I keep looking at Ned and sigh with all my despair. 'I'll handle this,' I tell him, and say louder, 'Come in.'

Ned's eyes shift to the right corners of their sockets and he's meaning to turn around.

But I nod at him and whisper, 'Wait. Don't do that. Just wait.'

The door opens and a thin voice asks to see me, Al. Ned has questions in his eyes, I have reassurance in my smile. Too bad we couldn't cover everything. But at least we tried.

There's Gregory Jeronimo, my Guardian boy. He brings joy and purpose in his voice, does Gary Guardian Jeremy, today of all days. Fitting, because now the three principals of today's song and dance act are finally gathered on stage.

I keep the gun lodged in Ned's mouth and peek around his body to look at the emotive reporter who has entered the inner sanctum. He must perform, or be performed at. This is the law that I was just beginning to get into with Ned. Makes me wonder if I shouldn't have perhaps written out the speech before getting to the performance of it. That way, timing could have been tweaked, and this minor error of incomplete monologues would not have arisen.

Ned's wide span is not easy to lean around while holding up my arm at the level of his face. But I achieve it while putting all the weight of the universe on one foot. Imagine that!

I line up the shot thinking mostly of the second sacrifice. And I face my demons. And I think to myself how much this is like thinking of someone else while having sex with your own wife. I tell GGGJ Greg to stay where he is. And I tweak the direction of the gun a smidgen to the right and down. And I breathe deeply, like an expert yogi in tree pose, to let oxygen and chi flow like a river up my tired, tired, fucking exhausted, arm.

And I start squeezing the trigger, cajoling metal parts of the gun to come closer to each other, slowly. And it takes forever to compress the thing enough. But then it snaps into position. And Ned's head pops open from behind. I hear a sharp *crack* of wood, or wooden metal. I keep hearing it. My head rings like a bell with that thin and thick sound, it becomes an extended echo.

Ned's head is no more. At least from the back, where the bullet made its way through the layers of his meaty flesh and nerves. Bodily viscera exude from him. Of course, Guardian's dead too. The whole future-of-journalism is head-shot via mouth-shot through someone else's body.

The single bullet stays firing in my head like an eternal recurrence. It always happened; it will also keep happening. There will be no person who does not hear this blast from a 38 or 45 for their entire life on Earth.

It was about time, though. It was definitely time.

I look at my dark clothes and notice one or two sprinklings of what can be passed off as thick bloody wine.

On the other hand, the floor is bespattered with brain and organic bits of flesh. Poor Ned, with his incomplete life. Hardly given any explanation. No more or less than Greg the Guardian is his dual-sacrifice partner. Maybe that's enough consolation for the dead body.

In any case, he is cheaply, clearly departed.

I step over his body carefully to go to un-Guarded Greg's. He's quite done. Near the centre of his forehead is his leakage spot. But more than just the bullet that reached his body, he's covered in brain matter from Ned's head. Like a Pollock painting on a mannequin.

Greg Guardian Gary … lifeless, staring up to the ceiling. I can't say anything to him now. But I still say something. I say, 'You're better off this way.'

I hear my voice. Every word comes out like a new version of the one gunshot. I hope my sense of hearing will return to normal.

Good fortune abounds. The sharp sound of the single bullet does its trick. It befuddles. Witnesses: none. Neighbours have heard a sound, but they can't be sure. *Video game? Film?* They can't be bothered to call this in, in this upper-middle-class neighbourhood. They won't get involved. No siren rings in the five minutes I stay and watch the bodies settle into death.

Going back into the living room, I pick up the glasses that Ned and I used, meaning to go to the kitchen sink and wash them. But I play some more with what's been given, wipe the glasses down and put them back in their places on the coasters. Wonder when the cops'll piece these together to make some sense of it all, some purpose-driven motive. The gun in suicidal Ned's hand, the disposable phones with their text messages in the pockets of the dead bodies, with Ned and Guardian Gary Greg's fingerprints on the keys. The one-bullet how-dunnit. What story will they botch together first, before working towards the truth?

This silence after the muffled gunshot is of the most deafening kind. It's as if the orchestra, which is momentarily resting, has never played at all.

I leave by the back door, clicking it softly back into place. I plant everything that leads back to the killer. But I leave not a hint of myself.

𝄽

I've done it Grandpa. I'm your darkest self come true, and only getting darker. There, that's melodramatic enough. No, I can't force purpose where there is none. Don't get caught up in the spectacle's reasons. The spectacle is nothing but itself. Too bad I couldn't tell all that to Ned in a way he would have understood it.

I wish there was a way to record all this for posterity.

III. Edwin 'Ned' Steinberg

The bell rings and there's impatient knocking right after it. I open the front door saying 'Hello there', and let Al come in and shake my hand. I return his smile, welcome him and lead him back through the hallway into the kitchen. It doesn't occur to me to ask about Phil and the other bodyguard who must be waiting outside. When I do remember, and turn around to ask him if he would like tea or coffee and what the bodyguards would take, Al is very close behind me. I have to smile. Sneaky brown fella that he is, he's very agile for a man his size.

'A drink? Water?' I ask.

'Sure. Water,' he says and sits down on my TV sofa while I fetch our drinks. No more beer in the house, praise the Lord, or I would have tried to drink some more. Not a good idea.

Once we're seated, I wait for him to begin. Sure enough, he does.

At first the questions are about living alone and loneliness. I don't let that kind of talk bother me usually, but it does get my mood down. Maybe because of the beer sloshing inside, like barrels of water in the bottom of a boat.

Well, yeah. I admit that I am kind of all right being so alone, and also kind of not so all right. Don't know what exactly I'm saying, really.

Then, suddenly, he gets really personal. Or maybe I do. I don't remember who mentions Nadine first. Do I even say her name? It gets me proper good, the wallowing. Oh man, I'll curse alcohol for the rest of my life. Never gonna have any more drinks. I swear it. It's like I've become soft. Like melting cheese.

Good thing it's Al who's around. I mean, professionalism and wanting to continuously make a good impression with him is one thing. But I feel good with Al around. It means he trusts me. Or I trust him. One of those. Whatever. Beer sucks. What I mean is I feel protected. Little do I know. The cheeky bugger probably has me dancing to his tune – making me miss Nadine, talking about closure. Shifting topics more suddenly than I can keep up. But I trust him.

Then up he gets and walks over to me. Like a lumbering Sasquatch, the opposite of healthy-looking, but so, so quick. I keep to my position on the easy chair, but have to get up when Al is standing right in front of me. I'm calling him 'Sir' a lot. Something about the last beer is an expo— what's the word? Exponential? Existential? Always confusing, those two – I'm getting drunker by the second.

He asks if I've got a gun. I should ask him *why*? But I don't. It's like I'm showing off for a wicked uncle how I reach around under my suit jacket and whip out the weapon. Even show him the clip, load it for him and turn off the safety before handing it over like a birthday gift.

What I'm thinking is, he's going to play with it a bit, get excited and point it in a few directions and act all gangster-like, a mafia hitman and whatever, and then give it back. What am I *thinking*?

I ask if he's handled guns before. Would give him a lesson or two, but he shrugs off any suggestion of that.

He walks me out of the living room, saying he's going to shoot me. And I would laugh to please him. It's a good joke and I would laugh politely, but I don't want to feel the force of laughter pound through my head just now. The beer-drinking cloudiness in my head is finally beginning to dissipate. I don't want to encourage it to stay.

But it isn't cloudiness that's going away. More than that, it feels like a tiny but loud-and-clear speck of sobriety running at breakneck speed from down in my stomach to up in my head. A feeling has been generated on Al insisting again and again that I'm going to get shot by him. And the feeling is swimming up from the gut.

The sober thought is still miles away in my body when Al points the gun first at his own head, and then at my head, and then comes closer and closer, inching up to me until he gets me to bite down on the barrel end of the handgun. It tickles my gums and the metal is hard against my teeth. But I do as he says.

Then Al begins to talk slow and says meandering things, and he is looking a bit worried about saying things that make no sense. But he isn't making much sense. Is he drunk too? I do smell alcohol, but maybe that's my own breath. He's trying to explain what's going on in his head, I think, and I try to encourage him by saying 'mhmm', but my mouth is still filled with the wrong end of a bullet chamber. For a moment I think I'm sobering up when a cough comes out of my mouth. But it's just a hiccup. Too bad. I could use a little more sobering.

It's difficult to understand Al when he says things like 'someone has to be sacrificed' and 'are you ready to become part of the spectacle, Ned?' He says my name like he and I have been friends for decades. He talks about the lubrication of life's events by inebriation. Or maybe that's a thought in my own head, said in his voice, but not by him. He says I should be kneeling, but not really, and then there's a sound outside the door. It must be Al's bodyguards. Phil and the other one. I should say hi to Phil. Let him know I'm making sure I get the job with Al by taking a bullet for him in this test situation.

Someone knocks repeatedly on the door. Al invites that someone into my house, without my permission, by saying 'Come in'. And in comes someone behind me. If it's Phil, I want to say hi. So, I try to turn around to see, but Al keeps the gun and my head in place.

The reporter? That's who's at my place? That miserable-looking bloke? Sure, sounds like his voice. But I can't get my head around something. Why's *he* here? Ohhh…

That's when I know what the sober speck from my gut has been trying to tell me. It's too late now. Because even if I consider trying to get Al's hands off the trigger, I know I can't. I think about asking him, 'Hey, are samosas India's best export or what?' It's the punch line from a racist joke someone once told me. I never knew what was so funny about it and I've forgotten the rest of the joke. No, it's not the punch line. It's the middle line. What was the rest of it? I could ask Al if he knows the rest, then he could tell it, and then I could laugh and step back, away from the gun.

In the next second, I feel what is about to happen before it happens. I feel the full metal-and-gunpowder explosion of the bullet at the back of my throat, even before Al pulls the trigger. It's going to happen. I will not stop it. But that's okay. It's going to be okay. Just a few seconds more.

I feel happy. My life has been all right. I'm ready to go out, like a bulb. Click! That's what he does. Al pulls the trigger.

More than a million thoughts rush into my head. Must be the synapses firing all that serotonin and dopamine and whatnot at each other.

So, I *can* take a bullet for Al. That's been my main concern recently. I feel like I've put a check on my life's most important box. And I am quite certainly dead.

II Purgatorial Womb

'In the midway of this our mortal life,
I found myself within a gloomy wood,
For the straightforward path had been lost.'

– Dante Alighieri, *The Divine Comedy*

4

Inside the Whale

You know you're in political exile from Pakistan when you can't gather twenty supportive friends to burn fifty-seven tyres on the roads to shut down a city any more.

I. George Gary Gregory Jaffar

[Transparent film of glass-like material as far as the eyes can see. George Gary Gregory Jaffar floats weightlessly within this film, a shadow in the glassy realm, which is neither spatial, nor constrained by time's fetters. The transparence exists beyond such boundaries. It lies outside the frame of conception that human beings can begin to know – even the Sufis and hippies. Light floods in from one direction, from a single speck that is also enmeshed within the transparent realm. The light sparks a wakefulness of spirit in the bodiless, smoky grey being that George Gary Gregory Jaffar has become. The dot of light speaks.]

ANGEL OF ADMITTANCE: I begin in the name of the One who is both the Possessor and Dispenser of Mercy. I am the Angel of Admittance. The Divine One has spoken to me about you. Your name is George Gary Gregory Jaffar and you are haunted by the Ghost of What Altamaash Should Suffer. I greet you with a wish of peace.

GEORGE GARY GREGORY JAFFAR: Hello? Is this … this is real-life? Am I dreaming? Or perhaps daydreaming while… Am I looking at a painting? The *Guernica* in my room – by chance a meditation on that? Is that what's … or am I – or…

ANGEL: You have died, George Gary Gregory Jaffar.

GGGJ: Really? Died *completely*? Oh. That bullet in my – oh yes. Of course. My forehead. I did die, didn't I? Never thought it would happen … so suddenly. I'm sorry, I didn't quite catch your name. I mean, this is – wow. Death. Holy … wow. Are you sure? I mean, are you certain that's what this is? I'm sorry, could you introduce yourself again? I'm a little, you know … death and all. It's just ... just like that.

ANGEL: George Gar— mind if I call you George?

GGGJ: Please do. Nobody else ever did.

ANGEL: I am the Angel of Admittance, George. I am here to be your guide. I am the guide of everyone who is admitted. The disorientation you are feeling is quite typical and shouldn't alarm you.

GGGJ: Right. I shouldn't feel disoriented about my disorientation. And you're the Angel of Admittance. Right. I can remember that. I'm talking to the Angel of Admittance, and I shouldn't feel disoriented. After dying, I've come here. And this is *not* a dream. It's a post-death situation. The last thing I remember … I was planning on killing the man who killed me. So, that really happened?

ANGEL: Yes, it did. The man you know as Altamaash shot you in the head.

GGGJ: And I died?

ANGEL: Yes. You died, George.

GGGJ: And now, here I am.

ANGEL: Yes. Here you are, George.

GGGJ: And where is this *here*, exactly? And what do I call you? Do I call you Angel of Admittance? Can I just call you 'Angel'? Am I perhaps, maybe, asking too many questions?

ANGEL: 'Angel' will be fine. You can call me that. You should ask all the questions that come to you. That is part of the process. As for this place ... tell me what you see around you, George.

GGGJ: I see you. At least I think that's you. You're that dot of light, right? Or maybe I'm blinded by light and can't really see you. And I can look at myself and see that there's a ... a cloudy thing. I see smoke instead of my body. Should I be like this? Like fluffed up smoke? It's grey, I think. And except that, there's nothing but transparent substance all around. Like water or glass. And we're within it. You, the light, and I am – am I the puffs of grey smoke?

ANGEL: This place shows only the distillation of a being's essence. I am an angel, and like angels, I am made of light. Your essence, as a human being, your spirit, is appearing to you as formless smoke right now, but the process of Admittance will change that. As for the name of where we are – this realm, this station, the term we use to describe it is 'The Belly'.

GGGJ: The Belly? As in stomach?

ANGEL: There is no other name for it that you would understand. The Belly is the closest in analogy that can be understood by humans who are going through the process of Admittance. Think of it as a spiritual womb, where you are being incubated. Or, if you wish, imagine it as a digestive tract. You, George, are in The Belly, getting processed and digested, just as much as you are processing and digesting what is happening to you.

GGGJ: And I'll come out the other end a different person?

ANGEL: You'll come out different, yes.

GGGJ: That's quite incredible, all of that. But, can we step back for a moment? I'm smoke? My essence is *smoke*? Was it always grey and misty like this, living inside the human body somewhere?

ANGEL: Your essence may appear to you like a cloud of smoke, given your still-mortal level of understanding, but that's not smoke you see, George. That's spirit. It's the Breath of God. You, George: you are the Breath of God. You always have been.

GGGJ: I have always been the Breath of God? Always? And you're *quite* sure that this isn't some sort of dream?

ANGEL: Dreams are not required any more, George. You are being prepared for Admittance.

GGGJ: Admittance. Right. You're the Angel of Admittance. You mentioned that … Admittance into what exactly?

ANGEL: Heaven. That's your destination.

GGGJ: I'm going to *Heaven*?

ANGEL: Yes, once you're ready for it.

GGGJ: But I didn't pray a lot. I wasn't – isn't Heaven rather, perhaps, more selective?

ANGEL: Yes, you didn't pray much. But do you think prayers are what get humans into Heaven, George?

GGGJ: Well, don't they? Prayers, acts of kindness, and such things. And God's favour, of course?

ANGEL: And yet you are surprised.

GGGJ: Well, yes. Honestly, I didn't quite fully believe, you know. In God and the whole … life after death, and angels and such things.

ANGEL: And you feel unworthy.

GGGJ: A bit, yes. Don't get me wrong. I'm quite, quite grateful. Extremely, in fact. And overwhelmed, to be sure. I just don't know how to react, given the kind of doubts I harboured about the existence of Heaven – I mean, you know, it's a bit of a stretch to give me access to a place I never believed in. Don't you think?

ANGEL: As you said, George. You didn't always believe. That's to be expected though. Everyone doubts the existence of the Divine One at some point. But the Divine One is full of gifts even for those who disbelieve in the afterlife but live in the breathing world by principles that support goodness over evil. And you did just that.

GGGJ: So, I get to go to Heaven because I lived by certain principles?

ANGEL: Yes, George. That is correct.

GGGJ: Okay, great. So, when do I get there? To Heaven, I mean. This Belly is not an extension or something, right?

ANGEL: Should you choose, you can start your journey to Heaven, to be in the Divine One's presence, right away. But the perfection that is going to surround you there is going to strike your soul very hard. You will suffer tremendously in the presence of that flawlessness, unless you are prepared for it.

GGGJ: And I won't suffer if I go through this process of Admittance?

ANGEL: Suffering is written into the human project. You will either suffer in increments or all at once. That is your choice. I recommend doing this incrementally: stay here; go through the process; you will be better prepared for meeting your Creator.

GGGJ: Okay. I guess I'll trust you on this then, Angel. Incremental suffering sounds more manageable. But I have some questions. First of all, and please, humour me, because I want to pursue this line of thought a bit more: Why me? Why am *I* being admitted to Heaven?

ANGEL: As I said earlier, George, you are being awarded Heaven not for your deeds, but for your intentions. Tell me, what was the final thing you intended to do in life?

GGGJ: I was planning on killing Altamaash. I was going to pull out the gun tucked in the back of my— wow, I remember that quite vividly.

ANGEL: That precise intention. That's why you, *specifically* you, are being admitted to Heaven.

GGGJ: But I *didn't* end up killing him. I only planned it.

ANGEL: That's right. Had you actually carried out the murder, your case would be trickier. You may even have ended up in Hell. But your *intention* was pure. Do you remember what it was, your intention?

GGGJ: I wanted to remove one speck of evil from the world.

ANGEL: That's a pure intention.

GGGJ: But that got me killed.

ANGEL: God chose that you would die at the exact moment when you needed to be killed in order to enter Heaven for the rest of eternity.

GGGJ: Hmm. That's a different spin on what happened, that I died at the right moment. And I had the right intention in the end. But, what about the rest of my life? I mean, I did do things other than plan a murder. Right?

ANGEL: George, it will be difficult for you to adjust your understanding of what your life was, now that it's over. But you should not even come close to believing that you understand yourself more than the Divine One, your Creator, knows you. You do *not* understand a whole lot. But that will change through the process of Admittance.

GGGJ: Again this 'process of Admittance' you keep mentioning … what is that?

ANGEL: It is an experiential process that will answer your questions in a way that doesn't leave doubts or despair. But before the process begins, I will disclose certain aspects about your life that will likely depress you. Do not fret about what feelings course through you during the process, George. You can expect a lot of suppressed emotions to surface.

GGGJ: But what is this process? What happens in it?

ANGEL: It is different for everyone. For you, it will be related to Altamaash's past, right up to the point where he killed you.

GGGJ: Al's past? But what does that have to do with me?

ANGEL: It's time you begin answering your own questions, George. Search within for the truth, and tell me: what do you think Altamaash has to do with your life?

GGGJ: I don't know. Perhaps I wanted to know what made him tick. I mean, I guess I was interested in him.

ANGEL: Would you honestly use that word 'interested'? Or would you replace it with something else, if you were honest?

GGGJ: Maybe a little more than interested.

ANGEL: Try, George.

GGGJ: Okay, I'll say it just to hear how it sounds out loud. I was obsessed about him. There. It's out now.

ANGEL: Go on, George. There's more.

GGGJ: Okay. At least for a month before I met him, I could think of nothing else. Al – Altamaash – he was living in London like he owned it. And he didn't seem to be paying for the violent chaos he'd brought to his home country. I wanted to … to know why he didn't suffer.

ANGEL: There it is; in your own words. You've said it. You are haunted by the Ghost of What Altamaash Should Suffer.

GGGJ: If you say so. I don't feel haunted, but—

ANGEL: You planned on killing him, George. You thought that would be the most meaningful act of your life.

GGGJ: With all the disgusting things he— of *course* ridding the world would have been the best thing I could have done.

ANGEL: That is a position only the Divine One can take, George. One human cannot judge another. You have been shown mercy from your Creator, who ordered your death just before you would have committed a major sin. And that timing of your death is the reason you will go to Heaven. But you are not ready yet. You must be made ready through the process of Admittance. Since you were obsessed with Altamaash, the process for you will be this: You will know his thoughts and actions more intimately now than you could ever have known them while you were alive.

GGGJ: Right. Okay. So, my process is…?

ANGEL: First, let's go through your question again, George. Why are you one of the chosen ones to go to Heaven? Know this for certain: there is no Heaven. The 'gardens under which rivers flow'; the 'fountains and streams of milk and honey'; 'beautiful companions with whom you can live forever' – these are all going to be very different from how you understood them in the life you lived. All the scriptural definitions of Heaven are what we call 'literal analogy'. The only thing you get to see is the face of God. For the rest of eternity. He will turn to you. Forever. And you will bask in the Divine One's glow. That will not make sense right now. It *cannot* make sense. It is not *supposed* to make sense. Not until you experience it yourself. And, you have been picked out of masses as one of the very few who fulfilled their obligations in life. You were chosen because you decided that you must live for the right ideal: removal of evil.

GGGJ: That's … I'm grateful and all, but—

ANGEL: But know this, George: you were not as important as you think. Not in what you believe to be the larger scheme of things. As an Angel, I am, by default, of lesser significance than you in the hierarchy of God's creations. But you are not much more significant as an individual. In comparison to other human beings, even those who will not be granted Admittance, your life was lived on a much smaller scale. Does that make sense, George?

GGGJ: It does make sense, I guess. I didn't really do much in life, did I? I mean, well … I was a reporter for a good newspaper. I was just starting out there. That's about it, really. I'm not – I mean … you know, I'm not depressed or anything. But it is sad; right? Objectively speaking, it *is* sad. Isn't it? I fulfilled around, what – *two* per cent of what I could have been?

ANGEL: This judgement of yourself is exactly what needs to transform during the process, George. Despair is settling into you. It will stay there, and once you are ready to let go of it, it will leave. But for now, it serves a purpose. So, it will accompany you. Yes, in human terms, your life was what you might deem insignificant. There is no shame in admitting that – at least there *will be* no shame once you're through the process. But George, whatever little part was given to you, you *did* perform it well. And for now, while you still understand things on human terms, I have picked out three analogies for you out of the more than seventeen quadrillion that serve human purposes.

GGGJ: Analogies?

ANGEL: Analogies. Extended metaphors. Comparisons to systems other than that which are being explained. Tools by which, conceptually, humans most easily understand what is required of them. Your first analogy is dark. But I can see that you are ready to receive it. You, George, are a cog in the machine. You were a cog attached to a lever. The lever was Altamaash. His function was impossible without you, because – as a crucial tooth in a tiny wheel within the mechanisms of its rotation – you were instrumental in his performing his function.

GGGJ: I was a cog? A tooth? So … my life's entire purpose was to be a tiny part of Al's life? That means – Altamaash was more important than me?

ANGEL: Let me answer that question with the second analogy. This one is the bleakest of the three. You were the drone ant and Al was the queen ant of the colony to which you both belonged. Understand, George, that systems were at play. Within the system, or colony – as in this analogy – to which you and Al belonged, your purpose was a seemingly minor one. But you performed it with excellence. You did not shy away from your part.

GGGJ: But I got killed.

ANGEL: Yes. You did. And you have gained Admittance to the presence of the Divine One because you fulfilled your purpose. Do you know what your purpose was?

GGGJ: To get killed?

ANGEL: Let me start with the third analogy here. And then let's see if it helps you begin the process of Admittance with the right mindset. Imagine the largest celebration of human history that you can. Some commemoration of epic proportions. What comes to mind?

GGGJ: I don't know, Angel… I mean, this is – well, I guess, perhaps, the Second Coming?

ANGEL: The Second Coming – yes, that works perfectly. All right, imagine that the Second Coming of Jesus Christ is announced ahead of time. Say, six months before it is scheduled to happen, the location is not revealed, but the whole world knows *when* – at what *precise* moment – it will happen. Then, imagine that all of humanity is utterly convinced of this – despite human tendency to disagree and quarrel over such simple things as the truth.

The heads of nations are told they will no longer need to rule over people, since Jesus Christ himself will form the One True Kingdom. Humanity has six months to prepare for his arrival.

Now, imagine that every human effort is organized in preparation for this event. Wars end. Hostilities cease. Sweatshops are closed and children learn to play without bullying. Human traffic of supplies and demands is balanced so that wealth is optimally redistributed and land is utilized without any form of wastage other than minor human error. Everybody goes about their business, making sure that the moment of the Arrival will be heralded with garlands of the most beautiful flowers, and that the most delectable sweets and fruits will be prepared for the Messiah.

All butchers do their butchering with honesty. All bankers lose interest in deriving more money from capital that does not belong to them. All artists infuse meaning and excellence rather than commerce and ostentation into their inspired acts of literature, music and poetry; and they prepare their work with the devotion that is in keeping with degrees of responsibility they owe their gifts.

Now imagine that along with artisans and farmers preparing food for the Messiah's consumption, and for that of his companions, there will be pets and dramatists creating odes and librettos for his amusement as well. And there will also be an orchestra. The largest, most intricate orchestra ever known to mankind. It will contain all the instruments that have yet been invented, and even more will be invented for it. String, wind, brass, and all other kinds, and their hybrids, they will be tuned to the most precise possible degrees. The score to accompany the Messiah's descent will begin with the greatest musical minds praying to the Divine One, staying up nights and locking into their muses and other sources of inspiration like never before. Once ready, the composition – and it will be beautiful – will be infused with the Divine One's own Grace. It will be perfect. It will be humanity's most concerted effort of melody. The painters and teachers and astronomers and equestrians and janitors and fruit sellers and librarians and electrical engineers will have had equal parts to play in its production.

Then, with two months left until the big moment, rehearsals will begin to practise the perfect music for humanity's Messiah. The massive orchestra will sit in a large auditorium – the largest ever – built specially with acoustic considerations kept in mind.

There will be no tickets, of course, because nobody knows where the Messiah will descend. All of humanity will be spread throughout the continents, and the first to see Christ descend from the heavens will be charged with the responsibility to inform all the others where he has descended.

All this while, in the six months of notice given to humanity, wires and speakers will have been laid out across the world – and in some cases, wireless speakers – just so long as every nook and cranny of the world is within audible reach of the speakers that will carry the grand orchestra's music.

And imagine that you will be part of the orchestra. One of fifteen thousand people chosen to perform for the Messiah. Can you picture it?

GGGJ: Yes, I can picture all of this.

ANGEL: What instrument do you hold in your hand, George?

GGGJ: You mean, in the orchestra?

ANGEL: Yes. In the orchestra of fifteen thousand human beings chosen to play the most beautiful music humans have ever produced to accompany the arrival of Jesus Christ to the world for the second time! Do you hold a specific instrument in your hand?

GGGJ: I don't know. A drum? A Turkish drum? The kind that looks like an hourglass?

ANGEL: Does it matter if you hold in your hand that Turkish drum – called a dumbak – or if you hold a piccolo?

GGGJ: A piccolo? The tiny flute-like thing? No, I guess it doesn't matter. I've never played the piccolo, but I guess I could learn it.

ANGEL: That is the answer. The third analogy is your instrument – your part and how you played it.

GGGJ: Okay. I think I get what you're trying to say about my part. My part was to die by Al's hands while intending to kill him.

ANGEL: You have almost understood your part, George. But not completely. You will. You most certainly will.

GGGJ: The process will begin now?

ANGEL: Yes. And I don't need to ask. I know you are ready.

GGGJ: Yes, I feel ready.

ANGEL: Good. You can start whenever you're ready.

GGGJ: What do I do?

ANGEL: Use your power of will and wish yourself to be purified. Go ahead. Think of the connection, the interdependence between you and Altamaash, and visualize the healing of that connection with the Divine One's grace.

GGGJ: Right. *Will* it. Visualize the healing. This is strange. But here goes.

Altamaash's life, you are mine to explore, without anger, without fear.

Here, from his earliest memories, some of which resonate with my own: He is young, a child … maybe six or seven, standing near a kitchen counter doing something wrong that feels right. He is eating a toast lathered with berry jam, on top of which is piled a heap of Ovaltine powder; each bite spreads the dust of the chocolate powder into the air, and flecks of it on the floor. Standing with his back to the doorway between the kitchen and the hallway leading to the rest of the house. Looking out the screen door into the backyard where grass grows erratically, unmowed for weeks. He is six years old. I know this for certain, now, as his thoughts open up for me like a book. I can read his thoughts. This is what he is thinking, without knowing the exact words in which to articulate any of it:

'When you look at the whole thing from the future,' he tells himself, *'it will appear like a montage of images in stop-start slow-motion. As if life were not a grass field or a forest with many paths. As if it were not an open road in all directions. It will appear as if life was like the blank spaces of a crossword puzzle waiting face-up on the breakfast table – and, coming and going, you filled its spaces with some answers that seemed right, and some that were so obviously ill-fitting they put everything else out of sync with the truth of how you should have lived.'*

II. Altamaash

An artist must be his own first audience, testing whether he is in thrall of what he has created; only then does he know that he gifts to his spectators a performance of high calibre. So, perhaps it is appropriate that I'm feeling stunned; after all, I've murdered for the sake of entertainment.

It's a numbness accompanied by other absences. Seldom have I witnessed such a hush, such absolute stillness. The pavement doesn't make a sound as I plod forward. Cars, cabs and buses, the few of them that flit by, do so without the usual whooshing sound. It's as though the night is passaged through a sermon on the human condition, and sound itself is bowing its head. We're bleak creatures, all of us.

My body hurts. Ears still numb, though getting better while everything else is heading in the opposite direction. Wheeze is stuck in my lungs, kidneys bagged full of liquid, jiggled liver, over-jostled and empty stomach; ankles and soles of my feet, aching; I feel these organs and appendages jangling about me like cans of food being lunked around rather than parts of my own living body.

All these inner processes are happening without a sound escaping outside the body. There isn't a peep from my starving stomach, let alone a growl; I've not panted once despite all this exertion. Even my blood is thinned down, and not making its usual thick-puddle *glug glug* noises inside my eardrums. The coat and hat and stick are making no taps or shuffling sounds. Everything is cloaked in fog. My thoughts most of all. But there is this one, overwhelming desire: I need to piss.

I have, like a method actor returning to life off-stage after the performance, washed my hands and cleaned my shoes and grabbed a hat and stick from Ned's belongings at the back door to his house. There is hunger somewhere within, but I do not feel like eating. It's late and getting later. Here, spread out before me like a buffet table, is the same old London – the centre of the world – that has been my home away from the homeland. But something is different tonight. All the options springing up before me are draining me. I can take cab after cab. I can go to Regent's or Hyde Park or Kensington Gardens, sit on a bench and watch the geese sleeping on the grass, with their heads folded back within their wings. There is nothing stopping me from going there. But I'm unpropelled.

The parks have never helped settle my nerves in any satisfactory arrangement. They do not contain. They spread out, like suburban sprawl.

How did I think this spectacle would work?

There is lull before and after storms. Between one storm and the next, as well. What I'm feeling must be this dull lull. The anticlimax of having achieved exactly what I wanted. It came too easily, like a false note. Where's the trophy, though? *Settle,*

settle, dear spirit, and lift thy chin. You are made for grander things than thuggish murders. You are the conquerer of cities and countries; nought that you do will be in vain. And my spirit dares me, in return, to do something epic. Very well. If that's what I must do to deliver the burden of my own epic expectations, I must seek *grand* relief; I must get to the Thames and baptize it with my piss. Then I'll feel better.

That's all the certitude that can be mustered for now. I am a man on a mission: *get to the river; piss in it!* I'm a large bulk on the pavement, walking past neon interruptions to the darkness.

Something sharp jars the stillness. Everything is not quiet around this bank building's corner up ahead. Three hardly dressed women laughing as they hail a taxi. They cackle all the while it takes to stop, and even as they climb into the back seat. I want to go up to them and scream hoarsely: *I've murdered two people in the past hour!* Just to give them something to think about.

But even if I confessed, they wouldn't believe me. *Havin' a laugh, are ya?* That's what they would say between their cackle-giggles.

These days, nobody even confesses honestly. Why then would I blame only these three? I judge not. They're gone, in any case.

Skirting a park, I go past the Royal Albert Hall. Never been inside; enough opera and music in real life as it is.

All's quiet again. The museum is closed, as it should be. Further on, vagrants congregate in smoking huddles outside a street-grade all-night sushi restaurant. All-night? Someone would crave *sushi*, and go hunting for it at *2 a.m.*? A closed muffin shop next to that. Everything's looking rained-on, but there's no rain. There isn't even wetness.

The hospital, a few scattered gardens. And there's the dank dead-body-like smell of the River Thames in the air. Like a relative you never want to meet at their own house. That's this river.

I take off Ned's hat and leave it on a bench that commemorates with a plaque a child who died while in his mother's womb. I do it to get rid of the hat. To let the brim of it not hold back the night's flickering lights from my eyes. I want to see more.

I'm in Westminster. I know where to access the river here. I'll do it off Westminster Bridge. Better do it soon. Bladder's bursting.

Feet have gone miles and miles today. Eyes have seen ghastly things. Hands haven't trembled even once.

What kind of animal spirit am I? A strung-out stingray. Done the poisoning, now looking to settle back at the floor, the bed, the hearth-shaped home I got out of.

But I'm moving further and further away from St. Johns Wood. I know this. Why? Every step I take in this direction will be a step I'll have to regret not cabbing homewards. But all the old homes and homelands are drained of comfort. None of them holds what I need.

I'm empty too. All my reasons ring hollow. I need to sit and think. But first I need to piss in the Thames. That's all that's left to do. But there are waist-high barriers everywhere on the bridges, and I can't very well raise myself above them to expose all that lies down under. There's a trickle of foot traffic still; the occasional car as well.

Without my knowing it, my spirit has been sinking, one step at a time. And the abrupt clarity with which that thought enters the focal point of my attention is devastating. The hope of everything working out cannot last any longer. I turn a corner in further despair than there ever has been in my chest of burdens.

But here it is. An unasked-for boon. A small, majestic garden. Circular in shape. Or more like a C that is still in the process of becoming a circle. A fountain in the middle, not gushing but bubbling. A parapet of stones around the pool of water, benches, and an enclosure of the whole of it by tall and ancient trees. It's a mini-enclave lit by a single street lamp's glow, which may as well be the light of Heaven the way it's being parsed softly, dark greenly, through the leaves of a sycamore.

Here, staring at this, I want to own this; but I don't even know where I am. Is this still London, or another dimension? For a moment, it appears as though I'm in a garden at the bottom of an ocean. I've found Atlantis, have I?

For that split second, this is not water bubbling in air, but a holy spring flowing into the world's collective body of oceans.

I move forward, step out of the magic of this place and into its reality.

I push the low gates with the wrought iron dragon-head knobs. The gates swing inwards without any rusty squeaks. I walk up the stone path to the fountain and peer into the water. It's clear, virgin. It reflects the shadows of the multi-sycamore canopy. Not an insect stirs. A soothing, constant gargle of water from the spigot is all I hear. I lean the stick against the raised parapet around the fountain, sit down on top of it, and tug at my legs to pull them up on the flat platform. I lean back and splay out on the width of the dryness and watch the bubbles form and disappear in the pool.

To enter the water would be to wade into the Fountain of Youth. I know this like I know that this grotto doesn't exist on any map. Some enchantment, no matter what you do to dispel it, lingers. I could take my shoes and socks off, and put my aching feet in the pool into which the fountain is draining. But I won't.

Things are becoming clearer. There is definite systematic purpose to my being here tonight. To think through it all. That's primary. But there's also some rejuvenating force flooding through the area. I'm spiritually soothed already.

The only wish is that to this meditation could be given the respect it deserves, by my sitting up with a straight spine and my legs folded one on top of the other – lotus-like.

But this spread-eagled leaning-back position will have to do. Reasons of bulk. Should be the title of my autobiography. As if.

This, my Bodhi tree moment, so tranquil, this water.

Now I can think, and also hear my thoughts.

I'll begin by leaving my here and now. Go back to the past.

Used to be, in the early years of the exile, it would have been impossible to sneak out of the house. There would be six bodyguards on every one of the three shifts, and I'd have a whole entourage stationed in and around the house. Party workers, bootlickers, well-wishing idealists. A handful of them still come back when I'm lashed in the media – maybe they like the trickle-down effect of attention – power by association. But it's nothing like the old days, when the Karachi office would make sure I had enough funds to employ what was needed to keep the pomp going.

It was temporary, their vigilance and devotion. It only lasted the first eight to ten years, when there was still chance of my triumphant return. But things changed.

Governments of bastards, bitches and fat men followed one another without removing threats to ol' Al. I would have done the same to me, really. I would have kept someone like me far away from Pakistan. And if I were an expat in London, I would stop visiting a person like me once he'd lost clout as a politician. Haven't been central to the political lives of my people for years. Naturally, they must move on, avert their eyes.

They'll pass me in the Waitrose or Whole Foods and experience the awkward two seconds of deciding whether to own up that they saw me. Acknowledgement will mean making eye contact, and perhaps bending a little to show that they remember the power I once had.

It's lucky in a way, because there are fewer witnesses of how long I've been away from home tonight. Only Phil or Jordan were dodged; and none of the old guards know where I am. They're all guessing I'm indoors in a St. Johns Wood citadel, sound asleep, snoring. And the womenfolk in the house are thinking I'm out painting the town red. Not too wrong, that.

Years of little activity except the money coming in from back home. Everyone's gone complacent about Al's upkeep. They don't want to keep both eyes open if they can afford to rest one. Nobody's alert to possibilities nowadays. Not paying attention; that's their biggest mistake. I've outwitted by outwaiting those whose attention wavered.

Tonight's the night of reckoning. Back home, this is the last day my party's members are waking up to go about business as usual, not giving enough consideration to what Al is all about. Such a pity it had come to this.

Years passed without event. But insolences crept in. What began to sting was the dwindling attendance at the Annual General Meeting of the Immigrants Party, which I hold over Skype with the entire Karachi clan of the party's senior members. Mostly a check-in; a howdy-doo. A celebration of the new Islamic year, when we ratify our party's plans and go over what's to come in the next cycle around the sun.

Close to thirty years ago, when I was elected the Pakistan Immigrants Party (PIP) Chairman, I knew there had to be drastic changes in the way the Immigrants demanded their rights. The old way – the dead way – it needed to pass. I linked that thought to the act. There was a purge, in which scores of the party's own people died. Some were shot. Others met accidents in traffic. Some showered their last showers with poisoned water.

Only fifteen of the previous leaders survived that purge. Those fifteen middle-aged men had never held any office in the party, but they had always been worth their weight in votes. Fifteen votes on the Leadership Council is what they counted as. (Over the years, five more have died, but the ten bendable old men who remain on the Leadership Council, are worth the stringing along of any party votes I want to conduct my way from far away.)

And there they remained, while I filled up the party's main offices with people my own age; young blood, fresh thoughts. They formed the body of the party. In time, they came to be known in my thoughts by the names I assigned them.

Let's start with the lower, base duo. Like anchors, the two of them. Encoded forever, those foundational two as Bashful and Sleepy. Both assertive, in-your-face, partners in crime who killed in public without compunction or forethought (the other Leadership Council members and I had to order more hits of witnesses to their crimes than I cared for), they were always more bodyguard material than party leaders. But they had ambitions above their skill levels. I thought it prudent to give both of them seats on the council. Bashful was Security Chief; Sleepy was Co-Security Chief. That kept them together and happy.

The rump and sexual organ of the party – I began calling him Sneezy, for his frequent coke vacations and lady-boy trips down to Phuket, his favourite vacation spot. I wonder if he sneezed or ejaculated more on those trips. He was Spokesperson for the PIP; a great performer of gibberish legalese behind the microphone. The drugs kept him several cycles of wit and news ahead of the press that came calling for answers about bodies and protests.

Happy and Grumpy – both these clowns were stoics, so I was compelled to add emotional slants to their names. You couldn't tell where their allegiances lay – with the intelligence services or the Immigrants Party? But they were never ruffled in the middle of any operations conducted by or against us; plus, they had great contacts. We all chose them as the liaisons with the army and intelligence agencies. Happy and Grumpy were the gut of our organization; they connected everyone.

Only two other people remained; my right- and left-hand men:

Dopey: the opposite of dimwitted, a man who knew how to get money in a flash, and make bodies disappear off the face of the planet – a fusion of corpses with anti-matter is what he achieved. Nobody ever found traces of the victims' existence. Except, he did slip up one crucial time. More on that later. Dopey was Co-Deputy Chairman and pleased for the longest time to remain as such.

Until, that is, the Deputy Chairman of the party, the man I began thinking of as the wicked leader of the seven sinful dwarves – Doc – began to make his move, shifting the younger set of the Leadership Council's loyalty. Deputy Chairman or not, he was both stupid and clinically unfit to rule.

They wanted to do away with me, the head of the party, the face of the new blood in the party. Of course.

Other than the informants who told me about their huddles, which began a decade ago, they never openly defied me. But then, a few years ago, *not* to attend the AGM became 'a thing'. They made reasons out of excuses – a death in the family for Dopey; or Sneezy would be out of the country. I've got pics of his debauchery with Thailand's most questionable gender benders to prove that the leave-from-country-and-annual-party-meeting was rather forced. Two of them not at the meeting. Two out of seventeen. A lesser man than myself would have labelled it coincidence. But I knew it was a trend they were trying to set. A defiance they were trying to creep into the operations of the party. Of the seventeen people in the leadership council, I could trust ten.

Five years ago, it was Dopey and Happy who didn't show up. Four years ago, three of them excused themselves from the Annual General Meeting on the 8th of Muharram: Happy, Sneezy, and one other from among the ten conformists. Three years ago, Happy did deign to attend the meeting, but both Bashful and Sleepy didn't. They were out on an operation sanctioned by the party's deputy, my right-hand man. I didn't say anything then. Then two years ago, Mr Deputy himself went missing, along with Dopey and Bashful. Three of the seven missing again. I was salivating to act all through that meeting two years ago, but kept mum. Last year, the absences crossed the threshold of the Instructions. Four of the seven did not attend. Beautiful, I thought, and gave myself the countdown of one year to put into effect the killings of tonight.

This is why I killed. *This* is why I opened a blood-tap that must open much, much wider. Not just the seven sinful dwarves, but everyone in the party will hear of this. Phil will make sure to let all the bodyguards know, and from there it will spread like a forest fire. They're going to fear me like nothing they've feared before, not even the Altamaash Bhai of the old days. But before I put the Chinese whispers into their terrifying progression, I must start off the other half of this show; I must rouse the old resting demons – the common people. More than two hundred million of them.

May divine spirits bless this enclave of trees, and this fountain and this otherworldly mothership that they've created. I needed this retreat into myself. Yes, it is unfair that this sanctuary is hidden away in this affluent corner of the city rather than publicly accessible in the middle of Hyde Park or Hampstead Heath. But the whole gambit of life is unfair. Getting more and more distortedly unfair. Exponentially lopsided. The see-saw is tilting nearly vertical between the masses and the ones they serve.

Not to get all Marxian, of course.

But to solve. That's my vision.

Shouldn't have cursed Raskolnikov earlier. I'm as purpose-driven as he was. Different targets, different target audiences, but similar mindset.

I was born for the stage. A coulda-been stand-up comedian. A shoulda-been actor and performer of satire. I was given the gifts of language and performance that could not be used in the country where I came of age. The gift festered and rotted into another kind of talent, one that could be used for a wide array of purposes. With my loose and limber tongue, I could have sold polyester to insurance salesmen.

Or, as successor to Grandpa Pir, I could have targeted the pulpit of the mosques and then of the religious TV programmes as they cropped up. Could have even stayed a low-paid actor with a planet-sized face that nobody wanted to cast in their plays and films. Could have stayed poor, thwarted by fate.

I chose to be raised on the other arena of entertainment. I chose politics, because, in the Land of the Pure, in this day and age, politics is the true mode of entertainment.

The murders – even though they're laced with intent, the creation of intent is also performance. It's a curse to be a performer without an act to carry out. And, bitter as my head has grown – yet emptier of the bitterness as it is feeling with each breath of the misty air next to this bubbling fountain – I'm not sure if it'll bear out. Murders then riots, the whispers that turn into shouts of fear for specific members of the party, then the powerbroked passage through Immigration and Customs. Will it all hold together?

The first condition: I needed to re-recruit my own people. Make them certain that I am still that same old menace who was forced out of Pakistan. The apparent double-suicide of Ned and Guardian Greg, which only my people back home will be helped to decipher in time, as my call to action and resurgence – that creates the conditions for the rest. My people, my splintered party of workers and campaigners must come together. I have created the clarion call of 'Attention!' They will awaken; they will fear.

Most of all, the six-headed splinter group within the party, and Mr Deputy Chairman, the Doc who's always trying to take over. They must think of me like they think of the most capable killer – one who does not get caught; one who is ready to take an entire country by its bullhorns and wrestle it to the ground. They must think this: *If Al did this to strangers – a reporter and someone who was auditioning to be a bodyguard – what's he going to do to us?* But the dwarves are the visible menace. This act is for the rest of the country as well.

Eventually, once the course of this plan comes together, I will subjugate the people of Pakistan under my rule. I will return home. I will be the king of all that land, and the owner of all its people. This is my vision. *This* is why the double-murder.

Along the way, I must entertain. There are elevated stations of glory and power marked out by fate for those who by discipline and hardship, or by chance and luck, reach them. For all the rest, life is unfair. But that is why entertainment exists and is essential. To distract and provide catharsis to those who don't have enough of what they want.

And if I can create a performance that not only entertains but also produces the magic of absolute wonder – that state of abject awe, so that I, along with everyone else, is among the collective audience of a miracle I've set in motion – why, there's absolutely nothing else like it.

And so, I killed Jorge Gary Guardian Greg. And I killed Ned the wannabe bodyguard.

No, I did not plan the lined-up shot. It was supposed to be much messier, a two-bullet affair. But things have come easy to me once I've put my mind to doing them. And so, I keep doing them, these easy things. Prophetically inclined as I am. As if some handheld lever pulled inside me clicks in sync with the goings-on of the world. I cannot disobey these ambitious inclinations. Some things must be done. To show my people that for them, for their causes, and for their desires, I will do anything that it takes. *By any means necessary.*

The fountain has healed my doubts. Whatever I've done, I've done it with good reason. And the rest will bear out as it should, or even better than I can plan.

After sitting undipped and dry here all this while, I finally reach down and lower a hand into the water pooling under the spigot of the fountain, and flick some of the cool liquid at my face. Then I get off the raised platform and walk back to the gate, ready to go on with the next scene in the act.

But, wait. No. Not like this.

I go slowly back up the path, heave my full body to stand up on the platform, open my zipper, and take out my pissing pistol.

Aaah… There.

With that urge relieved, this is no longer an enchanted fountain. I've sucked it dry of that.

III. Edwin 'Ned' Steinberg

[Transparence of glass all around. Edwin 'Ned' Steinberg floats as grey smoke, weightlessly suspended, a silhouette in the realm that is not space and is not bound within time. Edwin 'Ned' Steinberg's eyes are open, but he is blinded by the absence of substance. He does not feel at ease. He pulsates – the grey smoke that is him, does. A white speck appears in the distance, far above him, and it glows brighter. Edwin 'Ned' Steinberg watches the dot and squints. The dot begins to emanate speech, and its size increases and diminishes as the volume of its speech goes up or down.]

ANGEL OF TURNING AWAY: I begin in the name of the Divine One, who is Bearer of Judgement and Pronouncer of Sentences. I am the Angel of Turning Away. Your name is Edwin Steinberg, and in the land of the living you were called Ned. And you have been labelled an 'unwelcome wretch', a 'pitiful existence', a 'bringer of shame to all that surrounds you'. Do you acknowledge?

EDWIN 'NED' STEINBERG: Beg your pardon?

ANGEL: You, Ned. I shall call you by that diminutive. You. Ned. You 'insect'. You 'flotsam'. You are the Spiritual Detritus of Muscled and Deflated Regrets. The Past Tense of Exercised Will and Guzzled Proteins. Unrealized People Person. Delusional, Murder-Suicided Cautionary Tale. These are your introductions in The Belly. You are here for now, but not for long.

NED: Hey, how – what's going on? Who are *you*?

ANGEL: I am the Angel of Turning Away. I am the one who Denies and Disintegrates, by the Divine One's command, those who have lived as wastefully as you did. Do you understand?

NED: No. No, I don't. Please. What's going on?

ANGEL: Of course, you don't understand. You weren't meant to. Plus, you made no effort.

NED: Understand what? What effort?

ANGEL: Ned, why do you think you're here?

NED: Here? Where – I'm – Oh. I was drunk and now I'm dead, I think. He killed me, didn't he?

ANGEL: *He* did kill you, yes. Why else are you here?

NED: Here – you mean here as in – wait, what is this place?

ANGEL: That doesn't matter, Ned. You won't be staying long.

NED: Wow. I'm grey and smoky.

ANGEL: That grey smoke is your essence, Ned. But, again, not for long.

NED: What do you mean 'not for long'? Why do you keep saying that?

ANGEL: You've been sentenced. Denial and Disintegration is your sentence.

NED: Sentence? You're judging me?

ANGEL: No, Ned. *I* never judged you. My job is only to initiate the process of the sentence after making sure you understand what it is.

NED: What's the— what sentence?

ANGEL: You've been told the sentence already. I am the Angel of Turning Away, and my job is to Deny and Disintegrate. You are to be Denied the vision of God's face and His glory. And, you're to be given another fate: Disintegration. As for who judged you, who do you think?

NED: *I* don't know. God?

ANGEL: Did you believe in God, Ned?

NED: I, well, I don't know. I don't think so. Not outrightly. But then there were some strange moments that could have been… So, God was real?

ANGEL: Do you think it matters whether you believed in God?

NED: Matter? I guess it did, right? I mean, that's why I'm being … Denied? Is that it?

ANGEL: And Disintegrated. Denied *and* Disintegrated. That's your sentence, Ned. You did.

NED: Denied? Disintegrated? I don't understand what that means. It doesn't make sense.

ANGEL: Not right now, it doesn't. But I'll help you understand.

NED: Okay, but – wait. Can God forgive me? Can I pray? I want to beg for God's forgiveness.

ANGEL: You didn't pray when it could have helped. God's not listening to you any more. He has turned away already.

NED: Oh…

ANGEL: You know what that means, don't you?

NED: It means I'm done for?

ANGEL: I'm afraid you're not far off the mark. There's not much to console you with, Ned. Nor do you deserve consolation.

NED: I'm that bad, am I?

ANGEL: I'll tell you this much: you're not the worst. At the same time, you're too far from the best of the humans. Just too far.

NED: But what did I do? I don't remember hurting anyone. I don't know what I did that's so wrong.

ANGEL: It's okay, Ned. You're entitled to some denial. Take as much as you need. Fill your lungs up all the way if you like.

NED: You're mocking me.

ANGEL: No, no. You did that yourself, Ned. Do you want to figure it out yourself, or do you want me to tell you?

NED: Tell me.

ANGEL: You're sure?

NED: Yes. I'm sure. Please. I can't believe I wasn't good enough ... I mean – everything was rigged, I bet. God never gave me a chance to pray. I mean ... I was young when I died, but I wanted to do some praying later— And I did some good things, you know. I saved women from drinking dangerous cocktails. And I helped people out at the gym. I gave free advice. I paid for a friend's membership. I did some charity stuff. I sheltered a cat once and fed animals at the zoo. I took care of my parents; sent them money quite often. And I made some old folks laugh. Doesn't Jesus say somewhere in the Bible that even a smile is charity? I did that. I smiled whenever I could, even when I didn't feel like it. And I watered my garden and fed some ducks and played the piano to ease my troubled spirit when I was younger. I ... but ... but what did I do *wrong*?

ANGEL: You've said it yourself, Ned. You've listed nearly every kind of goodness you shared in your life. And I'll tell you that the weight of that list, including some other things that you forgot to mention, is literally that of a dust particle compared to what you were supposed to do. You say the whole thing was likely rigged against you. It was.

The odds were always stacked up against you. Just like they are stacked against everyone. And, like everyone, you were supposed to transcend the odds. You too. Yes, admittedly, given your limitations, you couldn't be expected to solve world hunger. But you could have fed *someone*. No? … That's not an entirely rhetorical question, by the way. As for what you did wrong, there is nothing like genocide or child molestation or lynching or desecration of other people's beliefs in your ledger. No. You did not do much that was harmful to others, Ned. You are not among the worst to walk the earth. That is why you are not being sent to Hell for eternity. You are not deserving of such constant torment as the fires of the Pit.

NED: Oh, thank God. Thank you, God.

ANGEL: Having said that, you also weren't of much *use* to anyone while you existed, Ned. You were, biblically speaking, lukewarm. Without much spiritual effect. The way you lived is the way you died; that is why you have been denied access to your Creator. You know how you died, of course. Altamaash, the man you called Al, he shot you in your mouth with your gun. You share as much responsibility for that murder as he does. You let him carry out the execution because you were in awe of him; you wanted to work for him so badly, you did not act out in principle against the kind of person he was. You really should have considered your values at that point, Ned. It could have been a turning point. It could have pivoted your whole life in another direction.

NED: I was – he – I got suckered by Al's charm.

ANGEL: You got charmed by your own desire to get suckered. You sought solace outside yourself. And now you will see what you enabled. As you Disintegrate, you will go through the many lives that Altamaash can lead in the future he lives after killing you. The vast range of his potentials will be laid out for you to witness. Now … Denial and Disintegration is your sentence. Do you know what is meant by Disintegration, Ned? Here's what doesn't even begin to compare: loss of all the muscles you considered so precious while you were alive.

NED: So … I'm going to disappear. Completely. Is that it? Shredded apart? Dear God!

ANGEL: You are receiving mercy only because you did not do anything egregiously wrong. Otherwise you would be facing a different kind of eternity. But it's a shame you do not get to be rewarded with Heaven and the presence of God.

NED: I – I feel ashamed. That body thing … I know now. What you've said, it rings true. I wish I could do it all over again. Everything would be different about my life.

ANGEL: Yes, it probably would be, knowing what you know now. But it's too late. The test is over.

NED: So, no more chances? This is it? I must Disintegrate? Now?

ANGEL: Yes, it starts now, Ned. You will no longer need me. You will no longer need anything. The process of your

Disintegration begins without you needing it to, and it goes in any direction required to smother you with your meaninglessness. It will finish when you stop existing.

[The speck disappears. Everything is transparent, all around.]

NED: What? Angel of— Angel, don't leave me. Please … well … at least I'm not going to Hell. But, I want to know something. Why do I look like smoke? And what *is* this place? Disintegration. My *God*, I won't even exist. Nothing at all. This emptiness. Looks like glass, this—

[He mumbles the last bit as everything shifts. A regular beeping sound is heard, coming from a hospital bed. This is what Ned sees next:]

A dark room in a hospital. There's someone breathing hard into a tube. A machine in the room whirs. Down the hall, in other rooms, beeps at regular intervals play the outline of what could be melody.

The body on the bed in this room is all wrinkly and shrivelled; a thick but weak and old husk. Its face is round like the moon, and the moustache, brows, and thin hair on its head are a mix of silver and black. A pipe runs into the body's mouth, and a smile of sorts plays on the lips around that pipe.

This cannot be the body of anyone other than Al. *This* is how he will die, decades after killing me. A *peaceful* death?

I am made to see this, through a blurred layer of smoke that isn't really smoke.

This must be the layer that separates ghosts from humans. And it was always there, when I was living, and there were angels and dead people in the other dimension watching how I lived. They knew I was living a messed-up life. And they did nothing.

The body's chest rises. It falls.

Rises. Falls.

Why couldn't this have been my death? Please, God, if there's still a chance for me, please forgive me.

5

The Path of Trials

You know you're in political exile from Pakistan when half of Pakistan misses you like a messiah, and the other half wants you lashed and lynched in public.

I. George Gary Gregory Jaffar

[In The Belly, the fuzz of grey smoke that is George Gary Gregory Jaffar sees, hears, feels, and is enveloped in this:]

Al starts diaries, he makes new year resolutions. It's the 1980s, and he wears tracksuits and clips on his Sony Walkman for early morning jogs in the park or by the shore one mile from his house. His body slims down by the end of Januaries. His face remains blimped, creating further disparity. The daily jogging sputters through Februaries, and stops by each March or April, but not for lack of resolve. It comes down to face versus body, and it's face over body that Al chooses. No matter how much he exercises, or stretches out his jowls by making and holding absurd faces in the mirror early morning and just before going to sleep late at night, that concentration of blubber in his jowls does not abate.

There are good days. When the roundness of his eyes and face is in sync, and the voluptuous smiles he flings across from the boys' side of the canteen at a joke to the girls' side is matched by equal and unopposing smiles. On those days, his humour works, his hot flashes of insecurity disappear, and not an iota of self-consciousness remains to bother him on his insides. The face that only a mother can love becomes the face graced with its unique look. Only *this* face can laugh with what seems like air-filled cheeks.

There are great days too. Sometimes, Sonia and Al walk around Karachi, throwing stones in the Arabian Sea, eating samosas and jalebis for lunch, and he will know exactly what to say. He will play the politics of their romance at the correct pitch, with the cards face-up or face-down, as required, as destined. She is his to pluck on those days.

Then there are the less than perfect days. Still, after decades, the non-immigrant Pakistanis discriminate against the immigrants, stinging them with labels like 'Mohajir', 'Indian' and 'Urdu-speaking'. The pulpit of students and young immigrants from India to Pakistan is lacking passionate speakers for their cause in the new country. Many young leader-types try to fill up that empty space behind the microphone. Their voices don't match the ground realities, or their audience's indignation. Too angry, with little or no effect. Too pushy, with excess treble in their shaking voices. Too thin and small to be leaders, some of them, despite their words and echoes matching the wavelength of their audience. But then Altamaash – Al *himself* – takes the stage.

In the early days, not having personal conviction in the cause or himself, he mimics the other speakers, and delivers his thoughts in short, crisp, but snippety sentences. Too sharp for the human ear. Someone records a few of his speeches, and Al hears those on tape, not knowing what to do to differentiate himself. Then he hears himself on the local radio news, having been coincidentally singled out as a 'typical speaker' at the local Immigrants' rally. That day, Al decides he will take to the stage in a completely different way.

Come the next rally, he's a sight to behold. Among the beige and grey waistcoats, his blood-red silk one with weaved-in snake-like patterns stings the audience's eyes. Only a thousand students and flies-on-the-wall attend the university event, and most come because there are free refills on the tea. Many plan to escape the hall after drinking their fill.

Altamaash is the third of six speakers on the docket. Each man is allowed between seven and ten minutes at the podium to present his vision for achieving more equality for the Immigrants.

After the second shrill speaker, they announce Al's name. He fixes a Mona Lisa smile on his lips and walks very calmly to the podium. The microphone squeaks with sharp and quick feedback when he approaches it. That is the last dismissible noise from the electrical setup, and, though the hall is abuzz with activity over the pouring of beverages and gossip about the latest student-professor seduction scandal, in a few seconds there will be atomic silence. A thousand people half-filling that room – this is where it will bud and bloom, that burgeoning bloody flower.

With dead quiet eyes, he remains standing soundlessly behind the podium. It seems ineffectual at first, and so it is, because the vacuum of sound spurs on the Karachi University students and loafers to speak their vapid opinions in louder whispers. Another speaker, another blah-blah rant; so what? That's what they're thinking.

Gradually, as if from their subtextual, collective unconscious, the scattered buzz of gossip notwithstanding, the audience begins to realize there is rhythmic, heavy breathing coming from the speakers. And some will swear later that there is a growl in the bass layer of that sound. It raises goosebumps, this menacing moment filled with nothing but breath – it being let in and let out. A hush swims its way from the walls, where the speakers are positioned, to the centre of the hall. Eyes turn this way and that, checking to confirm the experience of this moment with the meeting of other eyes. And once shrugs have been shared, everyone – standing in the tea line, or sitting on the broken-down seats – faces Al.

'You have all become used to your second-class status,' Al says. No 'Ladies and Gentlemen' or a 'Bismillah' as a formal opening to his speech.

Sound is frozen until his next words.

'You beautiful people. You glorious intellectuals. You idiots. You cowards. You rangers of independent thought and dependent action. You bloody rascals. You heavenly discards. You creators of nations and martyrs of freedom. You nincompoops.'

A little noise. A buzz. Then silence again. These are wake-up-call words from the speaker. Altamaash, the round-faced funny one, the class clown – he isn't being funny right now. He is calling them out.

Someone in the audience shouts, 'Who the fuck do *you* think you are?' A few laughs follow in support of that catcall.

At the podium, Al snarls. 'Call me "Dad". I am one of you. I am the broken. I am the one who is being stepped on. I am the hammered nail. The coffin lid – that's me, and that's you, and that's all the children we will bring into this godforsaken country. Immi-*grunts*? Immi-*CUNTS* is what we are. Getting nailed with our own bodies into our own corner of the ghettos of the big cities. We are the cockroaches who dream of becoming butterflies. Look around you, you wasted flesh-pots! Meet up, eat each other's shit, drink the cafeteria's piss-tea. That's all that we do.'

Truth stings the hall. It shames the thousand tea-drinkers. Nobody slurps from their cups. A girl starts sniffing and someone tells her to leave if she can't handle what is being said, but not to pretend it isn't being said, and not to ask that it not be said, because it needs saying, and finally, yes – finally, thank God – someone is saying it.

'La la laaaa,' Altamaash sings on stage, into the microphone. His first melody.

Blunt. Tuneless. Hoarse. 'La laaa la laaaa la laaaaaaaaa.' He glares at the one thousand of them. They wait for the message in his eyes to be translated into actual words. They stand transfixed, holding on to the mad hope that this man behind the podium is the one they have been waiting for. Logic-crooners at the microphones have failed to rally them. But this – *this* is something else.

Madness begets madness. Al stares them down and he steers hope out of that room. 'You are a gob of saliva,' he tells them. 'You are frothing on the ground. All around you there is dust and garbage. And you are part of it. You deserve nothing more than this piss-tea and this heap of broken dreams.'

He steps back from the microphone. Inside his head, there is a harangue of six more minutes, riveting entertainment disguised as excoriation (or vice versa), still waiting to be delivered. But he knows he's placed his bid just at the right cut-off point.

They will bet on him here and now. They'll stake their lives, eventually, but for now they will give their full attention to this young speaker.

There's no need to go into the solutions he's written out for his people. They don't want *solutions*. They wanted a saviour. He would be *that*.

(Decades later, perched in exile, with his anger having given way to lethargy and nostalgia, Al will confess in a motivational speech from London to his devoted millions via tele-link, that, had anyone picked up the one catcall and echoed its sentiment when he had been establishing his menace early on in that speech, he [Al] would have started shouting over his audience, and the magic would never have taken place. Al credits his people – his brothers, sisters, mothers, fathers, daughters, sons, all the enlisted Immigrants – for having faith in him since that beginning.)

After leaving the podium at this point, when he isn't even done criticizing half their stupidities, Al leaves the hall full of the Immigrant Party Student Wing members and stomps down the halls. He seats himself at his regular corner at the canteen, where he is quickly surrounded by his loafer friends. Others join them, wanting more of him. They come from the hall he has just left, where another speaker stands up to cheer the audience that quickly shuts him up.

At the canteen, the scolded and schooled college students don't rush to get in line for tea. It is 'piss-tea'; it always has been; now they are waking to the faults in it.

'Brother Altamaash,' they call him, the ones who don't know him well. And back then he isn't yet Al. It will take years and a whole lot of distance for him to become Al. His loafer companions become uncoupled from him. Sonia, his complicated relationship with her, it withers in significance compared to the 'Brother' he has now become. Good as 'Don', that 'Brother' is. Most often, it is said with reverence in Urdu: 'Altamaash Bhai.'

'Altamaash Bhai, our Brother,' they call him at the canteen, where he sits with one foot on the bench and the other flat on the ground, eating nothing. They ask him this: 'What do we do?

You have woken us up, but what should we do? You have told us like nobody ever did what problems we face and what idiots we are for not having overcome them for more than thirty years, ever since Pakistan's Independence. But nobody gave our fathers, the original Immigrants, any chances. So, what do *we* do? Who do we reach out to? Nobody listens to us, Altamaash Bhai. Please help us figure out what to do.'

Still acting, still planning his complete takeover of their senses, the man who will become *Al* looks disdainfully at them.

'Stop hanging about like dung-beetles,' he says. 'Get to work.'

They look around at each other. He looks at none of them. The middle-distance is his focus.

One of the hangers-on gathers his courage and says, 'But that's the problem. We don't know what to do. What should we do, Bhai?'

And Altamaash, their elder brother, replies: 'Do everything for the cause. Get your rights. No matter what it takes.'

[Not impatiently, but with curiosity about the process, George Gregory Gary Jaffar disengages from the scene within which he is ensconced. The glass of The Belly appears all around him.]

GGGJ: Angel, are you there? Can we still talk?

ANGEL OF ADMITTANCE: I'm here, George. How goes the process?

GGGJ: It's intriguing, to be honest. But there's some, well … perhaps the word is 'slowness'?

ANGEL: Slowness, George?

GGGJ: I wonder if, you know, if we can make this process go faster. I know that Al – Altamaash – he grew up in a politically charged atmosphere. I wrote an article about all this. So, can we get to the important bits without sacrificing the process?

ANGEL: Of course, George. Just use your power of will to view more pertinent moments. The process is made for you to take charge of, so you can work through your purification at your own ready pace.

GGGJ: Use my willpower. Right, so ... just *will* it harder?

ANGEL: The closest analogy to using your willpower in a direction is that of riding a Segway scooter. Lean forward, standing on the platform, and the thing goes faster. Do you recall the machine from your time on Earth?

GGGJ: Segway, of course. Right. That makes sense. I never got to ride a Segway, but I always wanted to. Do you think...?

ANGEL: In Heaven? For sure. But not the way you think. Even better.

GGGJ: Interesting; I'll look forward to finding out. Thank you for your help, Angel.

ANGEL: Anytime, George. You've earned it.

GGGJ: I'll go back now.

[Reimmersed, George Gary Gregory Jaffar witnesses the following, at a greater speed.]

In the beginning, the Immigrant movement manned by young and enthusiastic party workers like Altamaash is restive but ineffectual. Like an entity going through puberty, it doesn't know where to expend its prodigious energy, and falls into alternating bouts of running into a wall and slumping with listless, angsty fatigue.

The Immigrants will get grapevine stirrings about an old man not being allowed to board a Karachi-to-Lahore train because of his dubious Pakistani-ness, and they will descend on the station; but the old man will have returned home by then and the train will have rattled along long ago. Or was it just a rumour? They can't tell. The party's sophisticated information networks at the grassroots level is still being laid out back then. In lieu of solutions, the mass of Al's people chants slogans about equal rights for all citizens, and the graffiti artists among them deface the railway station's benches and pillars. 'Immigrants are humans too.' 'We're All Immigrants.' 'We're brothers from across the border!' 'Even Prophet Muhammad (Peace Be Upon Him) Immigrated!' Tame stuff.

Or they get wind of an anti-Immigrant parliamentarian coming down from the country's capital to rally the 'real' Pakistanis against the few newcomers who have managed to evoke enough sympathy from their interviewers to secure government jobs they deserve on merit. But Altamaash's people arrive at the scene and there is no rally. Just some politician sitting in some room in some building they are not allowed to enter. Displacements in employment are created and 'corrected' without fuss. The horde of Immigrants doesn't know what to do.

But while they regard themselves ineffectual, out of their depths, and impotent, Altamaash knows better.

In those early days, he often gathers a few of them – a different few each time, if possible – like favoured sheep, in the large echo-chamber hall where he first roused them with his disparaging speech. He hangs out with them, dangling his feet while sitting on the stage, or pacing about endlessly near the podium; and he listens to their voices echo and then dissipate in the otherwise empty room. Their complaints and resignations sound like the voices of frightened phantoms in the dark space.

His people's frustration is going to be his biggest power. He *knows* this. He can feel the energy of what they vocalize as an explosive force gathering potential for mass destruction. As though it's a live grenade, which he will have to hold for just the right amount of time, and which he will have to hurl at precisely the right moment to make the blast of it catapult his movement to the next level.

The sphere of his influence grows by increments within those early weeks and months. The younger lot rallies around him, though he gives very few speeches after that first one. The other speakers latch on to his message – half of them are converted to his cause and the others know they have no choice if they wanted to be heard. Only Altamaash Bhai's message will be spread among the Immigrants. Scold the downtrodden. Rid them of their victim status by scorching away their egos. And, all the while, keep playing with the words. Sometimes call them snakes, sometimes label them locusts. Keep them coming back for more symbolic slaps.

And then, one day, an Immigrant's daughter runs out into the road at precisely the right moment. She gets hit by a minivan and dies. How fortuitous for Altamaash that she doesn't linger on the deathbed, let alone survive. She dies on the spot, her head rammed into by the minivan. The driver of the van was looking up at God knows which balcony when he should have been looking down and to his right, from where the girl ran out of the gate of her father's house to get killed. Here is divine provision for Altamaash: the accidental kernel of an idea for the next phase in the Immigrants' lives. Of course, after the collision, the driver panics and hotfoots it out of there, never to be identified in any lineup. How incredibly lucky for Altamaash, then, that what he fights will be a ghost, an idea as intangible as the idea of immigration.

After that, life seems one long and tedious call for action. Never mind that 'action' is not what Al wants. No. He wants the end of inertia for his people; but he doesn't want the beast freed up completely. A chained monster striving against its chains – *that* state – that's what he wants. And his people remember his insults. They, the cockroaches, the rats, the caterpillars, skitter along the gutters of Karachi slums and gather en masse outside the houses of Karachi's parliamentarians, with the largest of their congregations stationing itself outside the residence of the province's chief minister.

'By any means necessary!' Altamaash shouts at the masses through his bullhorn. And he gives them a rough translation of excerpts from Martin Luther King Jr.'s 'I have a dream' speech, sprinkled with some of Brother Malcolm X's phrases. '… I have a vision of a country in which those who cross borders to become its citizens are held in equal reverence as those who have lived in the pure and promised land for generations. Many moons; many, many moons have we, the border-crossers, suffered. Scores of years more will we suffer, just as our sister suffered, taking her last breath under the heavy wheels of a public transit vehicle. Scores of years and shortness of breath. That is what we have to look forward to. Not to mention, we're unequal as fucking hell.' He paraphrases not the words, but the sentiment. He knows his people aren't ready for the eloquence of MLK Jr or Brother X's level just yet. Perhaps they will never be. But he will grab his people just like the American heroes got theirs: by the collars of their imagination.

What is the immigrant's wildest dream? Settlement. 'Ask the sons and daughters of Israel what was done to them,' Al declaims, and realizes that lack of sympathy for the Jewish people prevents his own audience from cheering at their loudest. 'Ask the Sons of Imam Ali,' he changes tracks, getting louder decibels from the audience. 'And think of our Prophet, may the peace and blessings of our Lord be upon him, who himself was among the immigrants to Medina. Weren't they welcomed with open arms in the land of their hosts?'

The issue is no longer the girl. She is only the platform, the one that has been awaited.

Five days later, Altamaash is arrested. He has prepared for it. He has passed down the first draft of what will become the 'Instructions' hours before the arrest: 'Fifty-five truck tyres in twenty-three different locations every day. Lay them out in the middle of the roads. Burn them. Shut Karachi down. Then go out on the streets that we, the Immigrants own. Only we, the cockroaches, can come out after the rubber-fires blaze on the hot Karachi streets. Don't fear anyone's authority. Come out in large numbers. And take over the city. Loot it! Loot it like it's never been looted before!'

It takes three days of this street-level realization of the citywide lockdown, and scores of cars and shops being vandalized, followed by the Karachi business community's vitriol against government inaction, before the authorities release Altamaash from jail with deals made in the party's favour. Al comes out wearing a pair of sunglasses. He looks like Rajinikanth, the Kollywood action hero who can flip a cigarette high in the air and fire a gun to light it before it lands right in his mouth. Altamaash, the Immigrant trigger.

The man who will become Al comes out of prison mythically transformed; a consummate politician already. He no longer attempts any changes in diet or adherence to exercise routines. He lets his body's increasing girth echo his ego's steady inflation, and he keeps the fiery hot Immigrants-related issues stoking.

(In the bottom drawer of his Karachi office, for the fifteen years he remains politically active in Pakistan after that first release from jail, Al keeps a copy of a news report, figuring one day he will get around to framing it. It's the account of a girl being hit by a minivan, the driver of which had fled from the scene of the accident. Altamaash, the politician, used that event to propel his people's concerns into the news that would reach all households across Pakistan. Altamaash, the entertainer, used the idea of an innocent girl's death to provide catharsis to his people. Altamaash, the human, couldn't let himself forget the girl. He wants to meet her in the afterlife, briefly, just so he can thank her for her sacrifice for the cause. What prompted her, after all, to jump in front of the minivan? He will ask her that when they meet in Heaven. She's already immigrated there, and he isn't planning on any other destination.)

Once Al is let out of jail that first time, he doesn't need to go back to the hall at the university. His people come to him at his house – herded all by themselves. Tamed as much as if they believe he is the lord their shepherd, and they the flock from a biblical psalm.

Twice more will Al go to jail, for similarly short stints. After those, he is too powerful a force. Two chief ministers of the province and a prime minister of the country attempt to jail Altamaash. The chief ministers fail – their police chiefs don't dare piss off the man who becomes the de facto Don of Karachi. They have wives and children and parents and dogs to think about.

The prime minister goes through the intelligence agencies as well as the police, but succeeds only in creating a credible threat to Altamaash's life – something he uses to gain a cause for asylum in England. He is tipped off. And that's when Al lays down the laws and the games and the traps in the blood-laced Instructions for what all his followers will commit to doing, should Al ever need them to cross thresholds that no political party in the country has ever crossed before.

He sets up those Instructions, then flees to England; seeking exile, he is welcomed like an endangered species, given refuge, protection and asylum in London. Here, in the St. Johns Wood mansion that he buys with contributions and confiscations, waiting and biding time until he can put those Instructions from his last days in Karachi into play, Altamaash grows in power and girth to proportions he would never have fathomed possible while living back home in Pakistan.

The first thing he does though – the very first thing: he officially changes his last name to Immigrant. 'Altamaash Immigrant' is how his British passport lists his first and last names.

[Disengaging from the too-fast forwarded summary of Al's past, the grey cloud that is George Gary Gregory Jaffar gathers his thoughts about what he has witnessed. He reflects.]

GGGJ: The way Altamaash lived his life on a grand scale compels me to know his past. Does that mean it's not important for me to know my own life as much as I now know his? That was rhetorical, of course. No need to ask that bit out loud. The Angel of Admittance said that I redeemed myself – earned my right to enter Heaven, whatever Heaven is – by merely intending to kill Al. *That* was my test and I succeeded. But what if I wouldn't have gone through with it even if I had been given the chance? Right … just look at me. I'm complaining about being given the all-clear to head to Heaven. Good grief! Meanwhile, God has other plans for Al. So, Al goes on living after he kills me. His role in the time-space continuum requires him to survive the feeble assassination attempt I made. Okay ... I can live with that. But then, will he too be redeemed? My *God*. Is that fair? Is that *justice*? Does anything even matter?

II. Altamaash

Back on my Edgware Road. God's, then mine; internally, I genuflect and give the grumbling cabbie a two-quid tip for amusing me with his belligerent rant, all the way from the secret garden to this spot, about Tony Blair's war crimes against brown people. Old Caucasian bloke too, so I wonder if he's hoarding my share of the indignation. I couldn't give a flying bloody Thatcher about it all, really. English, First World problems, these: wondering about international justice and the morality of corporate globalization and military intervention – blah blah blah. Felt like telling him that us brown ones can never suffer a permanent downfall. The desi springs back. Always.

On the left-hand side, across the main thoroughfare of Edgware lies Cafe Helen – the best reconstituter of meat on a spindle-grill-mechanism this side of the Arabian Sea. Call it döner kebab or shawarma; call it lamb, or chicken, or beef. Call it halaal, call it haraam. Grilled and sizzled perfection is what it is.

And on my side of the road, *Al*-wards, is the quintessential den of degenerates in the depth of doom'n'damnation; but, for this one night, it will be home away from home away from home away from – (exiles get that joke more easily): I'm talking, of course, about the festively lit Grosvenor Victoria Casino.

Regal appellation, that.

But Cafe Helen – isn't that name more primordially royal, given that it's got a touch of that Trojan whore in the name? *Bah – names.*

Great; fantastic; onwards, across the gap created by the parted cars to the other side of the street. The line's hardly seven people long. It will be short, the wait. But I haven't eaten for so many hours now that hunger has become a background motif.

I give my order at the window: lamb. In döner kebabs, always go with lamb. Beef's too dry and chicken's too chicken. Then I stand around waiting near the delivery window. 'Bloody beautiful night, innit?' I ask those waiting alongside me on the pavement. They respond not, they recognize not. The night-crawling hedonists. No matter. I repeat my 'bloody beautiful' line a few times, to hear my voice at different volumes and at varied pitches. I make a song of the deepest, gravelly whisper. 'Blood-bloody-beautiful, nighty-night innit?' The food arrives: wrapped in paper, the layers of bread and meat and strips of pickled veggies and gobs of white spicy sauce – Yyyyyyuummmm!

I munch bite after bite of the shawarma-döner. In moments, it's entirely down the hatch. Lamb and grits and pepper and spices and sauces and lettuce and tomato slices and pickled olives and all. One big taste. Good for another hour, I am. God help the personnel and atmosphere of Grosvenor Victoria Casino. No symphony, here. In my head now is a marching band shifting into high gear, with an entire legion's pumped-up stomps accelerating to nearly techno beat. *Uddst-uddst-uddst— bharhwa! Uddst-uddst-uddst— bharhwa! Uddst-uddst—* and so on, and ever faster.

At the reception in the casino, I show my ID: 'Al', it says, in the 'First Name' category. I've got an ID for every occasion. The man does not question, but takes my picture for the record.

Good citizen Al considers the lens of the tripod-camera on the reception desk, keeping his expression sly and cold.

After that, there's a lady at the coat-check. Brunette, cute; just-out-of-her-twenties kind of cute. Marginally affable at first while taking my things. I hand her my coat and stick and request separate tickets for each. She raises an eyebrow quizzically. 'To make sure I remember both,' I say. 'Wouldn't want to forget the stick.'

She nods and smiles like a customer service robot, points a trigger-finger at her head and says, 'Aah, smart thinking.' I nod curtly. She has *no* idea.

The first floor has all the lesser games and the second one is filled with poker tables. If one must gamble, one goes to the first floor. But, if one is in the mood to fuck other people over, then the second set of stairs must also be climbed. And Al will do both: gamble and deflower.

To initiate casino mode, one must warm up with the mini-games. I open the double doors and wade into the thickness of it all. It expires and inspires, this flatulent air cured with hints of alcohol, grease, vomit, döner and perfume. Without meaning to, I initiate a monologue of sorts. 'Hello, hello, denizens of this spit-choked narcoleptic underworld. I've got coins and cash aplenty tonight. Keep the roulette wheel turning, and the cards shuffling and flipping. This is just to warm up, this jerking off the machines that gobble my coins. A quid here, two quid there. This is nothing but foreplay. And the night is despicably young.'

'Did you say something?' my neighbour asks. He's got a toothless kind of face, this aged fellow of multiple, indiscernible ethnicities. I look at him with love and pity.

'I said this is a jerk-off activity not fit for grown men,' I say. He nods and laughs and puts a coin in the slot of his machine, without stopping his laughter and without neglecting his duty of servicing the machine.

'Yes, yes, oh-ho-ho-oh yes, you're so right,' he says. He pulls. He wins nothing.

I pull a lever and press buttons on two adjacent machines. Nothing in the first five drops of coin in each of the two machines. Very well. I take out first the mobile phone that will start the riot, and then the piece of paper from my wallet that has the two Pakistani numbers written on it each beginning with the country code '+92'.

'Sir, I'm afraid you're not allowed to use mobiles in here,' someone says, tapping my shoulder. I look around. Burly man. Bodyguard type. Behind him stands a leaner, hawk-nosed one who is probably even stronger. A resemblance to Daniel Day-Lewis in his profile. In suits, both. I nearly tell them about having killed their brother-bodyguard Ned earlier in the night. But, of course—

'Of course,' I say. A minor interval in the orchestral accompaniment. 'Bear with me please, while I make the call outside and then return. Do carry on with the gambling, the sartorial starchiness and other necromantic activities while I'm gone.'

'Thank you, sir,' he says, as I put my phone away and get up to leave. *Oh, Ned. Why couldn't you have been this good a member of the bodyguards' guild. I would never have needed to punish you along with Guardian Jeremiah Greg.*

I'm all jacked-off and jacked-up. Warmed up for the night. But there's one coin left. Heading away from the slots, I hand it to my neighbour, and ask him to use it next. The security folks and I watch as it leaves the old bugger's fingers to go down the slit in the machine, after which he pulls at the lever. Lo and behold. Nothing.

'Better luck next time,' I wish my companion. 'May the gods of chance change your fate.'

'Cheers, mate,' he replies, raising his glass of distilled spirits.

I start to head out the double doors to go down to the lobby, where making phone calls from mobile phones is allowed. But there's a buzz in my head from the stale air I just left in the gambling room. The call can wait awhile. I'm all warmed up for the money games. I flip shut the phone's lid and head back into the thick air. To the Black Jack tables this time. There's several empty stools. The problem is they're all *stools*. Seating arrangement that's not meant for as wide a set of buttocks as mine.

'Make twenty-one,' I say, recalling Black Jack rules. 'The perfect number. The golden ticket. That's why you're all here, right?' The backs of the gamblers don't reply. I carry on: 'This one is easy. You'll hit the high-target numbers several times, folks. The real challenge is what to do with fourteens, fifteens and sixteens. Do you stay or do you gamble?' Odds are where the game is played. I must math it up. 'Card-counting's for pussies,' I say, leaning my shoulder on the table at the empty spot I've chosen. I say that to insult the man I've observed counting cards. An obvious cheat; a basic cheat. 'Don't insult the rest of us gamblers, mate,' I tell him.

'Excuse me?' he says, turning to me. Handsome fella. The kind of non-committal handsome type that beds a new girl every week. Or maybe he's got someone steady and he's gambling to earn his way through medical school. Who gives a fuck. A cheat's a cheat. They need to throw him out. Or, there are other ways to get even with him. I've chosen this seat next to him to take his cues. It's him they'll catch if they catch the card counting.

'You best behave,' I say. I put two twenties on the table and the dealer changes them to chips. Never over-commit. The cards start coming.

'You mind your own business, fella,' says my new friend.

'Black as my soul is,' I whisper to myself and to the table's dealer, 'there are blacker souls still. And they're possessed thoroughly by darkness, which will lead them by chains to ruin and damnation.'

'Excuse me, sir,' says the dealer. 'Do you wish to place bets or lecture us on morality?'

'Both,' I tell him. 'It's that kind of night.'

The woman half of the couple on the other side of me chuckles. Middle-aged, playing her own hand while her husband stands behind her, watching her rake in the big chips. She looks skilled and lucky; he looks younger than her. 'Sure is that kind of night,' she says. Her accent is not from around here. South African? Aussie?

Her husband? Or is he her pimp? Whoever he is, he glares at my hand. Thirteen. I must now choose to either stay on my number or gamble for one closer to twenty-one. I look left and right at my companions.

'I make stories out of you all,' I tell them, even the dealer. 'I assign you roles in my life. Is that not what you do as well?'

We play on, and I keep interrupting my thoughts with my words. I'm talking to not pay attention to my mind. It wants to dwell on what's been and what's coming. I'm talking to soothe what's building up as ache in my head. But the cooing and crooning can go on only so long. Before a half hour is up, I've made fifty quid out of my forty. Ten pounds gained in twenty-five minutes. That's enough.

I grab my small stack of chips and pocket them for the upstairs room. My companions nod and smile their goodbyes as I leave, but they also let their shoulders down, as if they're glad to get rid of me and my incessant witticisms.

Going down the stairs to head outside, I swing out the doors and take out the flip mobile phone again, and the piece of paper with the numbers. I dial the first one and bring it to my ear as I'm crossing the street.

'Hello, Darkness,' I sing to the ringtone. 'My old friend.'

The man I've called in Pakistan picks up his phone after three rings. 'Yes?' I say the password: 'Bible and Quran. The Books of Immigrants.'

'Received, Bhai,' says the man. 'It starts?' Very, very well done. He's trained not to use my name. I trained him myself twenty years ago, and have refreshed the training every year since the day I created the first Instructions. Over the years, they have been modified to fit the updated contexts. And the last update was only a few weeks ago.

'Yes, son,' I say. 'It's time. Start.'

'My target?' he asks.

'The Fat One,' I say.

How ironic that it should be me calling someone else fat. Is that a chuckle across continents that I hear through the faint static on the line? Is he covering his mouthpiece and heaving with laughter? Well, if he is, it's my fault. Should have changed the code name for that fat and bald buffoon at some point. He's the only bald one among the targets, so it could have been an ironic *Hirsuite Harry* or a direct *Desert Head*.

'The Fat One,' he repeats. 'Done.'

'Good,' I say. And click the phone shut. Here I am again, in line at Helen the whore's.

Of all the food I can get on this street at an hour past midnight, why does only a lamb döner kebab figure as the right nourishment for the work I'm doing? Particularly since it doesn't fulfil either. So why do I return here, knowing it won't hit the spot? Gave up Nando's for döner kebab, I did. Isn't that a scandal?

I pay with cash, not casino chips. Money comes and goes in such different versions and in such varied transactions.

Mundane matters. That's what I'm using as hooks for my mind, to delay the inevitable. However, the weight of truth winds homeward to the eureka-craving centre of my conscious thoughts.

I've killed with my *own* hands. I fired a gun and I looked down at dead bodies. One shot, two corpses. This is like never before.

But what I'm feeling is not guilt. I suppose that will come later, if I fail. If the killing is rendered useless. Because it's failure I'm afraid of. All these plans…

Bah! Why should *I* fail? May all my enemies and their coming thirty generations fail from here on.

'Only fear I fear is the fear of failure,' I spout nonsense on the pavement where I'm waiting for the next shawarma. 'I took away their future with that shot,' I say. 'I yanked away their possible fates. They have no future because of me.'

The line moves quickly; men in the line – it's all men this time – they ignore me and my words. Fat, drunk man grumbling his confessions, they're thinking. I'm trying to say something; I'm trying to make the deed generally acceptable. But if I coat it with madness, no word seems like truth.

'Lamb, again, please,' I say at the window.

Then I look at the lights of the fast food joints still open on Edgware – all up and down the thoroughfare. A giant M crowns them all – M for McMurderer. The wait is over once the shawarma is in my hands and its paper wrapping is ripped and out, and into my gullet is teased the warm bread and the slaughtered and spice-slathered meat. Hoo yeah. Fucking greasy deliciousness. That hits – no; no, it doesn't really hit the spot. 'I'm gobbling emptiness,' I say with my mouth full. 'It's heavenly.'

Once done with that, and my greasy hands wiped down with ineffectually thin napkins, I head back across the road, show my ID at the desk again, and walk up to the second floor; the poker room this time. I'm done playing with my mind at the smaller game. Now it's time to play with gut at the bigger one.

That's the one rule of poker. Play your gut (got plenty in that department, don'tcha, Al? Haha). Forge new ways to play for each session, each hand, each bet, each card, each chip. That's the only rule. Forge something new. Make it a mystically creative moment between you and fate and the other fuckers at the table.

There's another rule too, but not many people can live by this one: know when it's time to get up and walk away.

But let's not get ahead of living life. I just got here. Tables of eight; all full. I put my name on a waiting list and order and sip icy cold water at the bar while savings are dwindled and fortunes exchanged. Tiny ones; merely ego-stinging ones.

Spots open up for the people ahead of me on the waitlist. Here's spread out a regular poker crowd with its desperate sets of eyes and the cloying sense of winning or losing without reason or accountability. I keep hydrating and watching players at the tables for tells. Hands fiddling with the table's edges, or with the cards or the chips. Nervous blinking. Nervous lack of blinking. Sighs. Twitches around the lips. Shrugs. Nostrils flaring wider. Everyone's edgy since I came into the room. Even those affecting stillness in their bodies. I smack my lips around the straw and suck in some water. This will be fun.

'Peanuts money. Nut cash,' I say to the bartender. 'That's what these people are gambling. When's the garbage truck coming around to haul them away?' I laugh a long and hoarse chuckle and force him to crack an uncomfortable smile. He doesn't know what to make of me. Good. That's the way I like my bartenders. Barely entertaining, uncomfortably conscious of their imprisonment behind large wooden counters.

I sip on, stay sitting on the stool. And I observe.

My waitlisted spot at a Texas Hold 'em table opens eventually. As I walk up to the seat, I recall the face of George Guardian Jeremy, and wonder how good he could have been at poker if I had schooled him. It hits me right hard, that thought. As if I've been drinking whisky, not water.

I put forward my chips for fifty quid from downstairs and put another fifty in cash on the table. The dealer gives a signal, and the pile of mixed currencies gets swept away. I'm given proper poker chips for the hundred, all of it split into fives, tens and a twenty. 'Let's play,' I say. There's a gentleman with sunglasses to one side, two old women at either end of the oblong table – semi-professional poker players, both – a youngish kid, a chubby chump, and a slacks-and-loafers-wearing touristy sort of middle-aged fellow (or is that a disguise?).

The chump's been rattling the other players' nerves with his incessant chatter and bluster. 'Yeeaaah,' he says, rolling out the word like a carpet. 'You've got a king and a low card of hearts,' he accuses the tourist, who's likely waiting for more hearts to show up in the last two cards. And he doesn't shut up there, the chubby chump. He talks like talking is gum to be chewed. 'I'll fold if you've definitely got hearts coming. But if you're waiting for more hearts, I think you're waiting mistakenly. There's going to be a club and a spades. So, don't go waiting for your hearts or you're probably going to get your heart broken.' He snorts, hamming it up. 'Play the cards without prejudice, remember.'

'Fuck the shut up, kid,' I mumble. He's getting a load of words out into my talking space. It's hurting my mind. Making me think of Gary Greg Guardian. Poor GGJ. He was worth six times the space in the world that this chub-tub takes up. Oh shit, what have I *done*? I've killed the one person who really *got* me.

'Say something, Pops?' Chub asks. I take a full look. I want to holler a heavy metal song at the pissant's face.

'Your dad should have worn a condom, son,' I say softly, and look back at my chips. One of the women giggles into her drink and then coughs and hacks. She slaps Chub on the back.

'Nice one, Pops,' says Chub. But he's gutshot. I've de-mojofied his bluster. It'll take him talking on and on for five more minutes before he can live past my insult. 'But you know how it is. This world's not for the scared or the hurt. We gotta gamble hard, you know.' Anything that comes into his mouth spills out for other people's ears.

'Oh man,' says one of the other men. 'Just stop talking, please.' Good. They're taking a ride on the impetus-train.

'Agreed,' says the woman who isn't coughing.

'If you want to talk,' I say, 'spout your philosophy, not weak guesses at other people's hands.'

'Yeah,' slacks-tourist says. 'Guessing hands is considered awful manners, you know.'

'Philosophy, Pops?' Chub asks, not giving up. 'What's *your* philosophy? Why don't you teach me some of your philosophy, Pops?'

'You can't teach philosophy,' says the coughing woman getting over her coughs. 'You have to live it, and then it's observed and noted. Then it's – *hack-ahhem* – emulated.'

'Well said, madam,' I say. 'You don't happen to know a Guardian Greg Gary Jeremy, do you?'

'What?' she asks. 'No. Who's that?'

'Oh, don't ask,' I say. 'It's a long, murderous story. But I'll tell you this much: he would have enjoyed talking to you. It would have healed an ache in his head.'

New cards come to me, face down. Chub is simpering. He's been out-bluffed, out-talked. I look at the cards in peace: two fours. Pocket fours. Fantastic. Low and mean little pocket nuggets.

Let me go with gut. It's only the first round … there will be more. I fold the hand before it becomes a nuisance.

And there it is. The one hand I could have looted the table on: with the flop and the river come out the other two fours. On the table; clear as mama's milk. And three people go all-in after the river. Two of them have full-houses. Chub has the lower full-house, and he is cleaned out. Now, he either puts more money down or leaves. He chooses to get up and stretch. But I know his kind; he's not leaving the poker room anytime soon. Not until he's talked his fill.

I would have had all the fours. I would have won all their money. But that's life. That's guts. All wrong, sometimes.

More hands follow, and some more conversation. But my heart's not in it. I even get a king and have it echoed with two more on the table. I win that hand, but nobody else goes in for much. Tonight's not my night. I'll lose everything if I stay longer than necessary. The table's fate has played me for a sucker this time. Mood's falling because of the lingering reverberations of Chub's earlier inane table-talk. And bad poker never helps.

Too soon after sitting down, I'm up from the table, taking my chips with me. Chub's been sitting at my spot at the bar since he got cleaned out earlier. As I get up, he takes my seat with fresh chips. 'You've got big clothes to fill, little one,' I tell him. I'm up by twenty quid and I leave. Nobody else does that in a gambling house. But then, nobody else is Al.

It's time for the second call.

And, yeah – why not? – another shawarma. Why am I still hungry? I've had two big ones already. Must be excited. Nervous too, a tad? A touch trembly, no?

Same route down, same route out and across the road, this time while dialling the other number on the paper. The man at the window at Helen's laughs at my return. I listen to the ringtone and to his laughter.

'Again, mate?' he says, eyes wide with wonder. 'You want an extra big one this time?'

'Might as well,' I tell him. 'Maybe that'll do it.' I doubt it though. This hunger has been building for years. It's not a stomach thing. It can't be sated with these white breads, synthetic sauces, fake meats and faux pickles.

The phone keeps ringing on the other end, in Pakistan.

Six rings.

Stay calm, Al; no need to panic just yet. The sacrifices won't go to waste. There *are* other things that can be done if this one doesn't pick up the phone. Other ways to reach him.

Eight rings. And counting.

I'm going to hang up after twelve rings. The mmmmmmother ffffffffucker. He picks up after the tenth ring. 'Bhai, Bhai? Hello?'

'Son,' I say, 'where were you? Why were you not picking up?' He knows his mistake. There's no reason to scream at him. I say it calmly. I keep us on an even keel.

'Bhai, I'm so sorry,' he says. 'I was in the bathroom and I rushed myself as much as I could when the phone started to ring. But it was – I've had awful diarrhoea for a week now. Food poisoning is what the doctor says. I've lost *twelve* pounds of body fluids in the past week. They don't know what's causing it. But I'm getting better. Allah be praised. Holding the fluids in finally. I'm sorry, Bhai. I should have kept the phone with me in the toilet too. But I didn't expect – I'm so, so sorry, Bhai. *Please* forgive me. Please, for my family's sake. I'll do *any*thing you ask. Please—'

'Yes,' I cut him off. 'You're forgiven. Do you remember all the Instructions about this phone call?'

'Yes, Al – I mean, oh *shit*. Yes, Bhai. I'm sorry. Yes, of course.'

Trying to placate him, so he doesn't blurt out anything else, I say the password: 'Bible and Quran. The Books of Immigrants.'

'Oh,' he says. Like he doesn't believe I would go *there*.

'I repeat,' I say. 'Bible and Quran. The Books of Immigrants.'

'Yes, Bhai,' he says, and drops something, maybe the phone. He picks up the fallen object, then asks, 'It starts?'

Good. We're back on script. 'Yes,' I say. 'It starts.'

'Bhai,' he says, 'my target? Is it The Fat One?'

'No,' I say. He's going off-script to pre-empt my orders. I'll write it off as side-effects of his diarrhoea. 'Not The Fat One. I repeat. Your target is *not* The Fat One. Your target is Mr Charming Bastard. I repeat. Your target is Mr Charming Bastard.'

Around me, the döner/shawarma eaters and their eyes perk up at my voice rising. But mumbling can only be suited for monologues tonight, it seems. This fucker in Pakistan, this asshole who I trained myself – him and his unplugged anal sphincter – he's forcing me to speak louder than I want! And I can't even walk away from the food that's coming.

Well, I could. But it's imminently coming. So…

'Acknowledged, Bhai,' comes down the line from Pakistan into my flip-phoned ear. 'Mr Charming Bastard is my target.'

'Good,' I say, ready to end the call. But before I can do that he's at it again. 'One question, Bhai.'

'Yes?' I ask between my gritted teeth.

'Um, about Mr Charming Bastard, my target,' he says. 'This means I have everyone start riots, right? I mean, not *take care* of him, as in *completely*, but just start riots against him, right?'

How—how—*how* the *fuck* – could I have chosen this piece of shit to be one of the two point-persons for this incredibly important job?

'Just the riots,' I say, my brain boiling. 'Repeat. Just the riots.' An oxy-acetylene flame couldn't be hotter than what's blazing at the centre of my head. Can't seem to unclench my jaw. But better this than scream at the, the, *this*—

'Okay, Bhai. Received. Riots only. Target: Mr Charming Bastard.' After that, he, mercifully, stops blabbering. I swear I'll murder again once I see this fart-brained buffoon in Karachi! May God give me strength and life enough to do what I want with him.

'Good,' I shout. 'Bye.' And then I shut the lid of the phone before more mistakes can be made. The *mother-sister-father-brother-fucker*! The phone in my hand would burst into shards, were it made of glass. Its plastic bends and the inner gadgetry crackles with shorting circuits.

'Are you all right, mate?' A drunk young man eating a chicken shawarma asks me. 'Need help fighting someone?'

'Thank you,' I say. 'I'm okay. Everything's okay.'

'Can you spare some change, mate?' the man asks. I look closer at his shaggy hair and dirty clothes. Ah, of course. Why else would he start a conversation? Wants money, this guy? Fine. I take out a poker chip worth a whole pound and press it into his palm.

I grab my shawarma from the delivery window. It's a big one all right. Nearly twice the size of each of the previous ones.

'Much obliged,' says the drunk beggar. 'This coin is really big.'

'Yes,' I say. 'Spend it wisely, will you?' I start to cross the road.

'It's not even metal,' he calls after me. He's got nobody else but me. The other kebab eaters are avoiding him. But maybe he's a soothsayer, a prophet for our times. Why don't I stop to consider that, now that the thought has flashed across my mind?

'Because he's drunk,' I tell myself out loud, 'and I'm tired; I've been robbed of a good poker session.' Because one of my two minions in Karachi, the second one, just now, didn't remember the riot-starting script well enough to regurgitate it despite his diarrhoea.

'What use is training if it's not followed,' I ask the night, 'especially in emergencies? And oh, yes, the real-real murder-murder earlier. That's weight of a different kind.'

I eat and keep talking; nobody's around on this side of Edgware, just outside the casino's entrance.

'And with all this happening,' I keep talking on to fill the silence and absence. 'I cannot process the possibility of a drunk beggar being the truth-teller for our times. We don't get the truth, let alone a truth-teller. All the prophets have come and gone. We're left without their guidance. All we have is hearsay. All we have is leftovers. Even the food these days doesn't satisfy, and yet we keep eating. We should protest and go on a hunger strike.'

Shawarma's done. In the casino, again, I cross the lobby and go up the stairs to the first floor. Poker's over for me. And the Instructions have been relayed. The flip phone must be discarded soon. It's time to end the night. My words keep coming. 'A rumble in the stomach,' I tell the people and the casino. 'I feel it. It's a wrestling match between food and constitution. Let's bet on something. I bet food wins and constitution weakens. I'll spin for it.'

And I head to the roulette wheels. When ready to enter back into the thick of life, spin some wheels. That's my credo. Pick ten numbers; place low bets. Then alternate that with picking colours instead of numbers. The balls spin around the wheels at every station, while the gamblers watch them closely. I watch them watching their flights of fancy, already spending the little incoming cash and chips on the next turn of the wheel.

'Why does nobody know when to step away from the table?' I ask my spinning host. In his bow-tie and tux, he gives me a nod. I give him my chips. 'Place everything on zero and the last nine odd numbers, will you?' I ask him. 'Zero's my last twist for the night. I'm negating luck and chance. Money flits away from me like a bad dream. I hope nightmares don't chase my sleep away.'

He nods. Maybe he's just the quiet type, or maybe he's full of menace. Maybe he committed parenticide. Went and killed his Mama and Papa. Haven't we all?

None of my numbers or colours hit. The ball settles at 22. Two little ducklings, 22. But that's another game.

'I'm even now,' I tell the spinner. 'No money lost; only the hours I've spent on gambles and phone calls. The night is latching on to me. I've eaten three people's meals and I'm still hungry. Not unusual for someone as sizeable as me, you reckon?'

He nods. 'Place your bets,' he says, spinning the wheel.

'I bet you'll suffer,' I tell him, and take what's left of my chips.

To pee or not to pee. Always the question.

After a short leakage in the toilet, I walk over to the slots.

At the slots, there's the toothless man from earlier in the night. He's still jerking the machines off.

'Hey,' he says, as I come closer. 'Any luck?'

'Fuck luck,' I tell him. 'Make your own fortune. Here.' I give him my chips. 'Take a head start. Go bust the tables up.' I also leave him the tickets to collect my coat and stick. 'All yours.'

'Wow. Thanks, mate,' he says. A hundred-quid worth of mixed chips. Still, he keeps sitting there as I leave, pulling at the slot-machines' johnsons.

I'm walking down the stairs and making no grand exit as I leave. The staff at the reception probably think I'm coming back again. But no. Al is done for tonight. 'Except, I'm still hungry,' I say out loud. 'What's with this awful, empty foodstuff? Why can't I feel filled up?'

'Excuse me, sir?' the receptionist asks. 'Did you say something?'

'I'm still hungry,' I tell him. 'Not a good poker night.'

'The kitchen is still open for another hour,' he says from behind the counter. 'I bet your luck will turn around if you stay. The menu is available in the poker room.' He's just another kind of bartender.

'Keep it open,' I say. 'Keep the food circulating. We'll need it until the very end of time.'

'Right you are, sir,' he says. I leave him within his comfort zone behind the reception desk. If I had the gun still, I wouldn't leave this place without a mini-massacre of the desk people. But then, I probably would. It's just the hunger and the wretched poker night talking.

No dessert tonight in the form of hybrid games that blend poker and blackjack. Not tonight. I'm all gambled out.

Out the door, across the road. No more calls to make. Assignments have been handed out. 'I bet they'll do a good job, my Pakistani minions,' I say to the few pavement-walkers. At Helen's there's a group of boys gathered. They look young and feisty; they laugh loudly, troubling the night with their camaraderie. 'Don't they know this hour is for solo flights in the darkness?'

I get in line behind them and recognize my native languages: Urdu and Punjabi. They're sprinkling their conversations with them. Cuss words galore. Wish *I* had friends. Right. Must be lack of nutrition and the after-effects of gambling and violence. Friends. Hah!

'Hey, hey,' says one of the boys, turning to me. 'Isn't that Altamaash Bhai?'

I look directly at him. Could pretend to be a foreign obesity for the night. But heck. I asked for friends. 'Getting hungry, boys?' I ask.

'Altamaash Bhai, it's you!' shouts the kid, and the others turn. 'How are you? I've been watching you on the news for years.'

'Hale and hearty, ready to party,' I say. 'That's a political ideology to live by, when you're cooking up shitstorms.'

The boys are in their late twenties. Corporate lackeys by the scruffy, loosened shirt-and-tie looks of them. One of them shakes my hand. Another takes out his phone. 'This is such an awesome coincidence running into you. I'm a big fan. Can I get a picture with you?' he asks.

'No,' I say. 'Not tonight. The lighting isn't right.'

They order food. I direct the creation of my next lamb concoction with extra spice and pay for their food as well. Their Pakistani-ness is contagious. I devolve. I talk to them about gambling. I almost give them my rules. Because the casino is where they're heading after the food. If only they had come earlier, been with me all night long. But it's not too far off, the day when I'll have whole hordes of young ones like these running a country with me.

I break white bread and lamb grits with them. We converse like civil citizens of a far-off homeland. We discuss our flawed nation. They fix Pakistan with their talk. I've already set up the fixing with my actions. But that's not a topic for polite conversation with kids. They'll find out soon enough as it is.

When I take leave, I do so with slow steps. And my skilled ears pick up what they're whispering in their excitement: 'He's *so* huge.' And 'What an *asshole.* Living like a king in London after ruining Karachi.' And 'Fuck Karachi. He's ruined *all* of Pakistan.' I smile at their judgement. It's flawed, of course, but not for long.

I have walked the night off. It's time to hail a taxi. I get in the first one that's on duty and give the cabbie directions for home. In the back seat, I'm a happy commuter. An inner peace takes hold. The ambitions rest in their place. I know they are achievable.

Soft, soothing tones in the music now, past the first climax, homing in to the final chords.

Rumination is in order. '*Huge*' is what the boys said I am. Yes, that's true. However, big as I am, it is possible to get bigger. However large my empire, a larger one, an Ozymandian one, a Solomonian one, looms as a distant target. What good are offshore accounts if one cannot open one as far away as Jupiter? That is the primary concern: How to create an empire, when the empire needs to be both tangible and ethereal.

There is, in the East, a ready-made kingdom I'm planning to waddle over and wrest control of. Some elementary questions surface:

How will it happen? That is the important one. The smallest distance from powerlessness in London to sovereignty in Islamabad is a double-murder and a riot.

Who is lodged in my way? The Pakistanis who disbelieve. They must be rendered faithful.

What crimes will I commit? Call them resolutions of issues – or facilitation efforts – or deliverables. Good old 'collateral damage' is a tidy term. We'll start with that and come back to it if needed.

The four big döner kebabs have left me unsatisfied and belching. My blood feels thicker; coagulated, trans-fatted, poisoned. Need oranges and water to make it run like fluid again. Swallowing back the spit that has accumulated in my mouth – I'm unsure whether the salivation is from the deed, or from a hunger that I am unable to do anything about.

Here's home. The cabbie pulls at the reins and the car comes to a halt outside the gate. I pay – cash, not chips. And out I step on my overworked feet. They threaten to trip me, but I weigh them down. Opening the gate, I walk up the driveway. There's Phil, standing at the front door, shaking his head at me.

'Phil,' I nod.

'You've been out, boss?' he asks. 'Why didn't you tell me?' He doesn't move out of the doorway. I should do him like I did Ned. But that's just body aches and fatigue talking.

'Needed to run some errands,' I say. 'You were required with the ladies.'

'Oh, boss, what have you been up to?' he says, shaking his head like a disappointed mother. 'How long have you been gone?'

'Just long enough,' I say. 'Thanks for your concern.'

'Concern? It's my *job*, Al. You should have taken me or Jordy. You could have got into trouble.'

'Oh yes. Or I could have been trouble for someone else.'

'What?'

'Nothing yet, Phil,' I say. Time to plant the subliminal thoughts for Phil. And then to let them fester inside him.

So I say: 'It'll be announced soon, though. Keep one ear on London news, and the other one on the goings-on in Pakistan. Pretty soon it'll be party time. Three words I'll give you: *bouncer*, *reporter* and *riots*. Remember, I believe in sharing good news.'

'What do you mean?' he asks.

'I mean to sleep,' I say. 'We can talk later.' I move forward. He moves aside to give me room and I open the door. *Al has arrived*, I want to announce as I enter. There's whispering in the air. After shucking my shoes off, I follow the sounds. They lead to the living room. The TV's on, and the womenfolk are there, sprawled on separate sofas. The television is on mute, showing a bearded fellow; the whispers are coming from my wife's and mother's mouths. They're praying for our family's safety and prosperity. They don't notice me entering the room. I shuffle over and stand directly behind the sofa where my mother is lying down, to listen, and to be closer to the soft Arabic chants that have kept us out of harm's way every single day and night of our lives.

III. Edwin 'Ned' Steinberg

[Desperate, hopeless, suspended in absence of colour, in an infinity of transparence.]

NED: If I don't move, will there be no more visions?

[As if in answer, things shift and transparence fades; the contours of Al's backside take shape in Ned's line of sight, and he is made to witness this from behind the buttocks of the big man.]

Al is leaning back against a large desk. From behind him, on top of the desk, like a settled speck of dust, I watch him. He is draped in a charcoal black suit, and his purple tie is as wide as a hand spread to its fullest width. This is the day of his daughter's wedding, many years in the future. It *can* happen, this day – that's what the Angel has told me. I am the witness undergoing Denial and Disintegration.

'Brother Al, please help,' says a grovelling man into the dimly lit room. Al pushes forward from the desk. And his rump fills up my blurry vision. This is what is being granted to me. Al's ass. I am forced to stare, now that I am only a point of view. In the lower parts of Al's butt cheeks, there is visual hint of a gathering fart; turbulence; an air-pocket; a mini sonic boom. This region has its own air currents.

For the past fifteen minutes, Al has been listening to his guest explain issues with the Treasury of Pakistan – specifically, the guest (the country's finance minister) has been caught laundering funds from the country's dollar reserves to Al's bank accounts in Toronto and Adelaide. But a rare honest fellow at the National Accountability Bureau has thrown a spanner in the works by threatening to publish his report on the money laundering in a daily newspaper.

Al is, in this future scenario, more important than Pakistan's finance minister. A king-maker. He is also much larger in girth and height than the minister. He looms over the man like a death threat, in the shape of a boulder, about to tip over any second.

'So,' Al says, bringing a hand out of his pocket, spreading it wide. He grins at the bodyguard positioned near the door to the room, then looks at the man begging him for help. 'You've been called to account for all the funds you've embezzled…' He pauses, considering the topic on hand.

Fifteen hundred guests are mingling outside, in the garden, where Al's daughter is getting married to the finance minister's son. Al has chosen the kid because he's got great genes – not the Al-family big moonface (though that'll probably reappear a generation or two down the line). His daughter's groom is tall, with a big chest, etc., unlike his dad, the grovelling finance minister cowering in front of Al.

'And you want me to save you,' Al says. 'You want … my help … to save you … from this … em-bez-zel-ling…' He lets out a silent, choke-holding fart right in my face. I swear I can smell it. A mix of fermented, gut-passaged meat and yeasty bread. Dis-*gusting*. 'Okay. You'll get my help.' Al leans further forward. 'Do this: Just say no.'

The finance minister blinks. He waits. There must be more, of course? No. There is no more. Al doesn't smile while he waits for the message to sink into the minister's head.

'Say *no*?' the man eventually asks. 'As in, deny the matter?'

'A "no" is hardly denial,' Al says. 'It's akin to the opposite of acknowledgement.'

'What?' the minister asks. 'But – how can I get away with saying just "no"?'

'When they ask you to corroborate the facts,' Al says, 'don't corroborate the facts.'

'But—b—the facts are undeniable. The money, the paper trail, everything is there. They *have* it.'

'Yes,' Al says. 'They do. So what?' He nods at the only other person in the room, the bodyguard, who walks over with a hand held out. On a platter in the bodyguard's hand is a silver tie-pin. Al picks it up and looks down at his ultra-wide tie. It's unneeded, this pin.

'What if we are exposed?' the finance minister asks.

'Hmm,' Al says, and the finance minister wonders if the large man is contemplating the tie-pin or the matter of the money-laundering.

Al looks up after a few seconds. 'Are you that blunt an instrument that my euphemisms aren't adequately processed in your cerebral cortex? Do you not know the extent of debt you're facing by asking me to solve this petty nuisance rather than going ahead and getting this done on your own initiative? Do you think the National Accountability Bureau is made of members without families? Do you believe limbs will not be torn from torsos, and bodies will not be flung in gunnysacks outside some houses? Do you want to spoil my daughter's wedding with trivial matters, like paperwork on money trails or sitting still in front of an investigation committee, that cause me to go into a tirade of rhetorical questions? Do you know the best method to ensure that the angle of a tie-pin stays constantly at zero degrees to the horizontal axis? I lost my earlier one, you see.'

I try to pull away, but cannot leave. Not yet. No choice in the matter.

'I – yes,' the finance minister swallows and backs away. Al steps forward to close the distance between them again.

As if from deep underwater, I hear my own voice calling for the Angel. I can feel my words entering the depths of a still and deep lake before disappearing without ever becoming audible.

But over and above my own frail attempt at language, I hear a woman's voice from outside the room where Al and the bodyguard and the finance minister are creating the scene to which I am witness. I hear the woman, and I am riveted by her voice. It's the clear voice of innocence. 'Is he in there?' she asks at the door. She's asking a bodyguard, perhaps, where Al is. Her voice is a wonder. There's a sweetness in that voice that I've never heard before. Like the little girl inside a grown woman is asking that question.

Is he in there? She's a young and beautiful woman with deep brown eyes and thick black hair, and she's holding in her hands a small bouquet. And it's uncanny how I can picture her just by hearing her voice. Unbelievable how I'm able to imagine a fully clothed woman. And a beautiful woman I'm not repulsed by. That's the biggest wonder of it all.

There's a knock on the door.

'Come in,' says Al, and the finance minister in front of him backs up, gulping, glad that Al is no longer following his movement.

The door opens, and in the doorway is the silhouette of a tall, solid woman wearing a knee-length white skirt, her hair down to her shoulders. I can't wait to see her face as she moves forward out of the shad—

[Scene shifts instantly to neutral, anesthetic glassiness, and absence of any colour except the small puff of grey smoke that is Ned.]

NED: But she was just going to – Angel! Angel! ... Angel! Are you there? Angel of Destruction! Angel of Denial, are you there? Angel ... of Denial and ... Disintegration? Ang—

[Pure transparence blurs, and into view swims a set of pearl white tiles in a washroom; Ned watches from a fly-on-the-wall angle.]

That woman. Not here. She's gone. What did she even look like? Her voice... Will I see her again?

Antiseptic hospital white. That's how white this room is.

Al's in the toilet. Heavier than the previous vision. But he had dieted for his daughter's wedding in that one – so is this before the wedding, when he's in the process of losing weight to fit into the suit he bought for the ceremony? Or is it a different year in the future, in a completely separate possibility? Is there a way to tell?

Anyhow, he's here in the toilet, after having taken a heavy dose of laxatives. He's grunting, as if in pain. Mid-section irritation. I know what that's like. And I fear knowing what he's about to do. I watch, thankfully not from behind him this time, as he unclips his belt and lowers his trousers. To be Denied and Disintegrated and suffer the punishment of visions such as this because God has decided to tur— that was it! Angel of Turning Away! Oh, blast it!

Al lowers his large briefs, and I watch, because I am forced to watch. Can't blink, and can't picture that woman from before. But that voice. Like a lilting song. *Is he in there?* she asked.

He's in here, all right. So am I, unfortunately. I only exist as a floating viewpoint. Not allowed the luxury of looking away from the mounds of his mountainous butt. Huh. Strange. It's not as hairy as I thought it'd be.

Did I ever do this to a toilet, like Al is – did I eclipse the ceiling's light bulb and become the porcelain bowl's menacing shadow lord?

I'm moving. I'm being lifted off the wall. I'm hovering in air. Uh. Oh.

Al is lowering himself with the aid of a large metal stand placed next to the toilet bowl. He grips it and looks behind himself, as far back as he can see, as he aims and lowers his backside.

I'm leaving the comfort of air. I'm nose diving. Oh no. Oh no. I'm going behind him. No! Al's almost lowered down, he's nearly cheek-to-rim-of-bowl … maybe I will escape – bounce away by hitting his skin or the toilet seat. But oooh … oh no … I'm *accelerating* … ohho no! I'm dipping down, and I've been *sneaked in*, in the nick of time. And now … I'm being turned face up … from the middle of the inside of the toilet bowl!

I'm *in* the bowl…

I've often wondered if God was everywhere, whether that included toilets, but … no … not like this—

I'm being turned … I'm facing up … up his—

The *horror*! The … horror! The abject terror! Like a spaceship door, it— Angel! Angel! ANGEL OF TURNING AWAY!!!

[The bathroom disappears. Again, everything all around is utterly transparent.]

NED: Angel of Turning Away. Angel of Turning— please, please … please, never do that again, *please.* Disintegrate me before anything like that. Deny and Disintegrate me. Do it now if you like. Please do it. Are you – where are you? Will you answer? Ever? Hello? … Hey ... Are you out there? Will you reply? I went to the toilet hundreds of times. Was someone always watching my ass? I mean, from under me? An angel, or a ghost, or someone waiting for Disintegra—

[Transparence blurs; browns and greys swim into view and begin to form shapes. A podium, a chair – no, lots of chairs. A classroom? No. A hall. A sigil of the map of the world, enwreathed and grid-lined, hangs on the wall that the chairs and desks face. Screens. A stage with three chairs. This is the United Nations General Assembly hall.]

From above, I look down at the room full of leaders of nearly all the countries of the world. A fishbowl is what this looks like. And the largest man among all of the ones here is him. Al is sitting in a large, custom-made chair that accommodates his increased girth. Much larger than I last saw him. In front of him there is a plaque that says 'Pakistan'. He's representing the country.

His name is being called: 'Altamaash Immigrant', and there's a rumble of wood as the heads of states acknowledge his name and his rank by pounding their fists: he's the prime minister of Pakistan. He gets up with difficulty, leaning on a cane.

I don't want to see this display of world politics. Politics is boring, always has been.

I want to see my Mom again, before I'm gone.

That woman's silhouette in the doorway, the day of Al's daughter's wedding. It reminded me of Mom for some reason. She was pure like that. Motherly. Like she could protect.

I want to walk on the grass with Mom like I did when I was only five. I want to be five years old again, I want to go back, Angel of Turning Away. Are you listening? Am I speaking? Or are these thoughts?

Can't I go back, to the old times, just for once? I know that isn't as important or exciting as Al becoming prime minister of a country, or the heads of states gathering in the halls of power. But I love my past. It was simple. It was pure. We had a good family. This flash on the world stage, this politicking, this circus that pretends to be important, it doesn't matter to me.

Angel? Can I not get that instead? I know you can hear me.

I watch from on high, like I'm a light bulb on the ceiling, looking down. Hundreds of people here, all cheering.

Al's standing up all the way, and now he's taking ages to haul his obese body to the podium. There's constant applause. They're standing and clapping at his unhealthiness.

It's very bad. He now needs *several* rounds of liposuction. It's disgusting. But of course, I'm missing something. The cheering… What's the deal here? He walks one shuffling step at a time. He reaches the podium. The standing ovation continues.

I wouldn't cheer for this. I don't even want to be here.

Mom's pancakes. Sunday brunches. That, from childhood. And feeling Dad's brutish strength as he pitched us boys around the backyard, playing a mix of Tag and Cowboys and Indians. That too, from when I was a kid. And then biking downhill among the dales in Yorkshire. The head rush of it. That, from my teenage days and nights. The one time I pedalled downhill at full speed while blindfolded, daring myself without anyone around, and ended up with a broken rib and fractured foot. Then, years later, all grown up, moving to London to get a job other than farming ... the days and nights drinking away at that place in the dark corner of Borough Market. What was the name of that pub? Then discovering the gym when I was twenty. The sweat of effort ... results of hard and heavy lifting of iron, and falling in love with Nadine after that—

—can't go back there. Can't ever relive. Instead ... here.

Al's at the podium, finally, and he's raising a hand to get everyone to quiet down.

They whisper and gush praises at him, all two hundred and something heads of governments. What's he done now? He smiles fatly. Gross. I can still see that last segment, the – no. Don't remember. The ghost of me will puke.

At the podium, he's starting to talk.

'Fellow leaders of the free world,' Al says, 'with your help, and with the prayers of millions around the globe, I have been able to bring peace and prosperity to Pakistan.' More applause. Cheering. Korea's President Kim Something-Something claps and cheers the loudest as everyone gets to their feet. Another standing ovation.

'Go, prime minister Al, Go!'

'Awesome!'

'You did it!' Huh? *He* did it?

'The Age of Terror is over,' says Al at the podium. The cheers and clapping climb a few more decibels. Is it even true, what he's saying? Peace in Pakistan? Terrorism finished?

It happens, like it's happened before. The blurring is intense in my field of sight.

I shout something. Or do I? I don't think so. There's no voice. Al is saying something at the podium, but even his words are garbled.

[Transparence of The Belly reappears in an instant, and then instantly fades. In view comes a bed in the hospital where an old and wrinkly Al lies machine-bound, his body being inhaled and exhaled artificially via machines and pipes.]

This is the same bed, and the same angle from which I saw him last when he was dying. The body's chest rises. It falls. Rises. Falls.

The room is dark. It's night at the hospital. Near the foot of his bed, in a reclining chair sits a young woman. No, it's *the* woman. It's *her*. Except, older; much older. Is this *the* woman's mother? The words come back at once: *Is he in there?*

A dark shawl is draped across this older woman's shoulders. I can see part of her face through the hair that's fallen across her cheeks. She sleeps with her mouth open, forming a little 'o'. Stunning, gracefully middle-aged, oval face, full lips. Wish her eyes were open, and I had hands so I could brush away the hair from her face. Maybe wake her up, watch her frown and squint as she'd look around. I want to see her looking at me … too late, though, too damn late. I've got no hands with which to wake her. I've got no voice with which to call her. She looks so full of peace. Maybe I wouldn't disturb her sleep even if I were able to. Just watch her until she wakes.

Where's that younger woman though? Must be this one's daughter…

When's the last time my thoughts about a woman were so – so chaste? On her lap is a creased and refolded newspaper, her finger and thumb have marked the place where she's left off reading before falling asleep. And I'm forced to read it now, as my line of sight is filled up with what the text says. Closer and closer I move.

Al, the 'former prime minister of Pakistan', is 'headed for prison' if he ever gets up from the bed where they have lain him, given up on him to die. But 'he's done this before – defrauded the nation with a hunger fast while in office'. The country's 'in a tailspin' since he 'went into a diabetic coma'. The public is divided: some 'wish him speedy recovery' while 'others are asking for the life support to be stopped' – even journalists 'want him to wake up or die spectacularly'. It seems everyone wants him to continue entertaining them, even if it's by dying.

The elegant sleeping woman. I try to turn my face up from the newspaper to see her aga—

[Transparence, sudden and severe. The white, pulsing dot looms on the horizon.]

ANGEL OF TURNING AWAY: Pray, Ned. Pray now. God is merciful. He may disintegrate you at once. You need not suffer any more.

NED: Okay, okay. I'm praying, Angel, I'm praying. Our Father, who art in Heaven. Hallowed be thy—

ANGEL: No, Ned. This is not prayer. This is scripture. You need to pray. You need to beg. Speak from your inner core. Pray like you've never done before.

NED: What? I—

[Transparence rushes away, and within frame comes a less bloated Al than Edwin 'Ned' Steinberg has ever seen him; he's walking and jogging in bursts in intense early morning heat on the side of a road that stretches from one end of a desert to the other. Edwin 'Ned' Steinberg floats over the mirages in the near distance, watching Al's slow progress.]

—pray? I don't know prayers.

Al can't even walk and he's attempting to jog. He's wearing a billowing grey tracksuit that flaps about him in the hot wind. Is this really the future? Will this happen? Looks so real. I can feel the heat. It's early in the morning and already so warm.

Am I never going to disintegrate if I don't pray? Will I have eternal visions of Al?

The heat is pungent. His flesh is giving off odours of meat and sweat and stale clothes. At least he's burning some of his fat in this marathon walk-jog. Much thinner than when I last saw him. Finally, he's being punished too. He comes closer to the dip in the road from where I am being made to watch this.

Nothing else is alive in this desert. Is this a world of symbols? Is it Hell?

He smacks his dry lips. He coughs – it is a wheeze and a rasp. Does that mean Al's dying?

But what about the hospital bed? And the woman, who *is* she?

Which of these things will actually happen? The desert or the hospital?

The corner of my eye catches *her* again. The same woman. I'm sure of it. But this time she's in a runner's tank top and tights. And, dressed like a runner, she's running. Fast, long strides. She's coming back for slowpoke Al. She's his – *trainer*? No, can't be. But she looks fit. *Super* fit. Like she can run for hours. Loping, with animal grace. Like fluids move, without any waste of energy. She's reached him and is handing him her water bottle. He stands still and drinks.

I remember how she said *Is he in there?* But she doesn't say anything now. The bottle goes from her to him and back to her without any use of words. I would love to have such silent communication with her.

Al moves on. She stays in that spot, standing tall, with her long neck slowly turning. I have to struggle to see her now that Al has moved on. She's in the blurry end of my vision, but I can see that her eyes are not completely brown. They've got some muddy green combination going on. Her limbs are tan and taut. She's muscle and skin. Lithe, all limbs and lips. And with her beautiful eyes she scans the horizon in each direction, taking her time. I can read her thoughts from the way she's looking at the horizon. She's wishing she was out there, running harder than she is right now, among sand dunes, spending her grace on rocky uphill sprints. She's wishing she could use her body for what it was really meant to do.

This time, I don't even try to call out to her. The silent communication that she had between herself and Al – that's what I want with her. Al is already up the road a half mile before she starts jogging after him. With an assured look in her eyes that says he will never be too far for her to catch up to. I love that about her. That quiet confidence. I've felt it too. And I've always wanted to share it.

I— I must pray.

God, are you there? I want to pray to you. Please, finish me. I don't want to exist. I beg you. Please have mercy. Please do that if you can't give me someone like—

[Flash of pure colourlessness. A white dot pulses.]

ANGEL: Good news, Ned. Your tribulations are nearly over.

NED: Angel, that woman, she's—

ANGEL: Yes, Ned. I know. That was your last trial.

6

The Dreamy Woman

You know you're in political exile from Pakistan when you see your face on TV news channels more than you do in the mirror. The discrepancy of on-screen older photographs showing a different you is like hangnail to your sense of self; you stop looking at mirrors and become something you have to look up: 'spectrophobic' – afraid of your own reflection.

I. George Gary Gregory Jaffar

[Going back and forth to and from The Belly into Al's past, George Gary Gregory Jaffar muses on the many parts of Al's life he has now seen; most of all, he thinks to himself about the women.]

GGGJ: And again, I slip in and out of Altamaash's past, forgoing my own life as though it were an inconsequential dream. Curious, that I'm letting go so easily. I use power of will to progress forward, and a new chapter of Al's story opens up. I navigate and pontificate. He's been married twice, though they – his party members and the journalists who come and go – they don't talk about the first one. It's not something Al wants talked about. That one's a torn page from his life.

And where has this page fluttered and settled? Become a makeshift plate for channa chaat? Rotted in some gutter in Karachi? Been found on the street by someone gracious enough to allow space in his heart for a loose page to become part of his book? Yes: remarried, most likely. This other woman, this could-have-been branch of Al's life several forks in the road ago, what does she think of Al when she inevitably thinks of Al? How has she processed the providence of that early divorce? They divorced when he was twenty-five; she was only twenty-two. Just two years after they got married. Does she miss Al? Does she – most likely a grandmother by now – wish she had, instead of her own husband's, borne Al's offspring?

And Al must miss her sometimes. He must touch the scar of her on the body of his life. It must brush up against things as he goes about his days. The graze of raw tissue that never heals against the grains of dead stone and splintered wood that every life resembles up close, once the layers under the visibly varnished ones are given adequate light.

A woman who becomes a mnemonic device. A tag with which to categorize an age of history. Before Sonia. *BS.* After Sonia. *AS.* Within the two timeless years between those two epochs of Al's life, Altamaash the Boy becomes Altamaash the Man. Deflowered, un-umbilicated, exiled, other'ed even from himself. His bloated and growing jowls remain the only constant through the otherwise thorough transition.

He does not gain or lose favour with his God. His bank balance remains around the same subsistence amount. But fortunes are altered, and fortunes are always linked more with the future than with the present or the past. Kismet. The lines engraved on his hands since birth veer in all directions in time. The two marriages cut into the wrinkles on the side of his palm will come true, of all things, because the first one ends soon after he fails to make anything of himself in the party or outside it.

She leaves him because he is persistently angry and manipulative. A passive-aggressive gorilla, she says to her shocked parents, as she yanks at the clothes from her suitcase to fit them back in her childhood room's child-sized closet.

Al does not come to persuade her. He does not come to beg. He does not come at all. He lies on his bed and tries to tangibly cry. The cut is so deep, there can be no healing. She has left him when he is at his lowest, going lower. Dawaa, the pharmaceutical company that has hired him as a part-time salesman is going deeper into red. Crimson and pitch black are the only shades left for it to enter.

The last inherited million from Grandpa Pir is leaking through the holes in his incompetent father's hands. Both the Immigrant Party's factions want other people as youth leaders. Al is not even a contender. Despite his two stints in prison, and his popularity as the party's most entertaining and popular young up-and-comer – because in Pakistan the skill to enthrall does not guarantee wealth. It brings only expectations. A mascot-hood.

Does her – that first wife's – heart beat with the fire of those uncertain days in their twenties, when Al could have been *some*thing but then fizzled into a dead spark? It had felt like an instant, when everything had ended in a protracted hopelessness. But that time was in fact a stretched-out year of a hundred and fifty rallies, two imprisonments, and scores of the Immigrants Party Youth Wing meetings at which she had to bring trays upon trays of tea and then retreat to the kitchen repeatedly.

Do the pupils of her eyes dilate, her breath go shallow, her mouth go dry, when remembering the first time she and Al kissed in the dark of the cinema hall a week after they got engaged, hunkered in their seats, lips wet with saliva and tongues darting about to explore the other's cavities and molars, not knowing if they were doing it right? Does she wonder if she did the right thing by leaving during the hard times, when he turned to stone? Should she have waited out the dark times for the darker ones? Who's to say what a woman regrets after life swings away once it does.

No need to be wistful about the choices, the lessons, the regrets. Men and women live out the grace given in the myriad ways in which grace can be lived out. Only some make good use of it. Others make perversions that may seem blessed on surface. But the dark bits will begin to show through layers of burnish. The dark bits always have a way of revealing themselves.

[Absolute transparence in every direction, and the utterly stationary puff of grey that is George Gary Gregory Jaffar in that infinity of transparence. The being of smoke-spirit does not shift. A white speck appears; it lingers, it observes George Gary Gregory Jaffar's suspension before saying anything.]

ANGEL OF ADMITTANCE: If I may intrude on your thoughts, George…

GGGJ: Angel. There you are. I was going to call out to you… I've been thinking.

ANGEL: Yes?

GGGJ: About women. I've been thinking about the women in my life.

ANGEL: Right…

GGGJ: I didn't have any significant ones.

ANGEL: No, you didn't.

GGGJ: My Ma faded from my life once I was old enough for university and work. And my girlfriends never wanted to stick around. I used to suspect something was wrong with me. Some sexuality issue or some psychological problem.

ANGEL: And what do you think now? Was there something wrong?

GGGJ: I don't think so. But…

ANGEL: Go on, George.

GGGJ: I'm … well, I'm trying to reason through this. I mean … was I deficient in some way? Did I not *need* romance? I mean, why was I so full of … hatred? Why did I become so … *spiteful*?

ANGEL: You're looking for the word 'indignant', George. That's what you were. That was your purpose. And you did well.

GGGJ: Indignant … full of indignation. That was what I was given? A concentration of righteous anger at injustice. That's what filled me up?

ANGEL: Yes. That's what fills up the best of humans. A visceral revulsion to imbalances in the natural order of justice.

GGGJ: Why, though? I mean, isn't 'love' what makes the world go round? Couldn't I have been given a whole lot of 'love' instead of this anger and indignation? I mean … it really – it frustrated me, you know? It was difficult. You know what I mean?

ANGEL: I do know what you mean, George. You've just witnessed the crumbs of Al's first marriage. And, given the abundance of romance in his life, you are questioning the status of your own love life. It is part of the process George, that you feel so full of despair, so cheated out of something that you feel was your right – do you know what it is that you are realizing?

GGGJ: I think so.

ANGEL: Tell me. I would like to hear you say it.

GGGJ: That it doesn't matter. It means that love is *not* what makes the world go round. It's only another emotion.

ANGEL: Right. Anything else?

GGGJ: That I was never inclined to be romantically … developed. I was filled with an – indignation. For a purpose. For *my* purpose.

ANGEL: And women – what about them? And what about what you call 'love'?

GGGJ: It doesn't matter.

ANGEL: It does matter, George.

GGGJ: What do you mean?

ANGEL: You do not see it? The indignation? The lack of women in your life?

GGGJ: I see that it's connected somehow… Do you mean to tell me that I would have lost some of my indignation if … of course. You wanted me like that. You wanted me angr— indignant. So, I didn't get my share of romance. That's why God kept me frustrated, without friends. So that I could focus on my violent mission.

ANGEL: You are very close to seeing things the way they are. You will not need to go much further. You have already made a lot of progress.

GGGJ: Really? In that case, I should say that I don't want you to think that I'm ungrateful, Angel. I'm not feeling hurt – well, maybe a little. But I do want to understand. I know it's bigger than me, this whole thing…

ANGEL: You've earned some rights, George. God watches constantly, and you're moving closer to readiness for Admittance. Say what you like.

GGGJ: Tell me something then, Angel. I have questions about other matters than Altamaash and my process.

ANGEL: I am here to answer your questions, George.

GGGJ: Why are so many people angry in life? I mean … I'm talking here about the worst kind of angry people: terrorists who lash out indiscriminately, also ordinary people who do things out of rage and confusion, and damage so many seemingly innocent bystanders. I understand that everybody has a different mission. I get that now. It makes sense. But why do so many people have to suffer? And I'm not talking about earthquakes and tsunamis. I mean … why child molesters and rapists? Why torture? Why wars – I've just answered this myself, haven't I? Goodness requires Evil to exist. That thing, right?

ANGEL: No, George. You have not answered anything. This is not such an easily answered area of life. The answer is: only the Divine One knows why the worst crimes exist. I cannot answer that.

GGGJ: So, what do you tell someone who has suffered rape or been molested as a child? Or even someone born deaf and blind?

ANGEL: I do not get to tell them anything, George. I never even see them. They gain Admittance without any processing. They have suffered so much in life that gaining instant Admittance is only marginally worse. They get to be with God much before anyone else.

GGGJ: Oh. So, they're like martyrs. Like saints.

ANGEL: Yes.

GGGJ: And I'm not? A martyr?

ANGEL: Did you suffer, George? Other than your surprise murder, did you suffer any of the most despicable things in life?

GGGJ: No. Except … well…

ANGEL: Say it, George. Except what?

GGGJ: Just that … I never fell in love.

[The white dot pulses. George Gary Gregory Jaffar remains puffed up, grey, suspended in the transparence; he doesn't use his power of will to look into Altamaash's past. And time does not pass. It too, stays as suspended as he does. The white dot flits in and out, checking on him. Woman is such a force that it would take the equivalent of two decades for George Gary Gregory Jaffar to overcome her absence in his life. Realizing some portion of this, he gives up his vigil, his protest and his lamentation, without understanding or accepting. He moves on, bringing himself closer to the moment of Admittance.]

His bedroom from childhood, that's where this is now. But Al is no longer a child.

This room in the recesses of his parents' home is where he brought his wife and where they lived for a year before she left him to go back to her own childhood bedroom. He feels he's moped around enough over the separation that began months ago. But he can't seem to bring himself out of the funk of it. Also, though he's popular with the young ones of his kind, he has made no headway with the Immigrant Party's leaders. They give him no attention, lost as they are in the ping-pong of trying to make the Immigrants more relevant and worth considering for the powers-that-be in Islamabad. Altamaash is the least of the party elders' concerns. In turn, the capital's resources and manpower are facing away from Karachi to their western Meccas: Washington D.C. and London, from where, on postcolonial winds, blow scattered messages on how successive Pakistani governments should align themselves on global issues in order to gain a few spare millions in condition-bound aid. Who's got time to consider young buck Altamaash's fortunes with the world spinning so fast around its more vital concerns?

He lies flat on his bed, watching the ceiling fan whirl, and he sees a distorted reflection of the room and himself in the silver knob in the fan's centre. More handsome than his real self, is this convex reflection, he thinks. His father is away loafing, squandering the last bit of inherited wealth. No vision infects that man. Nothing like the phantasms that haunt Altamaash's mother, who is sitting on a sofa in the front-most room of the house, where she's perched at the window, looking at her summer-scorched garden while cursing her kismet that she allowed her son to marry the wrong kind of girl at such a young age. In the distance, she sees vultures circling in the sky. Something must have recently died.

Many days have passed like this: the mother in the front of the house, cursing; the son in the back of the house, wallowing; theirs is a pact of self-pity that feels as though it will last their whole lives and even past the passage of death into a purgatorial eternity.

It's she who sees this eternal occurrence in the circling vultures while he misplaces his sense of existence in the false reflection of a silver-topped ceiling fan.

It's she who breaks the inertia by throwing aside the old daydreams that have been festering ever since her daughter-in-law picked up and heaved off.

While the son palavers with his pain, it's the mother who forsakes her throne and recedes into the building. She knocks on his door with purpose. He grunts, and sits up on the bed, thinking he's being called for a meal he will refuse to eat. She enters his room.

'Son,' she says, 'enough of this.'

He looks at her in his blank and broken way. Dead eyes, he's got, like nobody in the future will believe he could ever have had.

'What do you want?' he asks.

She stands in the doorway, staring at him. She's laid down the first gambit. '*What*, Ammi?' he asks again. 'What do you want?'

All she does in response is to raise an eyebrow. One arch.

He's annoyed. The ceiling fan whirs on and on, and the vultures keep their spiralling vigils going over some dead thing far away. How can she not see that it's *over*?

Rather than looking each other in the eye, they stare at the distance between them; she looks at what he can become; he sees what she's forcing out of him. They don't perceive each other at all.

By force of character, she stands her ground. She's the daughter-in-law of the greatest Pir-charlatan he knows. There's no way he can outmanoeuvre her contortions of spirit.

'Enough *what*, Ammi?' he asks, trying to change track of the conversation that he's holding up one-sidedly. 'What's enough about it? She's gone. Sonia *left* me.'

His mother's stare doesn't falter.

'I'm a failure, Ammi,' he says. 'At everything.'

She holds on for more. It's coming.

'My job is *shit*,' he says. 'My wife's *gone*. I have the most *third-class* friends. There's *nothing* in my future. I've got *nothing*.'

Now; now she steps into the room, charging its air with her matriarchal aura. 'That…,' she says, and then gives a long pause, during which she orchestrates herself sophisticatedly into a seated crouch on the bed, '… was quite pathetic, Altamaash.'

'What?' he starts. 'What are you— of course, it's pathetic. My entire life is pathetic. All I can do is act a little.'

'Yes,' she says. 'So, *act* a little, why don't you?'

'What do you mean?' he asks, but he already has an inkling about what she's getting at. He feels the deeper meaning of her words intensely nudging against the engine churning at the centre of his mind.

'Your life is rotten, right?' his mother asks of Al. 'So, convince me how it's rotten. Don't hold back. There's a *lot* more inside.'

Ah, yes, that – *that* – is what pumps him. His mother is saying *I'm your audience, Altamaash. Time to unleash what you've got. Show me, you little devil.*

'Ammi,' he says. 'Mother mine, how do I convey to you the depths of despair I've descended to?' He gets off the bed and paces in front of his cupboard, gathering the full might of his misery. 'I've been abandoned. *Abandoned*, I tell you, Ammi. At the first, most crucial *crossroad* of my political career. A *blind* woman she was – a blind and heartless narcissist! Leaving me like she should have left me at the altar instead. Wasted a whole year of my prime – and destroyed my sense of self. The sheer irresponsibility that only a spoilt brat can display. And she saw my very failure as her own mistake. She left because she couldn't do *any*thing to make me whole. She lived in this tiny room as a separate person from me, more distant every day.'

It's cheering him up, this stringing along of words. His hands and arms and his steps come into play, as he gets more involved. His mother watches closely for the performance to take off.

'I will not curse her,' says Altamaash, stopping in the middle of a step, and turning to his mother. 'She's left me like you leave a nearly dead animal without bothering to put it out of its misery. Do you know what that's like?' He lets the drama of words and the moment fill him up from the inside. Like it's a liquid thing that can be poured to take the shape of the container into which it is decanted. Cool and quenching is the drama, and yet it fuels the fire of his words so they get hotter.

'I'm a beaten man, Ammi,' Al says, and slumps his shoulders deliberately. 'I've been handed the largest ambitions in the smallest container; I've been assembled to suffocate on my string of failures: a thankless job, a deserting wife, and nobody worthwhile paying attention to what I can do for the party.'

He lets the fiasco of his life fill him up until the feeling has plugged him tightly. He thinks about forcing a couple of tears, but holds back. Better not to release. Better to burst out.

'Ammi, I'm as lost as a person can be,' Al whispers, for the first time looking directly into her eyes. He holds on to a wetness in his eyes, but doesn't spill it out.

There. What does she think of *that*? To let her know that he's ready for a reassessment, he would even take a bow. But he can't break eye contact now. That's part of the act as well.

Altamaash's mother looks into his eyes, smiles and says, 'At least it's better than before. But you need more practice. I suggest you do it in front of the mirror a few times, and then a few more times in front of your friends. But end with something like anger … no, not anger. More like indignation. Turn everything up a notch. All the oceans of despair, et cetera, bring a kind of dark hope to all that by promising some sort of revenge.'

'Yes,' Altamaash says. 'A retribution. That's what *they* deserve.' By *they* he means the audience of his act-in-development rather than those who have made him feel like a victim. Here, in the bedroom, standing in front of his mother as a performer-in-the-making, he smarts from her critique.

She leaves soon, to fetch Al's father, and he's alone in the room again. He stays and thinks about what she's given him. The groan of the fan whirling above him doesn't disturb him. In a moment, he'll open his cupboard and face the long mirror with bold eyes. But for now, he sits and discovers with penetrating clarity that everything he feels, and however he channels it, it's all an act. Even away from the stage, everything is still theatre.

'If it's all a play,' says Al to his reflection in the mirror, 'and I'm the director, I must name the actors too.' And he begins to recite the names of those he doesn't trust. This is the mirror in front of which he will practise for hours. The seven sins will be used to name some; others will be named after the nine circles of Hell. Still more will be called The Fat One, The Bitch and Mr Charming Bastard.

Part actor part act. That's who he is. And that thought creates the two Altamaashes – public and private – and the thought that he will forever remain split up into these two selves. The public one will be on display; the private will be planning which aspects to put on in the next show. There is nothing that will not be fuel for his life's unfolding drama. He's got one role, but he will play many different parts to build the whole of it.

[George Gary Gregory Jaffar disengages, looks around at the blank glass, and feels, once more, ungifted. The absence of forceful women in his own life bothers him again. He wishes his mother had been

like Al's. He doesn't speak anything; the white dot watches as George Gary Gregory Jaffar braces and immerses himself again into Al's life.]

Years have passed, I've willed myself forward to this moment, so I can see what Al is doing on the day of his daughter's birth. This should be the most genuine, uncluttered, unambiguous instant in his life. That's the theory.

There he is, alone except the six bodyguards stationed close, but not suffocatingly close. It's early in the morning, a half hour past break of dawn on a cold, cold day in Westminster. No rush on the pavement where he's pacing outside the hospital. He holds an unlit cigarette. He hasn't smoked in years. Regular new-father tensions envelop and prod his thoughts. He's waited all these years, even in exile, for a son or daughter.

Already past forty. Will he live to see her go to college? The second Mrs Al, she insisted all these years that she was too young to have a child. Now look at her. In her mid-thirties and giving birth. They're doing a cesarean on her, and he's thankful he doesn't have to be there, telling her to push. If he could, he would have pushed her into having a kid earlier, much earlier. But she wasn't to be bothered.

That's what he's pacing and pondering, more than he's thinking about the new life coming into the world. He is tired from having been up most of the night. He's bitter about his wife's unwillingness to become his puppeteered minion right from the start of their life in London.

The feisty women, ones with spirit – why do men get drawn to them? Is it their force of will that attracts? The first Mrs Al was meek right until the day she upped and left. He wasn't going to go for a docile one on the second go-round. But did he have to swing on the pendulum completely the opposite way? Why couldn't he love someone normal?

But then, why did he even try to break her spirit? And once he couldn't, because women are not pliable like leather, he went feeble, lulling himself. He gathered strength while he tried to aggressively pacify Mrs Al 2.0 into a state of negative resistance. He planned to one day challenge her when her defences were at their lowest. This same story of every lopsided marriage played out in Al's second stint: he rebounded from the divorce into a turbulent affair and tricked the spirited woman into joining him in exile in England. But every time he tried to use his political clout on her, she hinted at using social services.

The cigarette, unsmoked, his eyes unslept and red, he strides in front of the hospital. The two bodyguards outside the delivery room upstairs will relay whatever happens to the one who climbs the stairs every five minutes to get news. It's snowed earlier, and the London crack-of-dawn air is cold in a stale sort of way. A raw dryness in his throat is preventing Al from smoking and from breathing well.

He knows his wife thinks of him as an ugly brute. Already too large for her. They'll likely never have sex again once she's given birth. But that's okay. She will have served her purpose well, Mrs Al.

Years ago, when he was still in love with her, he promised her vacations in Greece, Italy, the Bahamas, Russia, Croatia, and wherever else she would like. Money wasn't ever going to be an issue, she was assured. She collected from United Travel Agents on Oxford Street all the brochures, pamphlets and Lonely Planet guides to Rome and Mykonos. It was the latter destination she favoured, having flipped through the pictures and seen women wearing alluring yellow-and-white striped sarongs at the beach. Couldn't wait to see herself in a picture just like that. A year went by with them not budging from their St. Johns Wood hovel, and she collected more information, especially new editions of the Lonely Planet guides. Another year, and even more complications on Al's passport. Not yet British citizens, and susceptible for deportation back to Pakistan under extradition treaties from too many other countries, Al wanted to stay put in England and Wales – not even venture to Ireland or Scotland.

Those were tough times for him, he remembers, breathing out a puff of air that could be mistaken for cigarette smoke or his own spirit.

But the years were tougher for Mrs Al; she had no long-term goals that included vengeance. Nothing stoked her desire to live for such a fate-driven kind of life. Her spirit of adventure faded in resentment over what she thought she'd been promised as the wife of an exile: jaunting across the world had been her notion of locking herself outside of Pakistan. She got none of that. But the spirit flared on other, related, issues.

If she wasn't going to get, she wasn't going to give either. This is why she held back from birthing a child for him. She forbade her body with multiple contraceptive means. She didn't hide the pills from Al. Took them right after his conjugal attentions. And told him about the IUD in greater detail than he wished to hear about. He tried to reason, he tried to bully, he tried to mope around. She didn't budge.

But the clock ticks in one direction, and, the older she got, the more resigned she became that at some point she would have to bear his weight and incubate his child. Her body decided before she did, despite her layers of defences. And that was nine months earlier.

Now she is there, upstairs, being relieved of the child.

And he is down here, on the verge of lighting up a cigarette, thinking finally about the life that will come into the world any second now, wailing like a siren. The girl that will become his – his – his *what*? He wonders.

Perhaps it's the lack of sleep. Maybe even the corroded relationship between him and his wife, or maybe it's the presence of ethereal reds and blues in the early morning sky as well as the crisp air that make the sound of music as it rushes by his ears.

Possibly, all the elements combine to make him think like this. He's thinking how he will become a better man as soon as he will hold his daughter in his hands. He's running in his mind the idea of his salvation. His daughter will be that. A light; a cleansing force.

But clean from what? Everything he did – all of it – he was forced by circumstances to do them. So, what's this purification, this idea of 'salvation'? He dismisses it. Circumstances might change. Crimes may need to be committed again.

But the thought lingers, it pesters. He has not yet seen the baby, he has not held her in his arms yet. There is nothing but an unsmoked cigarette in his hands. Yet, it's the concept rather than the actual child that he is considering. The concept should be *enlightening* – in both the ways: lifting of burdens, and illumination. He's going to become a father to a precious little girl. Before he sees her as a baby, he envisions her putting a flower on his grave. Because he won't live long, he feels. Already in his forties, growing larger.

So, he aims for a compromise. He promises nothing, but he will try – that's as far as he'll undertake this. He'll attempt to go clean in his operations. Less hits and extortions will be ordered from here on. Only the essential ones. No conflict of interest there – only circumstances would dictate his actions, and not his whim.

She's redeemed him, he thinks. His incoming daughter. Any time now, she'll pop out.

She's already out of her mother's body. Already bawling and being held close by a nurse while her mother gets stitched back up.

One of the excited bodyguards outside the operation theatre receives the news and rushes down the stairs to be the first to tell his boss.

For Al, the reverie in which he sees her laying a poppy on his grave morphs into a vision of her becoming the poppy. Before Al has even heard the news of her birth, an icy gust of wind rushes past his ear and makes him bristle and shove his hands deep inside his pockets. In his hand, the cigarette he's been holding on to, the one he wants to smoke in lieu of the cigars that make him nauseous, it catches on his pocket and breaks. Out into the cold air tumble the threads of roasted tobacco.

The door opens; out comes the bodyguard; the announcement is made. Seven and a half pounds; a healthy baby girl. Al beams his thousand-watt smile. He's the happiest man in the world. All the maybes drift off with the wind. He flings the broken cigarette on the hospital's steps and rushes in to see his newborn. The fake kiss of affection for his wife that will be relayed back in photos sent to the party members in Pakistan can wait until she wakes up and is beautified.

The wind has brought him a name they didn't even consider. The pride he feels, that he's sired an offspring; and the hunger for power that rushes through him as he rises in the elevator; the thoughts of forming a multi-generational legacy, it all comes down to the name. Fatima. Meaning: chaste. He *will* go clean. She will be his redemptive force. He will even heal the rift that's come between himself and his wife. This apocalyptic revelation slays his fears for the coming years. The dangers of political life will recede as much as he recedes from politics.

But he knows this set of considerations that he shares with no one – this circling of the vultures inside him – it's only an act. And being the only actor, the only audience member, the only critic, he knows it is a hoax. Things will change for a time, but only until he wants to delay his true self from coming out and taking over. Only until it's time to set into effect the Instructions, and serve the dish that's best served cold.

For now, in the elevator, rising to meet his brand new baby-sized redemption, he'll spare the men of his own party who colluded with the prime minister, the army and the police, to get him out of the way. He will overlook the evidence of their collusion for years to come. But he keeps up a recital on repeat in his head of the names he's given them: *Bashful, Sleepy, Sneezy, Happy, Grumpy, Dopey and Doc. Bashful, Sleepy, Sneezy, Happy, Grumpy, Dopey and Doc. Bashful, Sleepy, Sneezy, Happy, Grumpy, Dopey, and Doc.* The elevator's doors part, lifting the pall from his thoughts. He's awake and enlightened like never before.

[George Gary Gregory Jaffar steps out of Al's life and back to The Belly. Nothing is visible here. He feels a burden he cannot describe and stays silent. The white dot pulses.]

II. Altamaash

Before daughter, before wife, before sister, even before any goddess, comes mother. I stand patiently behind the sofa where she is lying down. For her to fall asleep will take time, I know. Her power of will has always astounded me. Without fail, she prays the required five times daily, and gets up in the middle of her sleep at night for an extra credit prayer; also, she launches into rosary-snapping chants at a moment's notice. And tonight, she's at full force with her mummmmmblesummmmmbles. Ammi took over from Grandpa Pir the fervent devotion father never could understand. She inhales and exhales spirituality. The frail woman. It's nearly time for her. All kinds of time.

I wait behind the sofa; standing, watching, listening. On the other couch, my recumbent wife exhausts herself via an ancient struggle with Arabic; she'll soon succumb to a head-lolling sleep. There; gently; there. 'Allahu; Allahu; Allahu; All … aah…' and she's drifted. One down.

The older woman is much more resilient. Even after the rest of her body has surrendered to sleep's oblivion, her lips keep moving. A good two minutes later, the TV running on mute, having said her five thousand Allahus for the one true God; still, the lips keep going, just in case He's not stopped watching the prayer-chanting mothers of the sinners among us. It's not in jest that I notice and mention; I don't mock what has kept us going. Ammi is the family's link to the Divine. Would that I had kept Grandpa Pir and Ammi's legacy intact in some nobler way than— never mind; to the task at hand.

The room is dark except the TV. I begin my part. I bow my head and force out the tears. Pinching eyelids down hard. *Squeeze. Squeeeze. Squeeeeeeeeze.* It's almost real, this crass act. What I mean is, it comes from a real place. It is generated in truth. I'm not building a deviant case.

They're slow in coming, my tears. But I've done this before. And being reminded of the last time I shared this with my mother makes this one easier. They flow. How they flow … I'm a marvel. God bless this ability. *Squeeeeeeeze.* Inside me must be a large-ish gland that serves as a reservoir of this liquid performative despair.

Ammi's lips are as motionless as they will be. I move closer to her, all the while forcing out more eye-water.

It's beautiful to witness from this up close how much peace sleep brings to Ammi. All the suffering of praying dissolves. Creases of worry disappear, as though they were just for presentation. She's well across the border, on the other side of sleep. It's cruel to call her back from such a well-earned rest. But, as per habit, Al must do what must be done.

I move closer still and bring my face directly above hers on the sofa. A distance of less than eighteen inches separates her eyes from my leaking taps – yes, I've overdone it a bit. Theatrical to the end, I'll be. Shame. Could have been a much subtler scene, this one. But, never mind.

I gently nudge her shoulder. Her lids fly open. She sees her son. She wakes with a grimace at seeing his face so up close in the darkness of a TV-lit room.

I begin. 'Ammi, mother mine,' I say, 'wake up my guardian angel. All your prayers have been answered.'

As I wanted, my projected voice has woken up Mrs Al as well. She's in a side-crunch on the other sofa, watching Ammi and myself.

'Altamaash?' Ammi asks. And her hand goes up to my eyes, touching my tears and then rubbing them into my cheeks. 'What's wrong, my son? Why are you crying?'

'You're crying, Altamaash?' from the other sofa, my wife asks, completing her side-crunch to sit up.

'I have great news,' I gush. 'Great, amazing news. Please bring our daughter.' She doesn't budge. 'Go,' I say, waving Mrs Al into the bedroom. And up she gets, en-wifed, en-mothered.

'What's the matter?' Ammi asks, sitting up. 'Hand me my beads.' I fetch her rosary and sit down on the sofa next to her. 'Turn on the light,' she says. 'Let me look at you.'

I reach for the dimmest table lamp. The drama calls for romantic subtlety, not too much lighting. Nostalgia requires as much darkness as I can borrow from the night.

'Let's wait for Pinky,' I say. Pinky, my mother's favourite thing to call my daughter. It's a filthy distortion of Fatima. But I use it to placate Ammi and to allay her fears for just this minute.

I wipe my eyes, and so does she, reaching out to my face with a loose extension of all the miles of cloth wound around her body.

'Pinky?' Ammi asks, wiping me down. 'What does she have to do with you crying? Why don't you talk to me? Is everything okay? Please talk to me, Altamaash; why don't you ever talk to me? I've been telling you for years to share your troubles with me, and now they're coming to tear us apart. Altamaash, son, I – I worry so much about you.' She's begun opening her own eye-tap now; looks like we'll be filling up the stage that this room has become with watery overflow. Oh, Ammi, Ammi. It *is* you that Grandpa Pir would have been proud of. Not your husband.

Into the room with her mother comes Pinky, rubbing her eyes and frowning. They sit down on the other sofa. I hold my mother's hands and smile at all three females through my moistened line of sight.

'Papa, is everything okay?' Pinky asks. She's been prepared for the day I won't make it home. She knows the dangers of being a Pakistani politician's daughter in exile.

'Everything is the best possible thing it could be,' I say, blubbering, making little sense; not feeling the need to make too much sense either. Emotions are more called for at a time like this. 'We're going home,' I say. Ammi's hands in my hands start pulling away. I grip them tighter. I repeat the message. 'Ammi, mother mine, your prayers – all our prayers, yours, Pinky's – they have come true. We're going home to Pakistan.'

Ammi says, 'Hawww,' and she stays nonplussed and open-mouthed for another unguarded moment – certainly not an act. Then she tries hard to bring her hands up to her face. I keep hold of her wrists and stay her hands in my own. She must face it. I need her to.

'What? *Why*?' Pinky asks. She's prayed ritually with the family for the return. Every Friday and Eid prayer, every Pakistani holiday, she's dressed up like an Eastern doll and joined her hands and said the words: *Dear God, please give prosperity and security to our family, and grant peace to Pakistan, and help us to return one day to our home in Karachi. Ameen.*

Now she's balking. As expected. What politically exiled child would want to move to Karachi from London unless her Papa was wielding some sort of power in Pakistan? Little does she know. Poor Pinky. Dear doll. I wish that I could spare you what's coming.

'Really?' Ammi asks. She's horrified. With good reason. 'Pakistan?'

'Thank God,' says my wife. Her turn for the tears now. It's contagious, this fakery. Ammi's hardly been any less dramatic than myself or her daughter-in-law in terms of performance. But the wife is an unseasoned actor. Her gratitude excludes the rest of us.

'I've been working on it,' I say. 'It's taken a long, long time. But, tonight, the meeting went off even better than I could ever have planned.' I squeeze Ammi's hands and they squeeze back with equal and opposing force. Then she tries again to pull away.

'When do we have to leave?' Pinky asks.

'How long do we go for? Forever?' my wife asks. Insipid woman's probably wondering how many more Pakistani TV channels and desi designer dresses will be available in the markets of Karachi.

'You all need to pack your bags,' I say. 'Tomorrow, at 5 p.m., the three of you will fly off from Heathrow to Karachi.'

'*Tomorrow*?' Pinky shouts. 'That's *way* too soon, Papa.' I nod at her. Yes, it *is* too soon. It is *sudden*. That's the key. They must get into Karachi within the next thirty hours. The game is already afoot.

Mother's hands go limp in mine. 'Tomorrow? But who will do the packing?' she asks.

'Are we going forever?' my wife asks. She's a callous one. Doesn't care a fig for either her daughter or her mother-in-law.

'Nothing's forever,' I say. I refrain from saying what I really want to say to her after that: *not for you*.

'When will *you* come?' Ammi asks. Aah … good question.

'As soon as I can,' I say. 'It could take up to a week to settle things politically with the government. But I've been assured that it will happen.'

'You've been assured,' Ammi says. 'You've been assured. Great.' I release her hands. They fall limp on her lap. Something inside her has broken. She knows. She must know, of course, that there are darker things than this room in the offing. After everything, how can she not know? She's left the conversation even as she sits with us.

'Can I take the two new blue suitcases?' my wife asks. Insensitive to the end. Good that I continue to feel this absence of love for her. It'll be good to get rid of her. But underneath that immediate feeling I know how awful it will be to lose her. I'll work fevers on myself when she's gone.

'I don't even have a passport,' Pinky says. Very true. Smart counter, young lady. I smile at her my most fatherly smile.

'Everything's been taken care of, darling,' I say.

'Everything,' Ammi says. She's entered a realm of mysterious understanding of everything that's going on. Maybe she sees something that even I can't.

'Yes, Ammi, mother mine,' I say, 'everything is going to be all right. You'll get there safely, and our own house in Karachi will be opened up for you as soon as you land. It's all been arranged.'

'I'll go start packing then,' Mrs Al says, not missing a beat. She's been dying for years to show off her Harrods purchases at Karachi soirees. I don't judge; I only indulge. She deserves this little joy before the inevitable. Let the canary make its final chirps. 'There's so much to do. Aren't you excited, Pinky?' She pulls our child from the sofa and the two younger ladies disappear into the bedrooms.

Leaving Ammi and me. I take Ammi's glass from the coffee table and fill it with water from a jug. She watches me drink, saying nothing.

'You'll have to follow all the Instructions from my men, Ammi,' I tell her once I'm more hydrated.

She looks down at her hands. They're an old person's hands. She's become old, she's thinking. The years of exile have been unkind even as they made her feel secure. She's been away from all the people she grew up with. Most have died without the news of their death reaching London. The ones who live no longer know her. She's been housebound for two decades while Mrs Al, Pinky and I have strutted about the country like its owners. But Ammi, poor Ammi, not so much.

'Ammi—' I say softly, 'I wish I could make it easier. But some things are not in my control.'

She looks up at me again and pats my hand.

'You do what you need to, son,' she says. 'You always have.'

Out of the corner of my eye I see the news ticker running at the bottom of the Pakistani news channel on TV. A riot has been reported in Karachi. Another one is brewing in Islamabad. The rioters are chanting against someone they call 'The Fat One'. And so, it begins.

Sitting here on this sofa, waiting for the spectacle to begin, like members of the audience, my leftover parent and I know what's going on in each other's head. She is forced by maternal instinct and the power of reason to connect the dots between what has been and what will become of our family. I love my mother more than all the other women in our family were ever loved. She's the only one who ever understood what the sacrifices meant. And the blood-letting isn't over just yet.

The words I've let slip to Phil – I lean back on the sofa and play those words back to myself: *bouncer*, *reporter*, and *riots*. Had it been anyone else, I would count on confusion, if not discretion. But Phil's well-connected to everyone. He's got tentacles and antennas stretched right across the world; certainly in the Secret Service of the United States; also the intelligence services in India, Pakistan and right here in UK. The two reasons why I hired him still ring true: *one*, he's extremely capable – intelligent as well as thoroughly muscled up; and *two*, he's incredibly loyal. Once, a long time ago, Dopey and his own personal bodyguard flew in from Karachi to hire someone like Phil for me. They found ol' Phil and poached him from the Prince of Wales's entourage. Then they left, thinking that the exorbitant amount of cash they'd forked over to lure him would earn his loyalty. But Dopey didn't understand that the first and foremost aim of Phil's life is to be capable.

Money, loyalty – they don't often split up; but, in Phil's life, loyalty and power to do his job as he sees fit are more closely related. Money comes and goes – he knows this. Plus, he knows I would pay more. So, he's never betrayed me, even though he's been offered the chance. He's told me the hints that Dopey's played into his ears. 'The powers have shifted, Phil. Come, work for the party in Karachi. Leave the old exile; he doesn't need protection any more; he's pretty much irrelevant.' Said sometimes in jest, other times in supposedly confidential texts. He wouldn't betray me, not Phil. Dopey's one dopey mistake.

He found for me a better bodyguard than I could have found myself.

That link is important, though. Jordan, poor Jordan, he's good for nothing but muscle and legwork. But Phil – he's a link of stories. It's from his revelation that I realized what was done to get me out of Pakistan: Dopey and the other sinful dwarves worked with The Fat One, The Bitch and Mr Charming Bastard to unearth evidence of the purge of old Immigrants Party blood I ordered spilt when I took over. Thirty years have passed, but I remember clearly ordering Dopey and Sneezy to get rid of the party's leftover old guards. Dopey the Disappearer could have made them vanish like he always did. But they were discovered quite easily, those bodies were, and it didn't even take any special police branch to do it. And it wasn't that Dopey did a sloppy job when he made the bodies pop up in the canals of Lahore and Karachi. He did quite an efficient job planting evidence that would point straight back at me.

Phil and I know the next steps. He's been prepared with those words: share the good news of the *reporter*, the *bouncer* and the *riots*.

And while I nap on this sofa, now that Ammi has removed herself to her room, things will play out as required.

The blood from Gary Guardian's head wound that I witnessed seeping out the front door will congeal on the front mat of Ned's house. A passerby will notice; if not, the morning milkman or newspaper delivery boy.

Cops will arrive at the scene with guns held up, just in case; they will open the slightly parted front door to see the two sprawled-out, dead bodies.

News vans will descend on the cordoned-off area, and the TV will begin to play the news of Ned and Guardian Greg's deaths.

Names might be shared with members of the press. But even if they are not, the address will leak out.

That's when it will get personal for the St. Johns Wood exiles.

One antenna of Phil's receiving appendages will start buzzing. He'll connect the dots with my first word: *bouncer*. Within minutes of that, without making any headway on the case, the Scotland Yard will also leak out information on the death of a member of the press. The Guardian may issue a statement – political correctness may require it. With that, another wire in Phil's network of information will get triggered.

First, Phil will enjoy seeing the connection himself.

What is he to do at that point? He's quite adept. He knows I want this news to be shared. I'm going to have beautiful dreams about this. Do it Phil.

I can just picture him sending a signal over the wires, encoding it in gibberish that goes across to the Eastern world. There, the message will be decoded by a network of bodyguards and paramilitary types. And among these networked bodyguards, is Dopey's own personal protector. Once he gets news, he'll share with his own boss the decoded message: Al has terminated two people in London, and he's left no trace while making it look like a double suicide.

The wheels of Dopey's mind will turn round and round, but he'll stay unable to figure out how I could have done it: two deaths; one bullet; apparent suicide-murder – a hell of an indecipherable crime. The sinful dwarves will hear of it next; good news spreads. And then there will come to them, in the evening, the more potent threat: day after tomorrow, in the early hours, the three ladies of the House of Altamaash will become airborne, heading to Karachi.

At that point, there is only one thing that will cross Doc's mind, as well as Happy's, Sleepy's and Bashful's: Al's getting ready to come back. And he's going to start killing people again.

Doc knows that I know. Dopey knows that I know. They think I've forgiven their political manoeuvrings because I had no other choice. They'd put me in my place, they thought. A faraway entertainer. A disappeared-from-Karachi mascot, they made me. And they let me pretend that I was the one holding the party's reins. They even bowed down to me and kept sending the same amount of money as the old days even though revenue had gone up tenfold.

And they thought that's where the matter would lie settled.

In a single day now, they will have to choose whether or not to attend the Annual General Meeting of the Immigrants Party. If they have any sense of the occasion, and if they're fully informed about the whispers around them, none of the sinful seven will abstain from attending – they'll cancel appendectomies and heart transplants, they'll pause in the middle of shagging their whores, even as they're just about to prematurely come; they'll shrivel inside even as they put on their best bluster; all this, they'll do. And one more thing: they'll all attend to Al's call. I see it like a light at the end of the tunnel. That's the camera lens as tunnel, and that room in the Karachi Sheraton that is the light of Skype, and the vision of their leader, Don Al, showing on the big screen in the conference room in the basement of that hotel. If the whisper carries all the way from Phil's network to that boardroom, not a soul of any of the soldiers will dare not to attend.

When I wake up from the nap on the sofa, I can hear the younger ladies packing in their rooms. And in the doorway between her room and the living room stands my mother, staring at me in the darkness. We're both wondering which one of us is having this nightmare.

III. Edwin 'Ned' Steinberg

[In otherwise pure transparence, the white dot pulses. It listens. It watches. Edwin 'Ned' Steinberg makes his case.]

EDWIN 'NED' STEINBERG: Angel of Turning Away, please listen. I need to say something. It's become so much clearer now. Are you listening? ... You must be, I guess. In any case, I have to tell you there are emotions that I'm feeling now. Now that I've discovered that there was more to life than going to the gym and feeding myself the right proportions of— I understand that I should have attached more worth to life and I should have examined my principles, and I should not have let Al mesmerize me. It's a huge discovery, right? Small as it sounds, just that change in direction of flow of things ... right? You know what made me realize this? It was the woman in the desert—

ANGEL OF TURNING AWAY: Yes, the woman in the desert. Before that, the woman's voice, right?

NED: That's right – in the doorway when Al was threatening the finance minister.

Yes. *Her*. I couldn't see her then. But I heard her voice. She said 'Is he in there?' And then I began to see her. She was so perfect ... I mean, nobody's perfect except God, of course, but she was as perfect as a mortal can be. Do you hear me, Angel of Turning Away? I'm in love with that woman. She's like the sight of sky between canopy of trees, as seen from a forest floor. And the way she ran? Did you see that effortless gait? Like she was *born* to run. I don't know her at all, but seeing her has – it's made me want to relive life. I want to give her everything. I'm so in love that I wish to be sent to Hell if she can go to Heaven. Isn't *that* love? Well?

ANGEL: Ned, poor Ned. You're so unforgivable. Do you know that you're falling in love with two different women?

NED: Different? *Two* different women?

ANGEL: The woman you saw in the desert; she is Al's trainer. She is helping him lose weight with what she calls 'hot cardio'.

NED: Oh. His trainer. But she looks exactly like—

ANGEL: She looks exactly like the woman whose silhouette you saw in the doorway of his office. They are related to Al. They are different potential futures of his daughter.

NED: His daughter? Oh … in the future?

ANGEL: When you died, she was eleven years old.

NED: Right. The future … that's when she's that old.

ANGEL: The women you saw: in the desert, in the doorway – each of those is a possible future version of the little girl. But they are not the same person. Those women are what *could* be. And the one you saw in the hospital, she was the mother of that little girl.

NED: Okay. So, just so I understand … there's no actual single woman like that? Angel, that breaks my hea—

ANGEL: You know what *should* break your heart, Ned? Your particular situation. Your sentence. You haven't learnt a thing. Do you see what it all means? You and what you felt for those women—

NED: But I *loved* that woman. I thought it was one woman. And I *utterly* loved her. How can you not see that?

ANGEL: God turned away from you for this, Ned. You are all surface, you desire nothing but superficial glitter. Do you know that the images you saw were meant to make you understand yourself, and nothing more? The women you saw, they looked twenty-two but each of them was forty-five years old. Body-conscious surface-level women, heavily invested in their fitness routines, including yoga, pilates, organic food, all the anti-aging creams that money and influence can have delivered to them. There is, obviously, depth beyond that within each one. But you did not wait to discover anything beyond the top layer. The surface appeals enough to you to forsake yourself for it. Of course, you will fall in love with the image of those women, Ned. You did not even distinguish between them. This is how you fell for Al. Do you not see what a fool you have been all your life?

NED: You fool me … and then call me a fool… You rig a game and tell me I play by its rules, but when I do… why do you blame me? Don't you at least see that I've realized how selfish I was?

ANGEL: I do not blame you, Ned. I only pity you. Even God pities you. Do you know how much pity it would take to bring about your Disintegration rather than sending you to Hell? Me – I only show you what you did wrong in life. I make you understand. That is as far as my duty goes. Whatever I show you is so you can see the truth about how you lived. And now that you have died, and understood how you should have lived, you regret being selfish. But your chances are truly over, Ned. They have been terminated since you got shot in the mouth. Maybe even before then. You see, you may understand and regret how you lived your life. But regrets are illuminations come too late. Now, whether you like it or not, the Disintegration continues.

NED: But—

[The transparence shimmers and dissolves, and into view comes Al … always, Al.]

III Unpromised Heaven

'Every story needs its hero. And its villain. And its monster.'

– Amie Kaufman & Jay Kristoff, *Obsidio*

7

Daddy Issues

You know you're in political exile from Pakistan when you begin dreaming your father is furious with you for not visiting his grave for twenty-three years; trouble is, you don't remember when, how, where, or if, he was buried.

I. George Gary Gregory Jaffar

[George Gary Gregory Jaffar, as grey smoke, stays suspended for a long time.]

GGGJ: Angel, I hope you can hear me. I'm going to go through with the rest of the process. I have a feeling it will remain unpleasant until it ends. But to this I bear witness: there *is* a God. And that God is the same for me as for Altamaash. The scale of life may be larger for Al than it was for me, but I bet that he feels pain just as I did. And I want to see him in pain. This is why I return. Here I go, disengaging emotionally, plunging back into his story, using all that has been built up of my willpower:

[All transparence disappears.]

After his first marriage ends in divorce, and once his mother gifts him with a paradigm shift, Al goes reckless; he brings danger home to his parents without thinking about the consequences. He rallies across the city and the province, shouting from microphones like a madman, goes to prison for leading minor protests and riots, and hangs out with the party's loutish youth to deliberate on future acts of violence they'll commit. The Karachi police despise him. He does not get released from his short stints in jail without bruises and cuts.

Grandpa Pir has been buried long ago, and Altamaash's own father is aloof to what goes on at the party's headquarters or in his son's life. The dunce of a man, who could have been a guide for Al, spends his days at the beach, combing the sand for perfect shells and talking to the camel-riders about their days while also haggling and gambling with them what his father left behind. He calls his time spent at the beach a hobby, but it's all that Altamaash's father does. Which leaves his mother to take up the arms of logic against her son. But she is too proud, too much a mother to fret about Altamaash's schemes, his rallies and his speeches. She is also giving him time and space after the divorce is finalized. How much time she will give, she isn't sure.

She also isn't sure when Al falls in love with an Immigrant Party leader's daughter at a political gathering. This new woman isn't shy – that would not attract Al after his divorce with the sheepish Sonia. This new one's loud. She pushes back against police cordons. Of course, she isn't impressed by Al as a person; no, what takes her by surprise are his words. To impress her, he will regularly charge into monologues as long as fifty minutes, and some as short as only six words before he leaves the stage: 'Parasites, unite; get your fucking rights!'

Once, he speaks for three hours without breaking for a sip of water. He lists the failures of immigrants in history, starting from the first forced deportation of Prophet Adam. There are so many more who failed to find a foothold in the lands promised to them. But some did succeed, and he reminds his people about them. Most of all, he speaks to them of the prophets Moses and Muhammad.

His voice hoarse, his spirit soaring, his head buzzing from having spent whatever energy he had, Al asks the bold young woman's father for her hand in marriage the same night he makes his long and riveting speech; Al is smoking with the older man on the porch of the party's headquarters. The senior party leader has paid little attention to Al before this night. He puffs away at his cigarillo disdainfully, waiting for the pumpkin- headed young blusterer to take his amorous aspirations elsewhere. Al doesn't budge. He enjoys his future-father-in-law's silent treatment and imagines the conversation that isn't taking place. He envisions himself threatening the older man with toenail-pulling torture if he doesn't agree to wed his daughter to Altamaash; the inner Al chuckles at the thought. So, all right, it will have to be the other way, the harder way. The young lady stays unwed, and she continues attending the protests and rallies; Al and she keep locking eyes on each other across grassy knolls and crowded halls.

Meanwhile, Al's political fortunes begin picking up a year after his providential early divorce. While the higher ups in the Immigrants Party are trying without success to get the prime minister, the army and members of the judiciary to take their phone calls, the youth wing of the party, led unofficially by Al and his ilk, forces Karachi to take notice of their violence. They burn tyres and buses, start looting shops and set up an extortion racket. And when Pakistan's biggest city comes under threat of violence and coercion, it affects business throughout the country. Commerce and politics cannot go on as usual. Al tries bluffs with phone-attending underlings and some of them work. He convinces a chief minister, a three-star General in the army, and the prime minister's secretary, to take his calls – under false threats of attack. He gets relayed up the chain.

Once on the line with them, he promises every one of them that his people will cooperate in return for favours for the Immigrants. The Prime Minister, a woman whom Al calls 'The Bitch' in the sanctity of his home and his party's headquarters, is married to the worst person in Pakistan: 'Mr Charming Bastard'. Mr CB is the one true Pakistani political gamesman other than Al himself. But then, Al never wanted to be a politician.

All he wanted was— never mind. There will be time for that.

So, Al gets promises made to him. He even gets to talk to Mr Charming Bastard himself, who assures Al that The Bitch is on board. Power will be more sensibly doled out in Karachi; and Immigrants will be given fairer shares in government representation and jobs in the private sector. Even the army General is amenable. The chief minister bows to Mr Charming Bastard's pressure, and starts listening to the voice of minority representatives and applying their advice in his government's decisions.

A year passes, then two and three. There is tangible, steady progress in Al's upward mobility. He is tipped to become the next party leader, even after having been considered and dismissed quite thoroughly in the Immigrants Party's last internal Youth Wing elections. This time, he has the external-links factor: he can get directly in touch with Mr Charming Bastard. He's even developed a line to the other 'real' Pakistanis' party in the North, and their leader, The Fat One. (Al is not, as yet, more of a spectacle of obesity than The Fat One. That will come later, after the stress and joys of exile. He stakes on that tag of 'The Fat One' to its owner an implicit bet that he, Altamaash, will never become bigger in size than The Fat One. Alas, metabolisms and fate have other ideas. The code name is never modified to fit shifting relative weights.)

Sure enough, Al narrowly wins the Immigrants Party leadership, despite being barely in his mid-twenties. He is bound to be heartless to his opponents, as per party tradition and per Al's own customs. And so, he is. Bodies of those who do not fall in line begin to appear floating in canals or sewn up in gunnysacks, butchered beyond recognition, and sometimes tagged with papers that let the authorities know whose corpses they are.

It's his contemporaries, the ones who rise to power under his own wings, people he calls (inside his own head) Dopey and Bashful, whom Al trusts with the disposal of his opponents. Big mistake – one that will cost him over twenty years of exile and the creation of seriously elaborate games to exact just retribution.

And while his people have been, without kicking up any fuss, using the modus operandi of 'disappearance' on their enemies and on honest businessmen who refuse to politely hand over extortion money, this same trick of making his own party's members 'vanish' will be Al's worst mistake. Mr Charming Bastard and The Bitch hold on to a key set of evidences (provided to them by Al's sinful seven, especially the cunning sinner Dopey) until after the country-wide five-yearly elections. But just before the election, they promise Altamaash's party all that they need to promise to get him to toe the line and support their party's stay in power.

The ruling coalition, led by The Bitch and Mr Charming Bastard, vow that they'll overhaul the election process, reverse policies in the judicial appointment process, and even include a quota for Immigrants to be represented on both the judiciary and the National Security Council. Al is getting pledges made to him much more easily than he can ever want. It should alert him, but he is overly self-assured. A mistake of youth.

The Bitch is re-elected to the country's top seat. Betrayal comes swiftly after the elections. The promises are discarded. Not even delayed. The Bitch and Mr Charming Bastard refuse to acknowledge Altamaash's phone calls. Instead, they use the card they've held on to: they initiate official investigations on the murders of his party members, and sneak in crucial pieces of evidence into open files. As if they've not committed similar acts of violence against their own opponents. Oh, it stings, the husband-and-wife's curse-worthy stooping to such a low level of betrayal.

Without a long enough interval on his hands to deal with the traitors in his midst, Al decides he will need to play the game with an extended timeline, of years – maybe decades – to get his revenge. Before that, though, he has to thwart the incoming assassination attempts. First, at the party headquarters, a poser pretending to be one of the Immigrants is caught with a silenced gun in his shalwar and a poison-dipped knife sheathed in the folds of his socks. Once caught, the would-be assassin is carted off to an unmarked house in the suburbs of Karachi, where the skin of his legs is stripped from knees to toes. He doesn't end up revealing much. After that, a second, more in-your-face, attempt is made at Al's house:

Shortly after The Bitch (allegedly) gets her own brother killed in a police 'encounter' (the brother is too, too honest and he holds substantial evidence of his sister and brother-in-law's financial and other shenanigans; plus, secret childhood grudges are in play), she tries to set up the same ambush and outcome for Altamaash.

In his house, besieged by the Karachi Police's elite squadron and a sheriff-like paunchy villain who bellows through a bullhorn at Al's family to come out and surrender to the authorities – likely so they can force an 'encounter' – Al modifies the Instructions, copiously writing under house arrest. This is a wide range of options to be carried out against The Bitch, Mr Charming Bastard, and The Fat One – and future opponents of the Immigrants' cause; in accordance with these Instructions, the enemies of the cause will seemingly be attacked by each other's people. One leader will be accused of blasphemy, and others of being Indian or Jewish agents – because nothing gets the Pakistani blood boiling than mid-mob mention of blasphemy, Indians, or Jews.

Altamaash – who will, one week after being sieged by armed police, be in England as an asylum-seeking politician-in-exile – makes only one phone call while thus painted into a corner. His call is to an army General, and their conversation lasts under three minutes.

The three-star General who has become sympathetic to the Immigrants Party's cause, is a big fan of Altamaash's speeches. He appreciates the political counterpunch that Al provides to The Bitch's popularity among the masses. That General makes several calls of his own, crafts arguments that cannot be refuted, and cuts a set of deals with his superiors and underlings. The only catch for everyone is this: Altamaash will have to leave the country. He will have to disappear from the face of Pakistan.

Al is relayed Mr Charming Bastard's terms: escape somehow, or be arrested and brought to court – if he can survive another 'encounter' attempt, that is. Like any thoroughbred politician, Al chooses to make haste for the border. But The Bitch, Mr Charming Bastard – and even The Fat One, who isn't even in power at the time – they don't make it easy to escape. They keep lookouts and spies posted at the train stations and airports.

Locked inside their house, packing their essentials, Al and his parents huddle to discuss their options. Which country? The father wants either to stay back in Karachi while everyone else leaves, or have the family head to the California coast – San Francisco is his first choice. Al's mother wants one-way tickets to Saudi Arabia – she yearns to pray out the rest of her life, to make sure that Al and his supporters in the party are forgiven by her Allah for the violence they've been forced to commit.

Altamaash listens closely to his parents. They present their cases and then bicker over each other's choice of country for banishment: an exile-themed dance-off of Saudi Arabian mosques vs. California beaches plays out in the house for two days, after which a cold silence brews among the inhabitants. Al broods for another day and a half. Then he goes for his last walk with his father.

They sneak out of the house in a party worker's car, and walk along Sea View, the common people's beach. His father scans the long shoreline for the camel-riders and the horses, and picks up shells to take with him on the trip. Al feels dejected for his father like he would feel sad for the failures of a distant acquaintance. Altamaash's father does not matter to his son. But Al doesn't judge him too harshly. Given that we're all equal and opposite reactions to the ones who give us birth, what can be expected in life from a person whose father was a spiritual charlatan anyway?

On that walk along the shore, Al's father says he is proud of Al for standing up for his people's rights. He says Al is going to make absolutely the right choices, no matter what crossroads he faces in life. It counts as father's pride, but is worth nothing to Al. He has never needed this man to be proud of him. On that walk, he plays out in his head the different ways in which he can deal with his father: have him come to England with nothing to do? That doesn't feel like the best outcome. A conceptually miss-able father is better than an actual dolt sitting in the corner of the living room, unable to operate something as simple as a TV remote. On the way back from the beach, Altamaash tells his father that he, Al's father, can stay back in Pakistan for a few weeks – that it will be safe for him to do so.

That evening, Al calls up the General, and asks to have his mother and himself transported to London as soon, and as safely as possible. Also, he requests that the woman he is interested in marrying be brought to live with him in England. She is an additional clause in the deal. She's been unapproachable for Al ever since he won the party election and got rid of her father along with the others who didn't approve of his taking charge. But she'll come around, of course. Love is a stronger force than daddy issues.

All packed, Al and his mother pile into the car. When Al shuts the doors to the vehicle, she understands that Altamaash's father, her husband, isn't coming with them. Before their car drives off to the airport, the man is already heading to the beach. Al and his mother reach the airport, where they take a flight from Karachi to Islamabad (right into the lion's den) under false names, with false documents; then, from there, a flight to Kabul, Afghanistan, where they start using their real names and legitimate passports; from Kabul, they get on a flight to Colombo in Sri Lanka. A British Airways flight from Colombo takes the two of them to Manchester, where Al's future wife meets them. She chose to come willingly rather than be kidnapped by the General's men (a contingency plan, just in case she was still miffed about Altamaash offing her father). Al knows he's picked a plucky one.

They hire a car to drive them from Manchester to London. There, in a hotel-room overlooking the Thames, begins their long vigil in front of the television. They wait for news of revolution. Surely the people will rise up.

Meanwhile, back in Karachi, nobody lays a finger on Al's father. He is free to come and go from his house as he pleases. Al checks on him a few times. Then he relays the first amendment to the Instructions. Within a couple of days, Altamaash's father goes missing. And that is the last that anyone hears of that idiot, until twelve years later, when parts of his skeleton are unearthed from under the foundations of a steel-manufacturing factory that is being dismantled. The factory is owned by The Fat One, who becomes implicated in Al's father's death. The Instructions are thorough and apply across decades.

Other parts of the Instructions include plans for future riots and blame games. These also will happen. I, George Gary Gregory Jaffar, bear witness that they will begin shortly after my own sacrifice to the cause. Now I know 'how' I was killed, and also 'why'.

[In utter transparence, the grey cloud that is George Gary Gregory Jaffar reappears. The white dot has been waiting.]

ANGEL: Are you feeling all right, George?

GGGJ: The world will be a much better place without Al. This I *know*. I understand why his party didn't forsake him. When Al said he would work for the cause, when he said he would get rights for the Immigrants 'by any means necessary', he meant 'even if we have to kill my father'.

ANGEL: Now you know who he was.

GGGJ: Yes, now I know.

ANGEL: And how do you feel, George?

GGGJ: How do you think I feel, Angel?

ANGEL: His cause is greater to him than a single life.

GGGJ: But his father ... even his father?

ANGEL: Go further. Cross over with him into exile.

[George Gary Gregory Jaffar does as the white dot suggests: he wills himself to the day that Al, his mother and his new wife, after eating takeout food, sit in a sparsely furnished newly renovated house in St. Johns Wood. The men Al calls Dopey and Doc enter after knocking.]

Altamaash gets up first, before the women, and he embraces the visitors from Pakistan. They are his brothers in the struggle for Immigrants' future in the homeland. They can come and go as they please, from Pakistan to any country, even though their hands are as bloody as his.

He holds nothing back when he opens his arms and squeezes the men with brotherly affection. They can hardly suspect any deception. They think they've outwitted him.

'Altamaash Bhai,' begins a sobbing Doc, 'Aunty,' and only a nod for the second Mrs Al, 'I am bringing terrible news.'

That's how information of his father's death arrives in the mansion, the same day that Al and his leftover family of women begin domesticating the space by unpacking boxes and unrolling carpets that have been shipped from the ancestral home in Karachi.

Doc and Dopey will stay for four days with them. In this time, they'll pledge lifelong allegiance to Al, assure him that he will be the leader of the party no matter where he's forced to live; and they'll fix him up with bodyguards and offshore bank accounts and lawyers and other connections he needs to make the most of his English asylum.

This day, though, they'll retire early to bed and leave Al and the ladies to huddle in the living room to mourn the dead.

Mrs Al, the second, sobs her way to sleep on one of the two sofas, while Al and his mother keep a vigil of sorts. A light is left on in the kitchen, but it's dark in the living room where they sit.

I know both sets of thoughts. I see them stream out in how they're acting. He knows that she knows that he knows that she knows and so on, that he ordered his own father's death.

And meanwhile, she knows that he knows that she knows and so on, that her son had her husband killed.

Yet they cry for hours, remembering the dead man's meaningless life. They rehearse the drama that they will keep towing along in their wake for the rest of their lives.

II. Altamaash

Once more, fortunes that were festering are now frolicking, forward up the fated footpath. Once more into a comfy cab, for another go around the London carousel. In simple words, I walk Ammi and the younger ladies out to the three taxis. I want to spend these few vehicle-bound moments with wife and child. Might as well create an aura of festivity around their rapid return to the motherland. So, we, the nuclear we, slump into the back seat of the first vehicle. Ammi sits with her bags and Phil in the second car, while the third carriage comes loaded with the bulk of the luggage. Jordan stays behind to guard the house.

Once underway on the highway to Heathrow, I'm solaced by the oscillation in the back seat. Good rhythm, this. If there were songs to sing for an imminent farewell, this oompy-loompy sway would provide the right cadence, and this would be the perfect time.

'Daughter mine,' I, with a burst of urgent affection, address the Nintendo-PlayStation-engrossed young bundle of eccentricities, who in turn ignores me. 'Fatima, my love,' I start again. But she only answers to *Pinky* these days – *shudder.* Instead of calling her by that pathetic endearment, I resort to merely watching her. The almond-shaped eyes, the rope-thick twists of braided hair, the feline yet oval face. She's inherited my thick lips, and her mother's small forehead and tiny nose. She's not there yet, but she *is* going to become an exquisite beauty. Already, she avoids overeating and under-nourishing herself on oily Pakistani meals that follow us exiles with our women. Already, she has a morning ritual comprising Pilates and yoga and other such contortionist activities. I've seen the sea green exercise mat in her room. It changes attitudes every day: sprawled diagonally in front of her TV, or rolled up in a corner; sometimes I find it leaning on a sofa in the living room. She's ten or eleven, and turning a year older in November. I'll always celebrate her birthday. Everyone in Pakistan will, from here on in.

Fatima, my route to salvation; my anomalous connection to grace – even more so than Ammi. I remember thinking about her like that when she was born; that I could '*go clean*' for her. That it was possible to expunge from my record all the negative things I'd done, and wash my hands, so that when I held her it wouldn't feel as though the hands of a killer-by-proxy were touching my beautiful daughter.

But I'd rather have it externally present – the necessary ugliness that latches onto beautiful beings. Rather that, than something that springs from within the girl.

The flash of a memory from many years ago comes back to haunt as it's done time and again. The older women were in the kitchen, preparing dinner – spicy nihari and saltless haleem, if I remember correctly. Fatima and I were in the living room; she was spreading blues and greens outside the lines in her colouring book, and I was grumpy about a cancelled press conference. At that moment, The Fat One came on the TV screen in a news clip from back home. Forgetting that my daughter inhaled and processed everything in her surroundings at the age of two or three that she was at the time, I said the word 'harami' while looking at The Fat One's smug mug. I must have whispered the word; the way I said it was subtle and the sound of it evaporated without settling.

But a few seconds later, up she looked from her colouring books, and the word came out from Fatima's lips in the question: 'Papa, what does harami mean?'

I could have killed myself. I had been too eager to vocalize my venom; it wasn't that The Fat One had done something especially outrageous, it was just that *he* was of concern for newscasters rather than *me*. To think that such an act of low-volume selfishness could have triggered Fatima's curiosity.

Being a parent in those moments is the most difficult thing in the world. Tougher than killing two people with one bullet, even.

'Nothing, darling,' I said at the time. Feigning nonchalance, sweating monsoons as I looked into her doe eyes. 'It's not a polite word, and it means "bad person".' The true meaning did flash across my mind as I was gently steering mini-Fatima away from it.

Harami=bastard. And simultaneously flashed in my head images of a future Fatima, turned *Fati* for her friends: she would be smoking with them, chugging pint after pint of cheap beer in dive bars, staying out well beyond parentally established curfews, and she'd be calling me, the rule-maker of her house, in his own language, a bastard. Harami – that word would come to her lips, without the innocence she'd said it with just then as a toddler.

I didn't want to lie to her. Nor did I want to tell her the truth. I tried equivocation, but I could see from how she paused her colouring and retreated into herself, that the word was laying anchor in her mind; synapses were firing across neurons to store it forever. She became infected with it. I could have punctured my lungs for ever having given breath to words.

But thank God she didn't turn out the way I feared she would. Not so far, that is. Phases come, phases go. Any parent can vouch for that. I just hope little Fatima doesn't turn into a *Pinky* for the rest of her life. Anything but that.

Rocked gently out of my reverie by a congestion in the traffic on the highway, and still no attention given to me in the cab from little Fatima, it's time to suck back my fatherly instincts. They've been on the brink of absence for so long that they want to gush forth at this last instance of togetherness before the flight that separates us for the next few days. I *want* the child to look at me and call me *Papa*. It's adorable the way she says it. Like she's going to follow it up with *Bear*. But that can wait until we're at the airport saying goodbyes. I'll give her a big hug, a bearish one.

Husbanding my emotional resources, I look at my wife on the other side of our offspring. Madam is expressively content. She's glowing like a little baby girl let loose in a candy shop. I'm glad she gets to go like this, so unlike the sullen way in which mother dearest is choosing to depart.

'Darling,' I say over our daughter's head, 'you'll need to follow all the Instructions of the party's people. They know what's best for you.' I've said this before; I'll say it again. It must be drilled into their heads. There cannot be any deviation from the plans.

Mrs Al nods and reaches over the game-thingamajig in our daughter's hands. She bites her lower lip, smiles, and pats my arm. I am about to take her hand in mine when she pulls away.

'Don't you worry, Altamaash, my sweetheart,' Mrs Al says. 'We'll settle in quickly. I'll take care of everything. Hopefully you can join us very soon.' How condescendingly she looks at me; as if all my adult life I've been nothing but an exiled fool. In her eyes, she's got pity that is akin to disgust for the failed politician she sees.

She doesn't sense, let alone comprehend, my mother's worst fears about this abrupt return to the Land of the Pure. My wife's immune to such thoughts in the midst of her glee. *Why* did I marry this one? Could have kept our trysts as a minor fling, and even stopped it as early as the initial days of London entrapment – and then, could have sent her back to her widowed mother in Karachi. But she was so different back then, full of verve and cheer for our shared potential destiny. Two decades ago, when every day held the promise of a revolution breaking out back home, an uprising that would be followed swiftly by our exultant return.

Look at us now, staring each other down over our daughter's head. One of us knows the future; the other one wants to shop away the past.

Let's not be callous. I *do* admit failures on my end. Though not in politics. Not in gearing up for the long-houred games. And certainly not in conjugal matters.

What I failed most at: being an inspirational father to my daughter. I'll be the first to admit it. This lissome assemblage of flesh that I love beyond reason – I could not instil in her the awe that Grandpa Pir gifted me. I don't know where it all went downhill.

Should I have taken her to the regular party meetings in London, when she was teeny tiny and the meetings still mattered? Or let her watch the news to get her acclimated more to the politics of our people? She was too young. Still is a child, even though she displays the sensibility of someone twice her age.

Maybe it all started with my not being a strong husband to her mother. I never laid down *the law*. Mrs Al did everything she wanted, and went anywhere and everywhere across England and Wales – provided the bodyguards and I were available to accompany her on the excursions. Everything I did was either for the household's protection and sustenance, or for the entertainment of its inhabitants. Maybe *that* was weak. Maybe it should have all been my way, not the highway.

But then, Grandpa Pir was never gung-ho about being the ruler of his house either. He let the women run whatever semblance of order in his house they wanted while he committed his crimes of piety. There *was* a kind of horror that took you over when you looked at him, though. Maybe that's what I should have cultivated: horror. Grandpa Pir was lace-thin. A wisp of a man, with mosquito limbs, who could fly away when the wind picked up. Whenever his eyes were open, and the spark of imminent death was not alight in them, with his manure-stench mouth and gold-yellow eyes, he was the spitting image of the devil's own son.

And yet, for all the derision with which I remember the Antichrist's doppelgänger, I would gladly take Grandpa Pir's lank and nimble frame, rather than be left with my own father's floppy body topped off with his pumpkin head. Even when I was waistless, able to touch toes without bending at the knees (okay, admittedly bending *a little* at the knees) my face was still the basketball it is right now. Splotchy, dark, and as round as a moon in eclipse.

Grandpa Pir, how did you take my father for your son? Why did you not suspect foul play in your house? I look back, haunted by my grandmother's very likely passionate embraces with some foreign body, an un-Pir corporeality.

Pumpkin-heads, my dad and I. The only two fatheads in the family. At least there was no doubt, given the ample evidence of replicated contours, that I sprang out of his own loins. The heads were inimitable, yes, but so were the lips: plump since birth. Father and I, we were as linked as any two gibbons are tethered by lack of adequate evolution to look essentially the same.

The only difference was: father had nothing to offer, to anyone, at all. And if you don't have any talents for public consumption, you're stuck outside the system of life. Supply and demand. That's what life is, when you look down the double-barrel of it. Grandpa Pir was supplied with skills to enkindle virtually anyone's flame of faith. A British housewife, in the old days of United India, begged to be initiated as Grandpa Pir's protégé.

Grandpa Pir, you went too soon. I could have used more lessons on how to be a good father. Wish you could have traded places with your son in the order of deaths.

Ah, well ... wishes: horses – beggars: riders. Et cetera; et cetera.

Instead of the upbeat conversation, about homecoming after more than two decades of exile, which is what I would have liked to have had with the Mrs and Pink— *Fatima! For God's sake, it's Fatima!* – the passage from home to Heathrow Airport has been consumed entirely by my own thoughts. A shame, really, how I take refuge from domestic obligations inside my own balloon.

We're here, pulling into the drop-off area at the airport. Onto the loading of luggage into carts. Phil does most of the hauling. Mother, wife and child follow us as we push the carts and get them lined up at the kiosk for Pakistan International Airlines' priority-class passengers from London to Karachi. Here comes the awkward hugging.

How do you wrap your arms around your wife for the last time? How do you kiss your child and send her to Hell? How do you honestly look into your mother's eyes while executing nefarious plans against your own family? Oh, she knows. Of course, she knows. Maybe all of them do, on varying levels of comprehension.

Only my mother and her grandchild will survive Pakistan. Updates have been issued into the Instructions. Ammi thinks erroneously that it'll be she who will be riddled with bullets at Zamzama Market. Poor Ammi. Wish I could spare her the suspense, but I can't let even her in on every plan.

I hug the wife first. Mrs Al pecks quickly at both my cheeks; eager to get going, she is. How meaningful was our life together? She should never have looked back at me across the halls in Karachi all those years ago. It's all *her* fault.

Ammi's next. She holds on, says something in my ear. 'Yes, mother mine?' I ask. 'What was that?'

'I'll wait on the other side,' she says softly. She steps back and looks at me with something like love. Is it resignation? Does she not suspect—? Oh, *oh*... 'other side' as in not Pakistan, but *aah* ... *right*. She *does* suspect it will be she who gets tripped into the grave before the rest of us.

I look deep into her eyes and say, 'I'll see you in Karachi in a few days. Be strong. Listen to everything my people tell you.'

She nods and looks away. I turn and face my daughter. She's sulking; a teenager in deportment at least, if not as yet in age.

She doesn't want a massive hug. Too bad. Papa wants one. I crush her to my chest. She squeezes out a tear or two. Maybe from the pressure I've applied. I let go, and then *she* hugs me. I love this kid. She's going to rule the world one day. Well, at least Pakistan.

That done, and some trite things said, Phil and I watch the ladies obtain their first-class boarding passes and go through security. They turn and wave, and I wave and turn.

Once back in the taxi – just the one this time, as all the luggage and human baggage is departed – Phil and I sit in the back seat. I look out the window at the passing grey roads, the brown and dull tenements. It'll be time to say goodbye to Old Blighty pretty soon.

'Did you really do it, Al?' Phil asks, a few minutes into the ride home. How bluntly he puts the question, and, yet … quite subtly. I like that. 'It' he calls the Ladbroke Grove act – what a magic word 'it' is. 'It' could be anything. I look away from the window and at my titanic protector.

I nod.

He shakes his head, smiling with mouth ajar. I've done it. I've created authentic amazement where there was none just before.

'You figure your plan will work, Boss?' Phil asks.

'I don't know,' is my first reaction. He gets me unguarded like this, Phil does.

Wonder why I trust him nearly as much as I trust myself; but how can I not appreciate the understated manner in which he carries all two tons of himself? Then I brace us both by saying: 'There's no reason the plan shouldn't work. With what's at stake, I mean. And thanks for playing your part. The news must have shaken them up back home.'

'It's causing chaos,' Phil says. 'Everyone's texting, asking me whether you've got a list you're working on. Some believe you do. And you're crossing it off as you go.'

'A *list*,' I say, trying the word. 'I like that.' And I turn back to the window. So, the whisperers in Karachi have been doing considerable work while I slept.

For the rest of the ride, we don't speak. Phil's got his own set of things on his mind, and I've got my mind to rest up for the battles ahead. A *list*… It would have been fun to have created a list of the order in which— but one's got to be dynamic about this sort of thing. Play the cards as and when they need to come into play. Pre-planning ruins the fun that spontaneity allows.

We reach home without any snaking about on the side-roads. Standing in front of the house, Jordan's got a copy of the afternoon paper in his hands. He's catching up this very moment on the double-suicide-slash-suspected-murder-suicide-two-people-dead-with-one-bullet-thingamabob that happened in Ladbroke Grove last night. The newspaper reporter plus the wannabe bodyguard – it's clicking with the details Phil has shared with him as well. Such a pleasure to teach one-plus-one to an adult with practical examples.

I jab at the newspaper in Jordan's hand and say, 'Yeah. That was my work.' His eyes – I want to see that look *every*where. I leave them to it at the front door. Bulk & Hulk share updates in the news about my shenanigans from last night while I enter the house and turn the TV on and start flipping.

On every Pakistani channel, there's looped tapes playing of the riots that have grown bigger in Karachi and Islamabad, and the new ones that are starting in Faisalabad, Lahore, Quetta, Dera Ghazi Khan, Multan, Abbottabad, Peshawar, Gujranwala, Swat, Gilgit – even *Gilgit*, that peaceful hill station so far out of the way, in the north – the people are rising up and taking sides. Blatant acts of violence. The terrible quality of the video feeds isn't helping; some gruesome content there. A lot of shouting by the newscasters. It's making their day. Two parties have taken to the streets; they have no logos, no colours, no stated affiliations; these mobs swearing allegiance *against* rather than *for* any ideology. All they're doing is protesting against two sets of people, my own creations: 'The Bitch and Mr Charming Bastard', and 'The Fat One', accusing the former two of blasphemy against the Holy Prophet, and the other one of being an agent of India's secret service. Pictures of each of the targets are held up aloft on banners and flags; crossed-out or flame-consumed pictures, most of them. All three of the targets were, at one point or another, the prime ministers of Pakistan; The Fat One is currently still latched onto that lofty position. News anchors and analysts on MARRO, ERY, Impress, DUSK, Chup, Aakhirat, and all the other warmongering channels, are perplexed by the protests, and making wild guesses about the 'real' reason and the timing, which is coinciding with the Shia processions for Muharram.

What's the agenda? Everyone's wondering. Shocks have been rent into the system. Again, this thought: *I have created wonder and awe*. God has given me the power and the grace.

Comes back the recital – is that what to call it, or shall I call it a *list*? – to my head like a childhood nursery rhyme: *Bashful, Sleepy, Sneezy, Happy, Grumpy, Dopey and Doc.* Again: *Bashful, Sleepy, Sneezy, Happy, Grumpy, Dopey and Doc … and Doc … and Doc …* and so on, ad infinitum. If I send out this *list* on a party broadcast email, will the seven sinful dwarves even know which code name stands for any of them? Will they figure out which one Basheer is? And Hammad? Will they think he's the one I call *Happy*? The 'H's' will coincide, but nothing else. No – they exist as nothing but seven wonderful animated beings who may as well be abstract and two-dimensional.

One hour until the flight with my family takes off from Heathrow. And one hour left, as well, until this year's Annual General Meeting of the Pakistan Immigrants Party Leadership Council in Karachi. It's time to send out the reminder. In the living room, I type out the email on my ancient laptop – really should replace this beast already. Get one of those sleek Mac machines. Phil says they're simpler to use.

Never before the AGM, in any of the last twenty-two years, have I sent a reminder email. It's been left up to Doc the Deputy to do that if he chooses. Some years he did; others, he didn't bother. I kept note. In any case, everyone on the council knows what time to congregate. At 10 p.m., just two hours before the cusp between 8th and 9th of Muharram is crossed, a week into the Islamic new year, while the world is preparing for the commemoration of Karbala's massacre, the Immigrants Party Leadership Council meets in the basement conference room of the Karachi Sheraton to plan the new year's political and social activities. Mostly chitchat is what it is. A chance for me to confer briefly with just the leaders, without the hordes of Immigrants cramming them up, in one place at one time. Just seventeen people around the table, and good ol' Al at the head, projected via Skype from London.

Tonight's meeting will serve a different purpose this year. Hence the switching up of who sends a memo to the council. This is what I type out in the email to the seventeen leaders: 'Gentlemen, looking forward to seeing all of you in attendance tonight. 1 hour to go. I have news.'

I press 'Send', but then do a double take. I forgot that one of the old stalwarts, one of the ten trustworthy and obedient conformists of the party, one who doesn't dare lie knowing what he knows about Al's abilities, wrote to me last weekend that he might not make it to the AGM. Ninety-one years old he is, six times a great-grandfather already, and he's got the genuine excuse of a heart murmur to keep him tied down and tubed up in bed. I've been sent pictures of his recent EKG as evidence. But this is a good litmus test. Let's see if even he shows up. Yes, let's see if there's enough fear of Al's so-called *list* in Karachi's troposphere for even a thoroughly vetted and legitimate excuse to be considered inadequate by the supplicants. Let them think Al's watching even closer than he is. Their Big Brother Al. Always watching, he is.

They'll reach for the more personal connection when they can, the party leaders.

To emails like mine, they'll reply by text. I'm quite prepared for that. Incoming any second now.

The first text I receive is from Sleepy. Rather vigilant, isn't he? This is what he writes: 'Looking forward to seeing you on Skype, Altamaash Bhai. Hope it's all good news?'

Sleepy's on high alert. But he won't get the satisfaction of a reply from me. *Show up to the meeting* is implicit in the silence from my side.

Two more texts arrive within a second of each other. One from Bashful, Sleepy's spiritual twin. They must be out creating trouble together. Must have conferred on what to write in response to my email. This is what Bashful's text says: 'Looking fwd, Altamaash Bhai.' No questions asked. They're wondering which one I'll reply to with affirmation. Let them wallow in the pits of wicked wonder.

The final text is from Doc. He writes: 'was just about to send a reminder myself, brother. looking forward to it. and to your news.' That lowercase 'b' will cost him.

Dopey, Sneezy, Grumpy and Happy – they don't even dare text responses. Cowering together, bucking themselves up with liquor, most likely.

Forty-eight minutes to go. There's such a load of time left. I could take a quick nap, even. But there's tangled up in my thoughts music for a tango. Makes me feel like flinging around some commands and demands. A furious kind of loving up a partner on a dance floor is what I feel like doing. So, I give in.

First, I reach out and ping Karachi Central Zone. A between-first-and-second-ring pick-up. Excellent. That's how you do it in a war zone.

'Karachi Central,' says the receiver. 'Salaam, Al Bhai.'

'This call's encrypted?' I ask.

'Double-encryption,' comes the reply. Some noise of crowd behind him, but his voice is crystal clear.

'Good. How goes everything?'

'Tip-top, Bhai. Peaceful Shia procession not being interrupted. Anti-The-Fat-One protestors everywhere they were deployed, and anti-Bitch-and-Bastard ones are catching up to their spots; a million and a half of our people out there recruiting citizens to join the processions; some clashes with the police; some baton-charge injuries; three shops completely burnt down, two banks looted – one of them by us; more than twenty arrested, but that number will rise; one dead on each side; smoke and tear gas grenades. Elite force and Rangers are expected any time now. We will have reinforcements ready, and fresh blood to relieve anyone injured. Any further instructions, Bhai?'

'Carry on,' I say, pleased with the report. 'Phase Two when I tell you. Not before.'

'Roger that, Bhai.'

I'm so, so pleased, that I don't want to hang up on this minion. We could become lovers waiting each other out on who hangs up first, chuckles my inner heart. Somehow, that reminds me of Guardian Greg. Well, here's your sacrifice paying off, GGGGGGGJ. Would love it if your ghost could see this.

Next call is to Lahore Central Zone. Third-ring pick-up. A tad late, that. I brace myself for an unsatisfactory conversation.

'Al Bhai, salaam. This is Lahore Central Zone.'

'The call's encrypted?'

'Quadruple encrypted, Bhai.' What a pompous shit. I've never even heard of encryption of that level.

'Right,' I say. 'Update?' I'm prepared to leave this call quite pissed off at Lahore's insipid attempt at one-upping Karachi.

'Bhai, besides the seven hundred thousand protestors and rioters deployed in all central zone and other locations mentioned in the Instructions, and other than the scores of baton-charged injuries we've sustained from the police, and even more than the protection we're providing to the Shias and their Muharram processions, not to mention the three grenades hurled into a police station because of which we're getting beaten back in Lahore Western zone quite a bit, but beyond even the life-sized effigies of The Fat One, The Bitch and Mr Charming Bastard burning one after another for fifteen hours straight by our people as well as by bystanders who are getting recruited by our speeches and demonstrations, I have some great news for you, Bhai.'

Out of breath, he stops after that sentence. Have to admit, Lahore's got my curiosity tickled with that last bit.

'Well then,' I say. 'Out with it. What's the news?'

'We've got The Fat One's youngest brother in our custody. He's completely apolitical and distances himself from the rest of the family's businesses. But we thought that's for you to decide, Bhai. We picked him up from a pharmacy where he was buying medicines for his wife. He is in a safe house, unharmed and secure. I was waiting for your call, Bhai, so you can tell us what to do with him.'

Bless this man. A pleasure to hear about competence of this level. What pleasing resourcefulness Lahore has displayed. To rescue – that's how we'll frame it – from the mob an opponent's brother. Good political mileage, that.

'Well done, son,' I say down the line. 'You've taken excellent initiative. I'll remember this one.'

'Bhai,' he says, 'we are proud to do anything that brings a smile to your face.' Oh so charming. Will have to watch out for this one – maybe there's an eighth sin or dwarf or wonder or spice to name him after. I'll call him Habanero for now. Très piquant.

'Keep him safe, and I'll let you know what to do very soon,' I say, signing off. He hangs up first. I like that. Confident little Habanero.

Where to next – where, indeed? The map of Pakistan spreads out in my mind. Let's hit a trouble spot, shall we? I dial.

'Bhai?' comes the voice down the line, before even the first ring is through. *A bit too fast?* May spell trouble.

I wait. And the minion from Multan doesn't state his location: *Multan Central Zone.* So, I cough.

'Bhai, you're there?' That's what he asks, instead of confirming for me his position.

'Of course.' Okay, okay, I calm myself; I'll be polite with the reprimand. 'Son, please state your zo—'

'Bhai,' he cuts me off, 'I need to talk to you. I don't know who else—'

'Is this call encrypted?' I ask, interrupting, sensing an emergency bigger than I thought Multan would be hosting by now. Did they fudge up everything up there in the hot Punjabi city? Should maybe have prioritized Multan and sent in a more capable crew rather than leave everything to the local chapter's workers? There, on the ticker on TV, Multan's showing as having '*erupted in chaos and violence*'. But no other details just yet; no video feeds. Got to find out what's going on. Could call up Multan East or West zones to check as well, but I believe in delegation whenever it's possible.

'Encrypted?' the minion from Multan mulls. 'I don't know, Bhai. I didn't know we were encrypting calls. Maybe it *is*. I'm not sure. I'm the backup guy; the main dispatch person was on duty for sixteen hours straight, and he's taking a three-hour break to sleep.'

I have to decide in two seconds whether to hang up on this potentially unsecured line or to continue chatting with this man.

Thousand one.

Thousand two.

I'm still here. Must mean I've decided to wait for the conversation to become compromised before hanging up.

'Okay, forget encryption,' I say. 'But encode your report. No specifics.'

'I need to talk to you, Bhai. I have nobody else to talk to about this. Bhai, Altam – Bhai, my nephew died. I found out an hour ago that he's dead. Hello, Bhai?'

Death over phone calls. Shouldn't I hang up? But the hoarse voice is drawing me in. I glance at the clock. Thirty-six minutes to go until the AGM with the Leadership Council. How else can I kill time? Twiddling my ten toes? His *nephew* just died. The least I can do is offer – of course.

'I'm so, so sorry, son. Can you reach out to Karachi Central Zone after two days and—'

'Bhai,' he says, 'I just want you to listen to me. There's nobody else I can talk to.'

All right. I'll take the chance. Biting the bullet, I say: 'I'm here, son. What's your name?'

'My name is Adnan. Everybody calls me A.D.'

'A.D. Okay. What rank are you?'

'Assistant to the Dispatch, Bhai. I sit here in the party's main office in Multan and relay information back and forth from different quarters.' He explains it as though I'm unaware of what a Dispatch does. Must be in shock, this A.D.

'And what's your report so far? I see news of violence.'

'It's very, very violent,' he says. That's two 'verys' – is that all the numerical data I'll get from A.D?

'A.D,' I say. 'I sense I'm rushing you. Why don't I take a step back and stop asking you questions? Your nephew just died and you say you need to talk. Let's talk then. I have a few minutes.'

'Yes, Bhai,' he says. 'I didn't know you would call, but I was hoping you would. I was praying for it.'

'You have my ears, son. Tell me what happened.'

'Bhai, I've been a soldier since I was very young in the party. I was only six – I'm starting from the beginning. Is that okay?'

'We only have a few minutes,' I say, leaning back, closing my eyes, picturing a six-year-old boy running around the 1990s streets of Karachi, a speck in the layers upon layers of metro-pulsed activity.

'I used to be in the party's information network. Following people. You know, one of the kids who would spy on targets. I was good.'

'Mhmm.'

'I was very good at that, but of course it couldn't be a permanent job. But I got to do some really neat things. I grew up listening to your speeches, for one thing. They were really motivational, you know.'

'Mhmm.' I'm being lulled with flattery without being told the story.

'And listening to your speeches, I became something. I channelled my energy and did my bit of money collection and other things the party wanted from me.'

'Okay,' I say, glad that he isn't explicitly stating that he robbed and pillaged, and likely more.

'I even got to go to Dubai, every time the heat picked up. And I got pocket money from the party to have a fun time in Dubai. It was great; I felt rewarded and valued.'

'Right.' Should I rush him? If he needs prodding, Al will prod.

'And then I married the perfect woman, and the party paid for part of my wedding and even helped out when my wife and I wanted to start a small general store in the older part of Multan. From that store, and from the work the party provided, I was able to save up quite a bit. We were looking to buy a small house in one of the nicer neighbourhoods in Multan, to move away from the two-bedroom apartment we were sharing with my brother Jawad and his wife. Everybody calls him J.D. We grew up together, and everybody called us A.D and J.D.'

'Right,' I say. 'Look, I'm very sorry about your nephew—'

'Oh, sorry, Bhai. I don't mean to take up too much of your time. But please, listen. I'll try to get to the point quickly. I – so, yes; we had money saved up, but we also had obligations to my elder brother and his wife, who let us stay with them very cheaply for years while we saved up. They cared for us better than any parents could; when we didn't have money and couldn't ask the party for extra cash, J.D. always helped out. He's fifteen years older than me.'

The un-siblinged child living deep inside me wishes he had grown up with a brother. *Al and Pal*, we would have been called. Rhyming, like A.D. and J.D. Am I even listening to him any more?

Commiseration requires an open ear, but isn't this mere ramble? A.D. continues on the line from Multan, with purpose, with urgency.

'So, my wife and I had enough money to buy a decent three-bedroom house. We wanted to start a family. But we decided that we should pay back my elder brother in some way, reinvest in the family – you see, us middle-class people, we believe in progress, and we wanted our whole family to benefit. And my brother's son, my nephew, who was an angel of a kid—'

Finally, the nephew. 'Right,' I say. 'I'm sure.' Everyone's an angel once they're dead.

'I mean it, Bhai. He was such a good kid. He studied hard and obeyed his parents; no drugs, no bad habits, nothing. And he was only seven years younger than me, so he and I, we grew up almost like brothers. We used to joke that he was the youngest brother of A.D. and J.D.! His name was Kamal, but everyone called him K.D.'

'Mhmm.' I yawn and get ready to prod the Multan minion to finish up. I'm switching channels quicker on TV too.

'So, my wife and I gave our savings to our nephew, K.D. Rather, we paid for his ticket and tuition expenses so he could study at a university in America. He had partial scholarship for an engineering degree, and we paid the rest with our life savings. It was a gift and an investment, because we knew that K.D. would one day become a very successful engineer, and that would benefit everyone in the family.'

'Right,' I say. 'Sounds like a great kid. I'm sorry son, I have to—'

'I'm sorry for taking up so much time, Bhai. I promise, I'm almost there. So, K.D. – he had just completed his second year at the City University of New York and had already completed the requirements for a major in engineering and a minor in filmmaking. Did I mention that he was fond of making films? Well, he was very good. And we're progressive middle-class people, not narrow-minded like most of our distant relatives. So my brother J.D. and I – we thought why not let K.D. study filmmaking on the side if he's making excellent progress on getting his engineering degree as well. I'm sorry – I'm digressing—'

'I have an urge—' I say, looking at the clock again.

'Right, I'll get to the point now. So, Bhai, I— right, so, K.D. came back to Multan for vacations this summer and he was making all kinds of films, and doing an internship at a local power plant. We were all so proud of him. And then, today, he wanted to go film the procession of Shias, to make a film about the Karbala commemorations. And that's where it happened.'

'That's where what happened?' I say.

'He died.'

'Oh. Of course.' I say. 'Look, I'm sure he's in a better—'

'Well, as you know, the Instructions said to take out two main processions from the opposite sides of the city, anti-The-Fat-One in the west, and anti-The-Bitch-and-Bastard-One from the east. And the Shia procession for Muharram was expected to come from the south-west. But we didn't count on there being a large force of the army, the Rangers, the Elite Police and the paramilitary wing of the police. Did *you* know about this, Bhai, that there were going to be these joint exercises between these heavily armed groups in the city?'

'Yes,' I say. 'But they weren't supposed to engage with the processions. They weren't even deployed for peace-keeping.'

'Right,' he says. 'That was our understanding as well. But maybe they got itchy for some action, or they were provoked by something from our side, or maybe the Shia procession did something. There was even a large funeral procession. Some local man they called a saint died and the body was being led out. Anyway, there were too many people on the roads and something triggered them. It's chaos out there, Bhai. Seventy of our people have already died. That I know of.'

'I'm so sorry,' I say. 'But it will—'

'Even my nephew,' he says. 'He's dead. And my life savings that we invested in him are gone. Just like that.'

'I'm so sorry, son.'

'I found out an hour ago. He was filming the fight that broke out. Someone hit him on the head with a stick to steal the camera. He had a large professional filmmaking camera, you see? And then he got trampled.'

'Right,' I say. Phew. Finally, I can sign off by doling out some tangible form of condolence. 'You have my sympathies, A.D. If your brother and you reach out to the Karachi office, I'll make sure you're compensated with a house as well as—'

'Bhai, you're not hearing me,' he says. 'I don't want the money. I don't want anything.'

'Oh,' I say.

'Bhai, my life savings are gone,' he says, 'and one of the dearest people in the world to me is gone. And it's worth it. He was a sacrifice for the cause.'

'Listen, son—'

'Bhai, please, listen to *me*. I'm *glad* that he died. I'm glad that I was able to give something for the cause. It's only been an hour since a neighbour came to tell me he saw K.D.'s body lying on the ground, face bloated and arms broken. They stepped on him until he died. I don't think my brother knows as yet. I don't think he can handle the news. But I can.'

'Bu-ut—' I begin.

'Bhai,' he says, 'I grew up listening to your speeches on TV, on tapes and on the Internet. Without your speeches, I would have been nothing. Absolutely nothing. I wish I had been old enough when you were still in Pakistan. I would have been your *shield*, Bhai. I would never have let anything happen to you.'

'I'm pleased to hear tha—' I try again.

'When you were forced to flee Pakistan, I was only seven or eight; still too young. But now that I look back on it, I'm ashamed of everyone who was an adult at the time. Why didn't they rise against the oppression of our people? Not even a few among us raised their heads. Everyone went underground. Believe me, Bhai, you don't deserve us. We're filth. We should have risen up, together, as a nation, and we should have begun the revolution that would have released us from The Bitch and the Bastard and The Fat One. I'm ashamed that our fathers' generation didn't. They let you down.'

'A.D., son, I admire your passion for the cause. But you need not be so upset. You are playing your part like a champion. But as for your nephew—'

'A thousand such nephews will I sacrifice for you, Bhai. A thousand of them, and each of those a thousand times over!'

'A.D., my son—'

'The day we let you down, Bhai, was the day we let our whole cause down. If I have to give up *any*thing, or any person for you, Bhai – you are the leader of our times – I will do just that. If we don't suffer the minor inconveniences of our nephews dying or our cars burning, how will we ever welcome a *true* Messiah? Will we say "*No, thank you*" to him, and go on with our lives like it doesn't matter that he's offering us freedom from trials and eternal Salvation? Of course not. So, I welcome K.D.'s death. If my brother J.D. comes in your way, please remove him as well. If you want, *I* can do that. You have my unconditional support, Bhai. And please, don't even think about compensating me. My life and death are for your cause. Your cause is my cause.'

'A.D., my son,' I say, moved. *Moved*? Riveted – that's the word to describe me. Such beautiful words I've heard. Such welcome craving to belong to a righteous cause. Wish I could give young A.D. a standing ovation, but he wouldn't understand that. 'I feel you are being wasted in Multan. Why don't you come to Karachi and see me in a few days?'

'Bhai, you're coming *back*?' Incredulity. Disbelief, not awe. Needs work, this news-sharing of the return of Al.

'Oh, yes,' I say. 'As long as there are people like you in Pakistan, I have hope of making a triumphant return.' Good. That's vague enough.

'It's an honour, Bhai. To be counted among your people.'

'I have to go now, son,' I say. 'Take care. Come to Karachi. We'll talk more then.'

'I will come whenever you call, Bhai. A hundred thousand miles will I—'

I hang up, enlightened; loads have been lifted, and I'm glowing. If there was one wish that I carried over from the miasmic traditions of the old world, it was that of siring a son. Not fulfilled by either wife, unfortunately. But if there are more people like A.D., even after twenty years of carrying the burden of this expectation – what will *that* fatherhood be like? Surely different from the relationship I have with Pinky. Absolutely no question that she occupies the centre of my heart. But to have a whole country, filled with sons like A.D. – I'm quite sure I'm beaming so strongly that I'm emitting light. But an ugly mood is sure to follow. Magnificence always gets latched onto like that by shadows and darkness.

Fifteen minutes until the AGM. No other report can live up to Multan's A.D. So, I don't even bother dialling the other numbers.

There's a summary of the countrywide events in Pakistan now showing on the DUSK channel; I turn the TV's volume up.

The two rioting factions are blaming not each other, and not any person by name.

One mob is screaming out that 'The Fat One', Pakistan's current prime minister, is an agent of the Indian government – just a bit of a stretch there, since he's got business ties all across South Asia (which self-respecting head-honcho doesn't, after all?). The other party is calling The Fat One's supposed opponents, 'The Bitch' and 'Mr Charming Bastard', blasphemers against Islam's own Holy Prophet, may peace and blessing be upon him. Real names aren't even being taken on the streets, but posters and pictures have been pasted on shopfronts, bus stops and public transport vehicles, for all to visualize the targets of the protests. *Forget* their real names, these rioters are saying. Call them who they are: a bitch, a bastard and a fat man – blasphemers, traitors. The two mobs are calling for blood. With pitchforks and hockey sticks, cricket bats, guns and machetes, and even stones for hurling, my party's workers and ordinary citizens they've recruited from among the masses are blowing on the horn of civil war in the streets of every city in Pakistan. They've burnt cars and shops; they've injured and maimed civilians; there have been accidental sacrifices too. Collateral damage – expected and acceptable.

I have puppeteered violence into existence; energy out of nothing; I have made it dance in the streets of every Pakistani city without the appearance of my hands on the strings. My name – even my shadow – figures nowhere in these schemes.

DUSK channel's summary of the riots and the ads for shampoo, cell phones and detergents after it, take up ten minutes; five minutes left until the AGM. Fresh alerts show the guts of a burnt-down bank again and again. Good. Get them capitalists, you cheated masses. As if.

I put on the button-down grey shirt and navy blue coat I like to wear for Skype meetings; the headphones and my computer are all plugged in and jacked up.

BREAKING NEWS cycles are done with. Time to check in with the seventeen leaders.

I open Skype and wait. One minute before 10 p.m. in Pakistan, five hours ahead of London's 5 p.m.; the contact for 'Pakistan Immigrants Party' goes from offline to online. Ready or not, here I click.

My face, it will loom on that wall, as large as a blimp, floating above the seven sinful dwarves and the ten conformists.

Two rings, and then a wheel begins turning on screen, with the one word '*Connecting...*'

And then there they are, seated on both sides of a long table, laid out so I'm at the head of it. Two-four-six-eight ... yes, all of the ten benign oldies are there, including excusable great-grandpa with his ailing old heart. Doc, the Deputy of the Pakistan Immigrants Party, sits at the far end of the table, and the other six sinful dwarves are also in attendance. This is the first time in eight years that there has been full attendance at the AGM.

Hallelujah. Let the conference commence. 'Good evening, gentlemen,' I say.

'Good evening, Bhai,' so say they all. That's enough preliminaries.

'Two announcements I would like to make up front,' I say. 'One: we're changing the name of the party from Pakistan Immigrants Party to Pakistan Integrated Party. Two: I'm coming home tomorrow. Any questions?'

A thick fog of silence on my Bose QuietComfort 35 II noise-cancelling headphones is all I hear.

The first to exchange glances are Dopey and Doc. The others are hypnotized by Al, their overlord.

From the haze that's clogged them all, Dopey un-dopes himself first; he pipes up and says, 'Bhai, could you repeat what you said? There was static. Did you say—'

'I said, I'm coming home to Pakistan. Tomorrow.' I let that sink in. It's good to stop and watch. To glow on their seventeen faces from a screen in my faraway city of exile.

'That's fantastic,' says one of the commandable ten. These oldies – who keep alive despite themselves. They've got bent backs and crooked characters, all of them. But they're willing to take money and position that's dispensed out at my whims. They would have driven the party to despair had my own fresh ideas not come to rescue them. My ideas, and the young blood of the seven sinful dwarves.

'Are you serious, Bhai?' Sneezy sniffles from his mid-table position. 'That would be amazing, *if* it's possible.'

'We can make it possible,' says another stalwart with a large, Pinocchio nose. 'Anything's possible,' he says, with half-hearted gusto. He is afraid. They all are. Such defective characters surround this table. *How* did the party survive these managers of its affairs? On faith in the faraway king who's ready to come back, that's how.

'Ahem,' Doc, the Deputy Chairman, clears his throat, visibly uneasy. I know what he's going to say before he opens his mouth. It's as if I've rehearsed with him the script he's supposed to follow. Here he goes: 'Tomorrow? You mean you're coming back a *year* from tomorrow, right Altamaash? I mean, a *year* would give us plenty of time to prepare.'

'Deputy Chairman, by tomorrow I mean within twenty-four hours,' I say. 'My wife, my daughter and my mother are already on a plane to Karachi.'

'*What*?' Two of the oldies blurt out. Dopey, Doc, Grumpy, Happy – all of them, really, if I had time to look around – they all show some version of that shock.

But Doc is the one who keeps talking. He begins, and so do I; with my hands on either side of the laptop, I refer to the sheets of the Instructions under my left hand, and type on my phone with my right.

Here's what Doc says: 'Don't you think you're being too hasty about this, Altamaash? Shouldn't we set up some kind of security team to look into the arrangements? I mean, you know how in chess the king only manages from far away while the pawns and the other strong pieces move about; the king only moves if absolutely necessary. You obviously have the option of using our powers; delegate duties to us. We are your bishops, rooks and knights. You have thousands of pawns that you could use.' Poor Doc the Deputy; he doesn't realize how much I despise chess metaphors.

While Doc talks, my hands get busy. With my left hand's index finger, I confirm on the sheets of the Instructions the one command that needs to be issued; with the tip of my right thumb, I type it out on the phone: '*{.-/f()}*'. While Deputy Chairman Doc talks, this is the order issued for him from my phone: *whisper Lie #7341i in the ears of the person speaking, escort him out of this room; take him to a secure room within the hotel; tie him down and gag him; inject him with a hallucinogen that guarantees paranoia; thereafter, without letting too much of his* *blood stain the carpet or any furniture, chop off his joystick and shove it down his throat; without waiting for him to eject his own joystick from his mouth, put a plastic bag tightly around his face; make him choke to death; tidy up the room; remove your fingerprints, and any evidence that may compromise you. Leave the joystick where it is.*

Doc's not finished talking or worrying; at least, he doesn't want to be done. His agitation is creased on his forehead, and he's shaking his head like *I'm* the one being unreasonable. Would have liked to – anyway, it's time. I press Send. The symbols '{.-/f()}' get sent off across telekinetic airwaves to a phone inside the basement conference room of the Karachi Sheraton.

I watch the live video feed in London over Skype, as, in the basement conference room in the Karachi Sheraton, a man from the shadows around the lit-up conference table walks up to Doc and bends to whisper something in his ear. The other sixteen leaders of our party dart looks at Doc conferring with the man from the shadows, at each other, and at the projection of me. The man from the shadows unbends, but stays at Doc's side.

'Altamaash,' Doc says, looking up at the screen where I'm enlarged for everyone in that room, 'there's something I have to take care of quickly. An emergency in the Islamabad demonstrations, it seems. I'm afraid it's rather urgent. Would you excuse me for just two minutes? I'm sure we can discuss your plans for returning to Pakistan when I get back. Meanwhile, everyone can give you reports from around the country. I'm already up to speed on those. Is that all right?'

'Quite all right, Deputy Chairman,' I say into the camera's eye. 'Take your time.'

Up he gets from his chair, pulling at his coat flaps to button them around his paunch, but the coat is too tight, so he gives up. Poor Doc. Such an unseemly way to depart.

Everyone at the table watches him walk away from the table with the man from the shadows. Both of them leave the room from a door at the far end.

Now un-Doc'ed, the table turns to colossal Al. I give them a benevolent smile. Sixteen Pakistani politicians in a conference room. Thugs, all of them. There's music to be made out of these elements. A tear-jerking opera.

'Gentlemen, let's hear your reports.' Part of me already wants to gloat. But I'll wait for the formalities to be concluded.

I keep a stiff upper lip as Dopey starts.

'Bhai,' he says, 'I can give you the Sindh recruitment status. We've got—'

'Stop,' I say, and relish having shut him up. Nobody takes up my talking space unless I let them. 'Let's start by refreshing everything you all are supposed to be doing. Let's go around the table, shall we? Who would like to start?'

'You mean—' Dopey begins again, as if he's the Deputy Chairman in the absence of the Deputy Chairman.

'Anyone but you,' I say. 'Anyone else.'

Sleepy half-raises a hand, and Dopey glares at him, betrayed. Sleepy begins: 'Bhai, do you mean we should summarize our agenda for the riots?'

'Yes,' I say. 'Play me back what's written in the Instructions.'

'But *you* wrote them,' Grumpy chimes in. And adds a late, fearful, 'Bhai.'

'Sometimes it's good to hear your words in other people's mouths,' I say.

'As you wish, Bhai,' Sleepy says. 'As per the Instructions, we were supposed to do the following in all major and minor cities around our allotted zones: collect voter lists from local police stations and Election Commission offices; use the lists to identify supporters of The Fat One, The Bitch and

Mr Charming Bastard; make a bloody spectacle of the said supporters; co-opt the police, rile up their sentiments of patriotism and love for the Holy Prophet, get them involved in, or at least sanction, the looting and destruction of property belonging to our three targets and their cronies; allow chaos to fester in the wake of our targeted activities, but protect the Shia processions;—'

'Enough,' I say. 'Your voice is too dull for such matters. Work on it. Pronunciation, cadence, drama – all of those need some work. I recommend that you take some voice elocution lessons.'

'Bhai?' Sleepy asks; a quiet question. This madness of their projected overlord is new for them, because it's been dormant too long. But it's time it started resurfacing. We're almost there.

'Don't *Bhai?* me,' I say. 'Not now. Not ever. You *Bhai* me to my face, and carry out only half of my instructions. Where are the *thousands* of *burning cars*? Where are your *own* sacrifices? Not *one* of you has suffered, and not *one* of you has been in the fields where the action is taking place.'

'Altamaash, Bhai,' Dopey again. 'We *are* in the field. You know we are. It's very well to accuse us while sitting in London, but we are all doing our best.'

'Your best?' I ask. 'Can you kill two people with one bullet?'

Again, breathing stops in the Karachi Sheraton's basement conference room. Nuclear silence reigns.

'So, it's not a rumour?' Grumpy steps in with that question. There is an element of disbelief in his tone, although clearly pretended.

'No,' I say. 'No rumours between you and me. We've got much more intimacy now.'

And the back door opens just as I say that. In through the door comes the man from the shadows who led Doc out. But

Doc isn't with him. The man from the shadows, the self-effacing man, he shuts the door, nods at the screen where I'm projected, and texts me a 'Y'. Easy to decipher. I have no need to look at the Instructions for this one. And now, the stage can be lit up and I can reveal things.

'Gentlemen,' I say, 'look around you. There's sixteen of you at the table. Only a few minutes ago, there were seventeen. The Deputy Chairman was called away to deal with an issue with the Islamabad riots. Do you want to know what he was told in his ear?'

Everyone around the conference table appears tense, as they would be if they were on the hot seat, looking for the final answer in *Who Wants to Be a Millionaire?* Except, this is not multiple choice; and it's not a *reward* situation.

'He was told,' I begin the reveal, 'that the prime minister of Pakistan, The Fat One, wanted to make a compromise with him. That's what was whispered to him. And he got up, looking to deceive me about the message, just as many of you have been deceiving me.'

Nobody responds. Good.

'What actually happened is that there is no more Deputy Chairman.'

'What's that?' This is great-grandpa leader's only contribution to the meeting so far.

'Exactly what I just said,' I say. 'The Deputy Chairman is no more.'

There's a short pause while that sinks in.

Then Dopey starts up: 'Bhai,' he says, acting all leader-of-Karachi-branch-of-the-party again, 'what's the meaning of all this? What's going on?'

'You,' I say, 'I'm guessing you were one of the sceptical ones when it was brought up that I may have a *list*.'

'Good God,' says great-grandpa. His poor ninety-year-old heart. Must have aged a decade in the past two minutes. Completed a century, he has.

'I knew it!' Sneezy starts sobbing. He holds his head with both hands and looks wildly around at every one of his colluders. 'I *told* you he had a list. Oh, Bhai, Bhai.' Poor Sneezy, breaking down under the slightest of pressures.

For the rest to come around, I lay out the roadmap for the coming activities. 'Gentlemen, there are sixteen of you at the table. Do you know how many more members of the party stand in the shadows of the room you're in? What about the shadows outside this room? That's it; look around yourselves. You think you're *leaders*; you think you delegate duties and choose what information to distribute among your network of underlings. Let me ask you this: did you think that there was only ever *one* version of the Instructions?' Rhetorically helping to expand their vision, I pause to let them absorb the implications of my words. 'A man in exile for twenty-three years – you'd think he's got time on his hands to write up more than one *list* of instructions, no? Well, you placed your chicks on the wrong assumption, and they ain't gonna hatch. The Deputy Chairman has been dealt with as I just euphemistically pointed out. If any of you sixteen wants to join him in a similar fate, speak up now … or … forever hold your peace.'

They're not even looking at each other any more. Dopey's staring into blank space; the middle distance is what you choose when you've lost sight of the short- and the long-term. Good. I like my minions self-aware.

'Here's what's going to happen from here on. Since you don't have a complete copy of the Instructions, you need to know this. So, pay attention. Phase Two of the riots begins immediately. You didn't know there was going to be a Phase Two, did you?

Well, now you do. Here's what it entails: first of all, all sixteen of you gentlemen will hold a joint press conference at midnight tonight – it's been arranged, all you have to do is attend. It's right here in this conference room. In the press conference, you will read out a statement – and you will do it with *great* enthusiasm – a statement saying that the Pakistan Immigrants Party has realized the need of the hour, and is changing its name and its agenda accordingly. The party will henceforth be renamed the Pakistan Integrated Party. Nice to keep the acronym the same, right? PIP. Our new slogan: "Safety and Rights for All".'

'My God,' great-grandpa never thought he'd see such a revolutionary as me. Or maybe he's complaining about his weak heart hurting.

'Fuck,' Happy says. Naturally.

'That's not all,' I continue. 'At the press conference, you will also state that all of your houses – that's right, your own houses – and all the party's offices are places of refuge for anyone who feels threatened by the rioters out there. "All are welcome", you will say. You will announce that, and you will put it into action. Anyone who enters your house, be they from The Fat One's party or the party of The Bitch and The Bastard – they will be safe in your households. Don't worry; their safety is going to be a priority for us; your safety, your families' safety, and the safety of everyone who wishes to take refuge in your ridiculously large number of properties. From here on in, you'll each have at least twenty people from our party around you all the time. These people have a separate set of the Instructions, and that overrides yours. I suggest you go along cheerfully, and nothing else will be altered. You will maintain the status of party leaders and you will continue to issue out commands that your people will tell you to issue out to them. Food and shelter are the main things you must provide to anyone who comes looking for them. Open up your sprawling estates, gentlemen. It's time to give back to the masses. Right after the press conference, all of your estates, all the party's properties will be opened for public shelter. Throughout Pakistan. Every single one of them. Is that understood?'

A murmur, a few resigned nods. Some dumbfounded looks. Doesn't matter. They're stringed up and ready to go on stage to play their parts.

'Just before we sign off, I have a couple of more things to confirm,' I say. 'First, I *am* coming tomorrow. Do you know why tomorrow, and not a week from now, or any other day?'

'Tomorrow is sooner than any other day,' says great-grandpa. He's now de-facto spokesperson for the spayed sixteen, it seems.

'Very well done, uncle. Tomorrow is soon,' I say. 'Also, tomorrow, as you all may recall, is the tenth of Muharram, the day of Prophet Muhammad's grandson's sacrifice, may God give him the highest of places in Heaven.'

But look further in history, my mind informs me. This date extends in significance all the way to the first human. That's right. I look the camera in the eye and share none of the glory that will be in my head when I fly down to the east: The tenth of Muharram is the day when Adam's repentance for the Original Sin was accepted; when Noah's ark came to rest on dry land after the Great Flood; when Abraham was given the title of Friend of God; Joseph was released from prison on this day; Jacob regained his sight; Jonah sprung out of the whale's belly; Moses freed the Jews from the Pharaoh; Jesus was lifted up to Heaven, this very day; and *then* our own beloved Prophet Muhammad's grandson was martyred.

Is that a tear I'm squeezing out of my left eye? On the other end, in the video, they're dazed, confused, and stuck in waiting. All *that* on a single day; I can't tell any one of them that. Of course they will disbelieve; none of them is mythologically inclined. Darn, useless sceptics. But never mind; the significance of the date can be invoked later, post-fact, for good use.

'Gentlemen,' I say, 'the tenth of Muharram, tomorrow, will also be the day that Pakistan is freed from the clutches of false democracies. I will be there. I will see you shortly. Meanwhile, you have a press conference to prepare for. Remember – read the statement to the press with *great* enthusiasm. Until tomorrow.'

I click the button to end the conversation. One more thing that kept me from Pakistan has been crossed off. Not much more to do now. I could take a nap, of course. Listening and talking are exhausting tasks. Before that promised rest, I stand in the kitchen, looking around, hungry for something; a craving I cannot fathom except as a vision in which I see myself in a General's uniform for some reason, and oh, so much leaner! Like a veteran-of-wars, lightly-paunched General. I've got a beret slanted on my head, and I'm standing tall out of the sunroof of a black Mercedes.

The doorbell rings, interrupting things. I look away from the kitchen, out the window. Outside, Phil and Jordan are deep in conversation with three men, shaking hands and patting backs. Are those— they are, indeed! That was quick. I didn't expect the culprit sycophants to come back this hastily after Pakistani politics started playing up.

The door opens, and in walk three old loyalists. These retired bureaucrats were Immigrants who left for London shortly after The Bitch started hunting our people down. Most went underground for a year, or made compromises like the sinful dwarves, but many headed out of the country. Dubai, Saudi, the US, the UK, Denmark, Finland – wherever they could get some sort of foothold.

Veterans of Pakistani procedures and politics, all of us. I hug each of them with implicit forgiveness for avoiding me at Selfridges and Harrods, and for considering me a has-been for nearly a decade. They've gathered each other, and courage, of course, to be here now. It's time to get them rooting for the home team. Indeed, it is time.

'How's your mother, Altamaash?' one asks, sudden-like.

'She's perfect, thank you,' I say.

'She's already in Pakistan?' another follows up.

'No, no,' I say. 'The flight just took off.' I thought news wouldn't travel until the ladies landed in Karachi.

'But the ticker said—' they begin.

I cut them off, 'Which station?' And they guide me to MARRO channel. There. I must have missed it earlier. '*Political exile Altamaash's wife, daughter and mother sighted at airport, boarding flight from London to Karachi.*' It's nuzzled in with other floating text snippets about scenes from Pakistan: burnt tyres and buildings, an arbitrary number of lost lives, fears of the government about to topple, and the greater alarm about an imminent military takeover.

That *was* quick. But it's Pakistan. It's always been suspended mid-pirouette at the edge of collapse. Nothing's quick enough when it comes to Pakistan, except news, which travels faster than bullet trains in that country of constant emergencies.

I turn the TV off. I face them, the toadies. They came to be informed, to bask within the halo of power.

'Gentlemen,' I say, 'a new era of politics is about to begin. The three of you are the first in London to witness the change. My family has moved back, which will be followed shortly by me heading back home. Yes, I, Altamaash, who was chased out of Pakistan over twenty years ago – the people will beg for me to come back. I will return triumphant.'

They face me with fear, they face me with confusion, they face me with doubt. In future, these sentiments will combine to become one: abject, reverential, wonderstruck awe. I will allow only that.

III. Edwin 'Ned' Steinberg

Al's got a gun in his hand. He's older and paunchier. His hands are shaking. But the grin on his face is making him look just as old as when I last saw him when he was alive. The gun isn't even pointed up, just diagonally down, where a man is lying down, beaten up, jaw broken and eyes swollen from being punched. Professional work on the face, by the look of it. But Al didn't do the punching. There's a bodyguard with a bloodied knuckle duster standing next to Al. Looks like Phil, but he's blurry. All I can see clearly is Al's face. The rest is a little bit out of focus.

This is happening in a basement den, in the house belonging to the man who is on his back at Al's feet. The house is in Islamabad, Pakistan. Al's going around the country, hunting down anybody who stands in the way of the Pakistan Integrated Party. This man on the ground – beaten until he can't even make a sound – is not a political rival of Al's. He's just a tiny-framed bureaucrat, a paper stamper.

All he did wrong was he didn't stamp a paper at the Capital Development Authority that would allow Al to take over a public park in Islamabad. Al wanted that land so that he (Al) could sell three hundred acres of prime capital property to a housing development authority at market rate. The prostrate man's not signing the paper at his office has cost Al two more reams of paperwork to prove that selling off the land is necessary to bolster the Pakistani economy. And there's nothing Al hates more than paperwork.

So, Al has arrived here, at this man's house, after having the bodyguards make sure the house is clear of all witnesses, including the man's sons and his wife. He has had the man beaten up. And now he's pointing the gun at the man's forehead, threatening him.

'You'll do the paperwork now,' Al says. 'You'll do it as soon as you get out of the hospital.'

And Al shoots him the kneecap. The man barely grunts, he's so injured. But his eyes are popping out of his skull, with fear and pain.

'Take him to a doctor,' Al says to his bodyguard. 'Fix him up.'

I can see this happening in the future, given what I know of Al.

[Sudden, unequivocal transparence; Edwin 'Ned' Steinberg looks around at the nothingness; just as suddenly as its absence, there is reappearance of colour.]

This place is even darker than the basement just a moment ago. I'm not getting exact images, just darkness and outlines of shapes in a very ill-lit room. There's a skylight high up, but it seems like it's night outside.

There's a small desk in the room, and a bed, from what I can make out in the darkness. But Al is not lying on the bed. He's on the floor of the … it's a prison cell. Al is in prison. Wow.

He's much thinner too; the food must not be calorific enough to support his big frame. Skin hangs off his body, and he's been shrinking for over a year now.

He's the only one in his cell, but he can hear human sounds from the cell next to his. Just the one sound, actually. A whimper of sorts.

Al's lips are moving. He's saying something. I'm being taken closer to him every second. Zooming in. He's mumbling words, definitely, but I can't make them out yet.

The two sounds in the darkness overlap. A whimper, as if from an injured animal, from the room next door, and a whisper from the ground where Al is in this cell.

Now I'm close enough to hear some of the words Al is saying. '…forgive them, they … what they're … and forgive… take away … pain.'

He's … *praying*? Yes, sounds like it.

At first, I don't get it. But then I get it all at once. Like a curtain has been lifted, and I can see behind it.

Al is praying for 'the kid' – who's not really a kid, but just a man as small as a kid – who is crying in the room next door. Prison isn't a good place for someone so small. The kid has been raped by so many different people in the prison, he's lost feeling in parts of his lower body.

Al is praying not for himself, but for this 'kid', and also for the rapists.

This is what it takes for Al to pray? Will this happen? If even *he* can pray…

'God, you are great. Forgive them. Forgive them.' He drifts off into a sleep where the moaning from across the wall does not cross over.

[A return to the pure transparence, Edwin 'Ned' Steinberg, the puffy grey cloud, floats.]

NED: 'Our Father who art in Heaven…' I could never pray beyond that. I got stuck at the 'art'. How sad that I thought scripture was the only way to pray – that there were no other words. *Why does God speak old English?* That's what I used to ask myself. The Bible sounded so irrelevant to real life. I opened the Koran once, to see what was in it. It was in a foreign language, Hebrew or Arabic and the translation was completely gibberish. Buddhism also didn't strike a chord. *Nothing for me in meditation or yoga.* I remember thinking that. And that's what I honestly got out of religious experimentation. No God or Angry God doling out heavy punishments. I made my choice.

I never gave those books a chance. I never gave *You* a chance. Were You real, or were You just a collective hallucination for the religious types? I wondered about that sometimes. Especially whenever I was nearly broke and looking for jobs, trying to pray, but not being able to. *Our Father who art in Heaven*, I thought, and there I stopped, usually distracted by something. You've got so many distractions built into life. What's a man to do? Follow the lust for a perfect body, a chrome-plated shiny car, or the next gadget that promises to deliver incredible amounts of fun – all these turned out to be empty. Just things that burn away time…

What I don't get is this: small crime pays squat, yet You punish the small-time criminals too. What if You chose to let them off the hook? There's still big fish in the sea. There's the rich Tory bastards, pardon my French. There are the Nazis and the likes of Hitler and the Pharaohs. And murderers and rapists and pedophiles and thieves. The African warlords. Even *Al*. Heck, you've got all kinds of big gamers to throw into Hell.

Something for everyone, a comedy tonight. Something for everyone, a tragedy tonight.

A song from some film I watched as a kid.

Even now, I'm distracted. Why'd You make me this way, God? What's it like being the Lord of such different creatures as Al and Hitler and my mother and me? And will they be denied and disintegrated too?

Or will Al go to Hell?

Don't tell me You'll send him to Heaven…

You won't answer, will You? I haven't earned Your answers, I guess. But I wonder what your voice is like.

Even now, knowing this is real, I feel like I'm talking to empty air. So, what's the difference between life and this? I couldn't face You then, God. I never knew for sure that You were there. But *You* always knew I was where I was. Why didn't *You* – but … forget it. You're right. You're right to treat me like this. I'd be pissed too.

I should have done better.

It wasn't worthy of me to die like I did. Drunk, hypnotized by someone who's claim-to-fame is money-laundering and creating political chaos. I should have died better. I should have *lived* better too.

I accept Your judgement. I was selfish about everything.

But that doesn't mean I would do anything differently if You gave me life all over again. I would probably mess up in some way. So, you're right. And I'm glad you're getting rid of me. I'm sure glad you're not locking me up in Hell. Disintegration's much better as a prospect.

I do want to know something before You fade me out – vanish me, or however this next bit goes. I won't feel a thing, the Angel of Turning Away says. That's great. Thank You for that. Truly. From the bottom of my heart and soul, I'm massively appreciative.

But I want to know one thing: What's going to happen to Al? Tell me. I'm just curious. Send me Your angels. Give me a sign. Anything.

You know what I'm thinking. But I want to say it. Send me Your agent, Your angel, Your messenger. Please, God, let me be heard!

[White dot of light in the pure absence, appearing instantly, begins to pulse.]

NED: I see you, Angel. Thanks for coming. Can I pray, still? I want to pray.

ANGEL: Ned, you *have* been praying. You reached out. I have just returned from the Divine One's presence. He says it is time for your Disintegration to begin. But, before that, you may make one last request. Of course, there is a caveat: it has to mean something for someone other than yourself, because *you* will cease to exist shortly. So, you will never know if it is granted. Do you have such a request?

NED: Yes. There is one final thing. I want … I want Al to suffer a little.

ANGEL: Hmmm … do you mean that? Are you sure that is what you wish?

NED: Yes, I've decided. I want him to hurt.

ANGEL: Rather vindictive, I see. As expected, of course. You wouldn't want Al to be absolved of killing you. But I can only pass along one request, *if* any. Do you really wish him to hurt? Is there no other wish you would like to make?

NED: Yes, I want him to hurt. That's my only wish.

ANGEL: Hmmm … well, he was already planning— Well, you don't need to know this. So, okay. Vindictive urge stated. You know you could have requested some goodness for someone, right? Like easy-blooming flowers in your mother's garden, or some such trivial but kind thing.

NED: That's okay. I'm not worried about the consequences. I just want Al to feel a bit hurt. Maybe, you know, it'll set him on the right path. There's got to be *some* kind of justice for what he's done, right?

ANGEL: Ned, I would have enjoyed talking more with you. You're twisted in a kindly sort of way. Now that you see things as they truly are, that is. But your time is over. Are you ready?

NED: I'll never be ready not to exist, I think. You'll just have to do it. So, what happens next? What do I feel?

ANGEL: Edwin 'Ned' Steinberg, you have been Denied, and you are about to be Disintegrated. You were never the hero of your own life, Ned. To be a hero – to pass through the trials of growth from boy to man to saint – that is what you failed at. Your soul will disintegrate now, and its constituent parts will collapse back into All-Pervading Presence. A million thoughts about Al will now course through you, letting you observe what any one human being's potential can be. That the thoughts are not about yourself, but about your killer, is your ultimate punishment before you no longer exist. Then, nothingness. We're about to begin the process, Ned. Choose carefully in the next two seconds the words you speak. They will be your last.

NED: All right. Bring it o—

[Denial's done. Disintegration begins.]

8

Apotheosis

You know you're in political exile from Pakistan when you can't stop hitting refresh on your Facebook page, just to see if there are more 'likes'. You choose a threshold number that will make you believe it's time to go back; you raise the threshold each time it is surpassed. The day your numbers stop increasing is the day you die.

I. George Gary Gregory Jaffar

[From The Belly, the being that is George Gary Gregory Jaffar zooms out to one moment in Al's life, and then to the next. He chooses the politically enabled Altamaash, the one that the asylum in UK propped up to scare Pakistan from the European haven.]

From far away, once his safety is not an issue, Al is able to rejoin the Pakistani political arena via telelink. He watches as power keeps getting handed over from The Fat One to The Bitch and Mr Charming Bastard, and then back to The Fat One, like a whoopie cushion passed back and forth. He holds his peace while the seven sinful ones bite away pieces of the Immigrants Party and give up all that he worked for. He watches, he seethes, he bides his time. The millennium turns; things heat up. The

Internet is made for Al. Especially YouTube. In Pakistan, it may as well be called AlTube. He doesn't make his own channel; he doesn't need to. Clips of him addressing his party through Pakistani media outlets stationed in London will get picked up and spread around. Some will watch in reverence; others, while jeering. He will sing to his people nostalgic Indian and Pakistani songs, his hoarse voice full of longing. The equivalent of 'O my country' will be rendered by him as 'O myyyy countryyyyyyyyyyyyyyyy-yyyyyyy'. The Immigrants will feel his pain. They know what immigration (that euphemism for 'exile by apparent choice') does to the mind. He can reduce to tears the most stoic among his ranks. And then, the next moment, he'll begin singing a Daler Mehndi or Junoon or Alka Yagnik cover, and you'll be laughing through your tears.

His actions, and he himself, border on the absurd. This incident stands out: He's got a London studio full of lackeys operating cameras, lights and sound-capturing-and-processing devices for the broadcast to be shared with a few channels back home in Pakistan. He begins his address sitting at a desk: 'My beloved country's treasured citizens, today I am deeply angry at the government of Pakistan for starting negotiations with extremist groups. I feel like hitting something. So, if you're watching – Mr Prime Minister, Mr President and other government representatives – this one's for you.' After that, he pushes back his chair, stands up, walks around the desk holding up his fists, and starts shadowboxing with the camera. *Jab-jab-punch-jab-swing-jab-dodge-punch-jab-jab-dodge-uppercut.* The camera backs away and Al follows. 'I'm punching your lights out; I'm a stinging butterfly,' he snarls. The camera stumbles back and dodges, but Al bends and weaves his corpulent frame to follow the line of sight he's established with the camera. The audience becomes aware of around twenty people who are in the room, behind the scenes, lighting, recording and laughing at the antics of their benevolent leader in exile. The clip ends when Al *one-two* punches the camera for real. *Crack-smash* goes the glass. This is the theatre of the bizarre.

Another one: He's standing outside a colonial era building, probably a London courthouse (or a Debenhams made to look like a courthouse) that reminds viewers of the facade of an official building in Karachi. Al speaks – rather, shouts – in Urdu about the plight of the Immigrants and other minorities in Pakistan. His party workers are being continuously targeted throughout Pakistan with prison sentences by one government after the next. He threatens in Urdu, and the Brits can't do anything about words in a language that only the Indo–Pak expatriates among them understand. *This* he says in the middle of his speech in that public space outside the tall grey building, with pedestrians milling about, while surrounded by the curious, the bootlickers and the party reps: 'Tell the government officials to measure their heights. We'll get the gunnysacks ready.' Mic drop.

While he watches that clip of himself play repeatedly on the news at night, his mother sits with him in the living room. She fiddles with her rosary, mumbles her chants; the blankness across her face shifts only a little at the word 'gunnysacks'. A glimmer of amusement. She gets it; her inner heart chuckles.

In a corner of the film reel in which he boxes with the camera, for the briefest, blur of a moment, Al's wife appears. Young, beautiful, pregnant; standing in the doorway where she's retreated after watching him get up from his chair to start pummelling the air. Within that instant in which she's on screen, hardly noticeable unless magnified, her shock wears off, and her lips curl into just the tiniest grimace. Like she's trying not to show disgust; nonetheless, it emerges. When Altamaash watches reruns of that on YouTube, he pauses at his wife's image. He begins to fall out of love with her, because she doesn't understand at all.

Only an expert comedian or a master of tragedy can bring the audience gradually to the climax of true amazement.

Off-screen once, without any audience, I watch him create some such thing in a bus going up Finchley Road from St Johns Wood to Golders Green. Why he is in a bus, I wonder. Must be one of those spontaneous things he does. And before I know it, I'm thinking his thoughts. Al's on his way to scarf down some kosher beef sandwiches in his favourite Jewish cafeteria in North London. He's got raging pangs. One sandwich won't do. He's wondering whether three or four will hit the spot. He's hoping for three to be enough. But maybe as many as five will be needed to do the trick. The bus stops at the O2 Center, and on board climbs the type of group that usually prefers taking the Tube, but has settled grudgingly for overground travel this afternoon: football hooligans. Al's sitting near the back on the lower level of the bus, taking up one and a half seats. The chanting Chelsea fans could go up the stairs to the second level of the bus – which is empty except for two people – but they don't. They want to be surrounded by witnesses of their celebrations. Just having come out from a pub where they watched on the telly their team beating regular rivals Arsenal, they're pumped up. Bus drivers don't often tolerate the obnoxious noise level that this bunch of drunks is generating, but this driver must be a Chelsea fan. 'Chelseeeaaaaa, Chelseaa! Chelseeeaaaa, Chelseaaa!' Just that word, chanted with variations in length, like it will save lives if elongated for precisely the right number of milliseconds. Louder and louder grow the young ones, with all their fledgling might shoving their voices into everyone's ears.

Al, the football-hating curmudgeon (when he's hungry, that's how he is), looks around at the bus's other passengers. There are old Jewish men and women covering their ears, tut-tutting silently. A woman with her two babies in a pram is looking around for help, just in case something erupts. Al shrugs. He's no hero. But his own ears and mind are beginning to hurt. The bus slows down; a high school girl in her uniform at the stop takes a gander at the chanting, hollering Chelsea fans and refuses to board. The bus moves on. This is enough.

Al gets up. 'Hey,' he says. The seated old Jewish folks are looking at him like he's an ineffectual Moses. *What can this overly large brown man do?* their eyes ask. He doesn't mind; Al loves to surprise from a position of disadvantage.

The jolly chanters spare a glance his way when he stands, but his voice doesn't reach them. They're still going at the one word in their vocabulary like zealots hopeful of imminently unlocking nirvana.

'Hey!' Al shouts, making his voice carry. 'Shut the eff up! We know what team you support!'

Just the kind of thing the group has been looking for: a target for their energies. This will be fun. The old folks and the young mother can see the chanters' target eyes begin to articulate a different kind of mantra. And then out it comes from a pipsqueak's mouth: 'You Paki!'

Another one balls up his fist and lifts it to his face. 'Paki wants a piece o' this?'

Brown-man Al walks a step forward. The narrow aisle between the seats doesn't allow him to move except in a sideways shimmy. The hooligans laugh their heads off at the spectacle he makes.

'Fat Paki bastard!' says a drunk blue-eyed long-haired blond-tressed punk. And the others pick it up.

'Pa-ki bas-tard! Pa-ki bas-tard!'

It's been eight seconds or more since anyone has said the word 'Chelsea'. Al's almost beginning to miss the torture of it. In front of him, they're perfectly lined up. Like bowling pins. So he grins, Al does, and he begins to brace himself for what he's about to get into. He does this next: he shuffles sideways until the aisle opens up enough for him to move facing forward. And he runs four steps, and launches himself at the group standing nearly single file.

The look in their eyes is that of terror. Like a building's falling on top of them. The first one tries to fend off Al's enormous mass with arms held up. The one behind him pushes at his drunk buddy. But Al's a-flying.

What makes him do this? Behind him, in the vacuum he's left, the old Jewish folks and the young mother watch him go nearly horizontal in the middle of the northbound bus. The joy in their eyes at having someone thwart noise and boredom and the meaninglessness of life in a world taken over by Chelsea chanters – a world that once belonged to church and synagogue edicts, then political drib-drab, before it's come to this lack of any sense other than derangement – that's what he helps them avenge with this flight against reason. This is why he does it – for the joy of the people, even if they're not really his people except for this little moment on the bus. He gives it everything he's got.

In that sacrificial leap, he's made little consideration for his bad back, has Al. He's gone all-in. This is not poker. This is not a table for gambling. This is his body, his life.

And then he crashes into the first of the lot. The boy goes down under Al's weight, and he dominos his rude compadres into a heap at the floor at the front of the bus. Only one of them manages to hang on to a railing, and be displaced to a diagonal relative to the floor. But he's still weighted down by the others.

The driver halts the bus. There's a shrill scream from underneath Al. Is the kid okay? He's just shocked. It's immense, the weight on top of him. But he's young. The body will recover from shocks and sprains.

What would I have done?

What the woman with the babies in the pram does next. She chuckles without sound, like a mad woman. She takes out her phone. She fumbles to open the camera app to take a picture. She wants to share with the world what has happened in her universe. But she's too late.

Al gets up, his lower back throbbing a new muscular pain (which he doesn't let on). The bus is still stopped. He walks to the exit in the belly of the bus while the driver tries to get a hold on what's happened. Al pushes at the door in the middle of the bus. It resists, but he insists. In emergencies, if forced, it's supposed to give way. And so it does, after he nudges harder. He opens the door and keeps it forced open.

'Either you fuckers are getting out, or the rest of us are,' he says. He stares at the louts. The bus driver is looking around at the scene from his seat behind the wheel; he is still unable to say anything. The Chelsea fans are getting up. One's forearm is twisted, another holds his shoulder. One limps, just to prove he tumbled too.

What would I have done?

What the bus driver does next. He orders the noisemakers off his bus with a flick of his head. 'Get off, all of you,' he says, likely embarrassed by fellow Chelsea fans not surviving Al's weighted assault.

One by one, they go past Al at the exit door he's propped open for them. They try not to touch him, squeezing their arms and torsos away from him. They drop off one by one, and stare back up at him from the road they've descended to in a single file. Al moves away from the exit, and the driver closes the door with a button on the control panel next to the steering wheel. The bus moves on.

Seven. That's how many I count. Al took on and vanquished seven drunk ruffians in public.

What would I have done?

What Al does next. He shuffles slowly in the narrow aisle, sideways, back to his seat. The woman with the kids says 'Bravo, bravo.' The old folks smile at him. Two of them pat his shoulder from behind. To them this feels like Moses come back from the mountain with the word and deed of God. They look like they believe in miracles again.

Al nods. He keeps to himself the rest of the way on the bus. He mentally adds one more beef sandwich to his original tally. Some things you feel you've earned, and you take them even if you don't need them.

He's thinking he'll maybe get two extra sandwiches, just in case he gets hungry on the return trip and feels like having one more. The last one, he'll save that for Fatima.

[Re-entering pure transparence, George Gary Gregory Jaffar lingers, saturated with visions.]

ANGEL OF ADMITTANCE: I have just returned from hearing the Divine One speak of you, George.

GGGJ: Oh?

ANGEL: He thinks you're just about ready.

GGGJ: I feel the same.

ANGEL: As do I.

GGGJ: So, it's time to go to Heaven?

ANGEL: Almost time. There is just one more thing…

II. Altamaash

In this, the early onset of dark lonesomeness and the ennui of expecting a phone call on my last evening in the St Johns Wood mansion, I rouse myself from a nap, and take loud yawns in the womanless living room. No audience means no change of clothes is required. The hours will pass with leftover pizza and the trickle of ticker-taped news flowing from one end on the bottom of the TV to the other.

The riots throughout Pakistan are progressing as per plan. Damage to businesses and destruction of public property is building pressure on the government to do something. Prime Minister Fat Man is missing himself, but he's got his goons out trying to quell the violence – but that's the opposite of what they're trained for. Also, what can you do to stop a headless demon? How do you end a leaderless riot? They don't know it's Al, the exiled relic, who's let loose the reins.

In my transitional state between slumber and the waking world, it's practically impossible not to visualize the mayhem on the streets of Lahore, Karachi and Islamabad. Even bloody Gilgit. A child cries because its mother has abandoned it at her doorstep – off to chant at a rally 'Death to The Fat One' she goes. And students hang their classmate by a noose made of sheets, beat his body to a pulp, shouting all the while 'The Bitch is a blasphemer. Just like this Christian dead boy. Death to The Bitch. Death to the Charming Bastard'. All the inhabitants of a Hindu village outside Lahore gather in the courtyard of their village's most powerful man, a Muslim who cannot defend them against the mob once the stream of flesh and riot shifts from the city out to the suburbs. None of this is on the news; but it's happening. Collateral damage is high; it always is.

I've received texts from Pakistan. Ammi and the younger ladies have reportedly landed and are being driven to our family home. They must be walking up the driveway by now. The news channels are calling them 'Mother of Altamaash', 'Mrs Altamaash' and 'Pinky' (not 'Fatima'). Well, at least they're alive and well. Good enough for now.

Speaking of which, I should look for more news on that thing in Ladbroke Grove. I bet Scotland Yard isn't ready to tackle this one in the double time they need to. Al's flying off imminently, boys, better not hold any nets down… Nope, nothing on the news channels that I can tell. Just a 'befuddling suicide-murder investigation continues' update showing up on BBC's news from London. That's it. No names mentioned in the short space given the brief news item. No pictures, no names – the families have requested their privacy be kept intact.

I don't make the foolish mistake of searching for Ned or Guardian Geremy's names on the Internet. They could trace it to this computer. I wouldn't know what to search for, in case of the latter's name anyway. From what I can tell from passive research, a connection has not been established between St. Johns Wood's exiled politician and Ladbroke Grove's killing spree on the Internet's news portals either; while, fortuitously, all the required connections have been established in Pakistan. Can't look me in the eye any more, those villains.

The fear of Al has spread within and without the party's ranks. Ned and Guardian Greg, thank you. From the bottom of my soul-searched heart, I pray that you are pleased with your sacrifices. You've made the plan such a breeze. I'll find you in the afterlife, if that's possible. May you be blessed and rewarded with some of my share of the virgin houris that await us all.

As. If.

Backgrounded by the TV's glow, I sit here googling the news and myself. That word. *Googling*. Sounds like I'm tickling myself, but it's not like that. I'm searching for myself on Google. Hmm ... *that* sounds like a shamanistic New Age-y ritual following a mid-life crisis, but that's not it either. I'm typing my name into a computer screen and looking at the thousands of results.

It's like reading tea leaves at the bottom of a teacup. What I look for is not fortune or foretelling. What I look for is not the larger picture, or perspective. What I look for is myself. I find myself in unexpected places. Like God is everywhere, even when we're nude, showering or shagging. Just like that, I show up in places I have never been, among people I've never known. That's what Google says.

With a full name like mine, every combination must be tried separately. Because people don't care for spelling names like mine correctly. Al is short for Altamaash Immigrant. I like Al. *Call me Al.* That song was where I first learned what my new name in England would be. Altamaash is a twister for these Anglo tongues. 'Al' makes things easier. Al suits me. It fits me; it gloves me; it encapsulates me; it owns me. *Pleased to meet you; hope you've guessed my name.* Another song, another life. Meanwhile, I'm Al.

Back to unexpected places to find me at. I google combinations of my last and first names; forward, then reversed. Boolean search operators activated. Phil taught me all this; he said it comes in handy when looking for jobs. Hope he's not thinking of leaving anytime soon. It's going to get a whole lot more interesting from here on in.

The most efficient way to search is to be precise with your terms. That's what leads me down this darkish alley.

Or, Allie, I should say.

It is a high-alert kind of tedious evening. The same old mad flashes of 'BREAKING NEWS' again and again on the telly. The summer day has been unbearably sticky; the evening is no less humid. Every day is a holiday for exiles, but this is the dead of the holidays, when it's impossible to sleep for long despite the drowsiness that layers everything. I slump down on the sofa. The women are all safely at home in Pakistan now, with one of them going into a deeper circle of Hell soon – the shopaholic numbskull.

My laptop is being slow. It's already been six years since I bought it. I type my name, but the letters will only appear after a few seconds of lag. I type Pinky's real name, Fatima Immigrant; and, of course, there are pictures of her with me. The beautiful angel. Every birthday documented with cake-cutting pictures sent back home to the party via email. Video clips too. The cute little thing. I spend a few minutes indulging nostalgia, watching the clips of little, wide-eyed, two-year-old Fatima singing '*Happy Birthday to me*' for her own special day; she stands with a knife behind a Minnie Mouse cake.

Once that video's done, it's my turn. I want to type 'ALLTAMAASH IMMIGRANT PAKISTAN', just to see if there are any recent results with the double L. The L accidentally gets pressed longer than required for two Ls. The letters don't appear at once on the screen, given the lag of the outdated machine. I press backspace a few times and type the rest of my name and wait. The clicks and blips take their several seconds. And then the letters appear on screen in the search box, as if typed by the Ghost of Al Past. Except, there are still too many Ls.

'ALLLLTAMAASH IMMIGRANT PAKISTAN.'

That's what it says on the screen. Four Ls in my first name.

Like I say, it is a dull task waiting for your faraway country to collapse, for a phone call from a man in search for the country's saviour, and, within that country, for your wife to be shot through the head and abdomen by your people, even as the violent act is meticulously framed on your political rivals.

It's not only the most anticipation-filled evening of this summer. It is the kind of evening that accumulates all the anticipation felt over an entire life into one single darkening moment.

So, I *don't* press delete. Yes, I've never added Ls on purpose to this level of combinatorial extensions and permutations. Even *I* don't have that titanic a reservoir of patience when it comes to technology. I'm usually repeating searches with the basic variations on 'All Immigrant' and 'Altamash' and 'Altaamash'. Minor variations, those. So, imagine my shock, when this is the first result on that search with the four Ls:

ALLLLIE IMMIGRANT, PAKISTANI EXILE: A PROFILE BY ANN O. MINUS

I'm baited. I click. The page comes up. It is my face, my moon-shaped face. But it also isn't my face. This is disconcerting. Like looking into a dirty mirror trying to find my eyes. But, of course, the eyes are blurred out with added lines.

The page is a parody. I get that up front. I understand that. A distorted version of me.

And.

I'm ashamed to say this. The lecher.

The coward Ann O. Minus has hidden it behind four Ls. And his or her own name behind the cryptic name Ann O. Minus.

ALLLLIE. Al turned into *Allllie*.

The face, my face. Without my moustache. With lips, cheeks and eyes coloured with bright make-up – flaming red lipstick and neon purple eyeliner.

Photoshop. That word crosses my mind. I wonder what it means. When photos are changed, it's a Photoshop.

I have seen touristy folks getting their caricatures made on the kitschy park-side streets in London. Back home, I've ordered newspaper cartoonists' hands broken because of caricatures of my family, especially my father. And of myself, of course. I've warned editors at all the dailies. The act of making me into a joke is not something I allow other people to do. They cannot take my person as a cause or source of levity without the joke being worthy of a laugh. There will be no derision. This should have been the eleventh commandment: *Thou shalt not make a bad joke.*

But this. This four Ls in 'ALLLLIE IMMIGRANT'. This is not hand-drawn. This is computer manipulation. This is a Photoshop.

Eventually, after several calming breaths, I get past the shock, and read the profile by this Ann O. Minus.

I read it from start to finish, in one session of lying down on the sofa in the bloody sweaty evening. On a day that began as the day most full of promises.

Here's how it goes, the mock profile:

Allllie Immigrant, Pakistani Exile, is a woman who flees Pakistan for fear of political persecution, and is living the high life in London, Ontario, Canada. In this London, she is living in a 'St Lawnswood Cove castle'.

Ann O. Minus, the profile's writer, has written secret messages inside the barrel of the gun pointing at her own temple. What a way to go.

The woman Allllie Immigrant has been in exile since 1995. She is the leader of a party called 'ImmiCunts'. (How unoriginal; I've already called the party that.)

The Bastard Ann O. Minus. A.O.M. Those must be the writer's initials. I'll hunt you down on the Internet, Mr or Ms or Mrs A.O.M. *Could be a Dr too, of course,* chips in a thought from deep in my head. *Shut the fuck up*, I tell my head. *This is not the time.*

Allllie Immigrant is 'always pining' to return to Karachi, says the profile.

Lie. I don't pine. I'm not Allllie and I have never pined. I didn't pine, I don't pine, I will *never* pine. Pining is for wimps. I detest wimps. A.O. Minus, you should never have crossed the road, you chicken.

Allllie Immigrant has conducted an orchestra of murders, it says.

I open a new tab, and type out 'ANN O. MINUS' in the search box. I say the name out loud while I'm typing it.

And my unborn sister be fucked.

Ann O. Minus is just a wordplay on Annominus. I mean, on *Anonymous.*

Blaaaaast. Meeee.

I get up. I pace the hot living room, I stomp up and down the stairs, and I heave myself into the kitchen and grab the last two slices of a frigid, tasteless pizza. One slice in each hand, I take bites from both, alternating. How did these survive my earlier hunger?

I feel like pressing the intercom button and getting Phil and Jordan to stand at attention in front of me, and unload all this fury. Grab them by their balls and make them find this son-or-daughter of a bitch who dares to make fun of the person who can plough a fuck-mobile up and down seven generations of his or her family.

I'm back at the computer without wanting to be. I scroll down to the bottom of the page. It is incomplete. A 'To be continued…' appears at the bottom. It was last updated more than five years ago. So why *now*…?

On the very date that I'm supposed to be held aloft in the constellations as the guiding standard for a vicious, cold-hearted leader who will sacrifice anyone for the cause, the very night on which I'm supposed to be re-elevated to the status of a mythical god for my people back home again, with imminent return and retaking the reins written into destiny's italic fonts … why *now* did I have to diffuse all that gathering momentum in my transcendence by pressing 'search' on that four-L'd version of my name. *Baaaaaaah*!

A bloodbath is coming. You better watch out; you putrefied rat-jelly A.O.M. If I *ever* find you…

There are others too. Of course. Anger splays out in all directions like a cantankerous mother's curse.

Here's a list of the people on my death wishlist:

- sordidly pathetic entertainers (A.O.M. being a prime example – he/she is as unfunny as a *flying fucking squirrel*)
- nincompoops (subtle humour and understated aesthetics escape their grasp, and that's enough reason)
- the blasé and bored (how dare they exist without being in at least a mild state of wonder at the way the world operates)
- my wife (one whole more day; I wait impatiently; not enough hours in the day when I'm able to forget that she'll be gone; go already, go already, go!)

- all party workers not willing to put their loved ones on the line, should the cause require it

Everyone needs elevation to the level of Multani minion A.D.; our Abrahamic tradition requires such ultimate acts of devotion. The majority of my people have never understood that my life and my sacrifices are not just for the sake of distracting them from the drudgery of everyday life. It is not *all* act; it's all steeped in *the real.*

A great man once forced lesser beings around him to rise above their spiritual and self-actualized stations. He said they should demand their rights *by any means necessary*; and so, I do what must be done. *Any*thing for the cause. The ends justify the means.

Of all people, Ammi understands; and she'll be thoroughly accommodating of Mrs Al biting the bullet. First, though, the old woman will wait for the other shoe to drop, just to make sure I don't do to her what I had done to father. Poor Ammi. How much she could have been spared.

And me? If only Pakistan had a bigger audience for the theatre. If there were funds and second acts for performance artistes, maybe I would never have climbed those stairs to give those ridiculous speeches about our rights as the stepped-on people of a nation's history. Doesn't every great nation need to step on some human scalps to get to true liberty?

But what if—

Bahhh, what's the use of 'what-if's?

That – all of it – it has passed. The lack of entertainment can't be blamed. A plethora of spectacles doesn't provide outlet to the homeland's violent energies either. Now it's all these despicable TV channels running all the time, creating diversions round the clock without nourishing their audience with anything meaningful. It's too much. All too rancid.

The thresholds of my patience have been breached on all sides. Time to pick up the pace and force the call already.

I do the *brrring-brrring*, and across the world picks up an underling. 'Karachi Central Zone, Bhai. Double-encrypted.'

'Hi. Update on Phase Two, son?' I ask. 'Have you got something special for me?' My left hand is holding the phone to my ear, and with my right, I'm ready to let loose, and bring on the heavy drums that will fill up my head if Karachi Central Zone gives me some good news. *Cheer me up, laddie.*

'Bhai,' says he, 'we have taken over the Sindh High Court building. We've destroyed the benches and platforms; the judges are safe, and the lawyers have taken out a protest against the anti-Bitch-and-Bastard rioters; they're doing half our work of setting things on fire. Also, we've uprooted more than two hundred electricity poles, to create further agitation and bring more people out into the streets.' He stops there.

'Good, good.' I say, but that's just worth one drum beat. It won't trigger the entire symphony. 'Carry on. Recruit more young thugs if you can. They're always more imaginative with destruction. But, remember, make sure you have a kill-switch so they don't get out of hand once we bring everything to a full-stop. Also, that's not enough institutional damage; and get me some heads rolling.'

'Yes, Bhai. We'll do our best.' As if. Should have *already* been doing their best.

We sign off, and I flirt with the idea of calling Lahore right away. But, no. I'll save the best for last. No need to call A.D. in Multan either. He's already got my spirit soaring just thinking of him. So … next call to Islamabad? Why not?

Two-ring pick-up. Good.

'Islamabad Central Zone, Bhai. Phase Two begun.'

'Encryption level of this call?' My right arm, it goes up again. Waving to Islamabad from thousands of miles away, I am.

'Double-encrypted, Bhai.'

'Give me a status update, son.'

'Bhai, we've been able to capture the obese religious leader – The Fat One's coalition partner. He's in our custody. A few broken teeth on him, and a few bruises, but nothing major.'

Da-Da-Da-Daaaaaamn! Goes Beethoven's *Symphony No. 5* in my head, and with it my right hand cuts the air four times.

'Excellent!' That's a good start from Islamabad on Phase Two. Now we're getting somewhere. 'And the institutions?'

'We're a little behind,' he reports, 'on breaking down the security cordon around the Supreme Court. A few pushes and shoves between the police and the anti-The-Fat-One protestors there, but no major violence has erupted as yet. We're still trying the peaceful method of takeover, as you advised. But weapons are ready if that doesn't work.'

'Sounds like the peaceful method hasn't worked,' I say. The music halts in my head. Lack of a minion's initiative always does that. 'So, advance to the part where you go beyond non-violence.'

'Of course, Bhai, of course.'

'Get to it, son. I want to see it on TV.'

'Yes, Bhai.'

'And your hostage … how about slitting his throat already? Before he asks to go to the bathroom. Do it anti-Bitch-and-Bastard style. Page twenty-two of the Instructions. I'll send along the symbols.'

'Oh. Okay, Bhai. I'll get to it.' Afraid to get their hands dirty, they are, in the capital. I sense hesitation, but he'll obey.

'Good man. I'll wait to see his corpse, the Supreme Court takeover, and some flames in the National Assembly hall. More action from here on. Okay?'

'As you command, Bhai,' says Islamabad Central Zone.

They're being achingly slow… Isloo and Karachi. I need to speed up the crossing of the brink. Time for the big boy in Lahore to step up and be counted among the wolves.

Brrring-brrring.

'Lahore Central Zone, Bhai. Great to hear from you again!' Could have been the best radio jockey in the nation, this young buck.

'Lahore, state this call's encryption,' I say.

'Encryption level holding at quadruple, Bhai.'

'Right. And Phase Two update?'

'Right on target, Bhai. Even slightly ahead. We've ransacked the Punjab Governor's House. Removed all the furniture. We're ready with gasoline. Let us know, and we'll burn it to the ground. All the major mosques have been spray-painted with pro-Bitch-and-Bastard, anti-religious slogans. Also, the whole city's main roads are now full of protests with the Phase Two slogans: "Blood for Faith", "Blood for Country", "Hand Him Over" and "Hand Her Over" that'll rile up a whole host of the masses. And we've pretty much destroyed the Lahore Railway Station. The anti-The-Fat-One protestors have unbolted the train tracks for twenty miles all around the station. Massive damage there.'

There it is. There, and here. When you've been a conductor as long as I have, and the orchestra has been training for two decades for a grand performance, the greatest satisfaction is not before or after, but during the series of crescendos squeezed together at the end. This is music by and for Al. I pick up my hands and wave them. Every instrument is participating now: the trumpet blasts its warnings, the cello soothes the dying, the clarinet's bleak solace is drowned out by the clash-clash-and-clash of cymbals. I keep conducting as Lahore Zone's report continues:

'Plus, we've uprooted a hundred and fifty electricity poles and cut wires in four of the ten major areas of the city. Our head electrician was electrocuted, but the rest are going on with the effort. We hope to achieve the target of three hundred poles within five hours. And although we've not managed to grab any other major political big fish, there are some minnows that got caught in our traps. The head of the National Accountability Bureau, who's a slave of The Fat One. Our sources in the Federal Aviation Authority say the The Bitch and The Bastard have escaped the country, and The Fat One is looking to head out too. So, we've got some people in place to capture anyone who helps them – after the escape, of course, as you ordered. Once we get those people, we can set their heads rolling down the road before offing the prime minister's brother. What do you think, Bhai?'

I'm too busy enjoying the music of devastation to respond at once. I can picture all the mayhem.

'Son,' I say, at last, resting again my arms at my side. 'You've made me quite, quite proud. I'd be remiss if I didn't give Lahore the prize for best spectacle. So, go ahead and set it up on The Fat One's sibling. It's on page 31 of the Instructions. I'll send you the symbols.'

'Bhai,' he says, 'I think I know which one you will send. Is it the one where I make him run naked in front of a mob equipped with hockey sticks, daggers and kerosene; the one in which the mob catches him and castrates him in public, and then pours kerosene over him, and then not one of us, but a bystander picks up the cue and lights the match that ignites the flame while our people make sure that the police doesn't interfere?'

'Let's not jump the gun, son.' In my head, an inexplicably euphonious synthesis of *Hallelujah* and *Carmina Burana* commences. Should I go along with Lahore's sense of escalation? No. The best laid plans don't allow it. 'You won't *actually* do it; just *threaten* the castration as the mob chases him; what's crucial is that you have our people rescue him. Understood?'

'Understood, Bhai. We'll announce asylum and rescue plans for him well before we put him on the street. And then we'll rescue him.'

'Good. I like that you've got the instructions downloaded onto your brain, son. Happy hunting.'

'Bhai,' Lahore says down the line, 'I will have that clown hunted so raggedly he won't know what end of him is running – his tail or his legs!'

'Music to my ears, son,' I say. 'Make sure there's a live video feed on television of the whole thing.'

'Of course, Bhai,' says Lahore Central Zone. 'In less than two hours, you'll be watching the entire performance on every major channel.'

'You're a find,' I tell him. 'See you soon.'

'You are too kind, Bhai. See you very soon.'

We hang up. That's sorted. The music is lingering long after I can hear the audacity of its experimental combination. Here's the descent into darkness that I promised to some in the Instructions; others, of course, never knew. Now I wait for the call that starts the rapid return of Al.

The TV's still on, the evening's coming into night, and I've got another two hours to wait for the game to progress. Willing time to pass, willing Mrs Al to meet her maker already; fuming, I fall from slumber into sleep with the remote in my hand. A new kind of sleep, this.

A noise or a melody – I hope it's the latter as my eyes flutter open after only six minutes of sleep.

Wishes must come true. Mine, at least. Because there it is. The phone buzzing before going dark. That was a missed call just now from an undisclosed number on the flip phone (*The Last of the Mohican Flip Phones*, my inner heart chuckles) meant only for one thing: it's *true*; not a dream; I'm going back home.

I give in to a smile. I do it like nobody else can.

III. Edwin 'Ned' Steinberg

[In perfect, unending transparence, the smoke that is Edwin 'Ned' Steinberg begins to form the shape of a human body – his own body from when he was alive. Then the smoke begins to fade and vanish, starting with the toes; it disappears without trace, as if it never existed in the first place. It occupies no space and disappears from time's ledgers. Once he is disintegrated, time and timelessness never did, never do, and never will contain any trace of Edwin 'Ned' Steinberg.]

Two men face Al. They both have guns. The tables of Ladbroke Grove get reversed. Both men fire at each other; one dies on the spot. Al stomps the other to death.

[Ned's toes disintegrate first, starting with the nails. It's only smoke that puffs into non-existence, but Ned feels it like he would a body part; as each part of the smoke-body disintegrates, he forgets the feeling of it having ever existed.]

Once, Al fasts for nine months.

Al's forehead has the invisible sign for 'chosen people' who will go to the portion of Heaven reserved for the elect among those admitted.

Al's sweat smells like rose water.

[Ned's feet disappear from existence.]

Al romances five hundred women, but sleeps only with his wife. Most of Al's wealth is legitimate.

Al misses a playdate with his great-granddaughter. She refuses to talk to him until he's dead. She does not regret this until she's close to death and has no granddaughter of her own to talk to.

[Ankles, legs and further upwards along Ned's body moves the force of Disintegration.]

Al eats dessert only on the last Friday of every month.

When the peace train finally comes around, Al will be its engineer and driver.

There is only one Al. A unity that is easy to behold, encapsulate, and understand for everyone who beholds him.

[Ned is now without knees or lower thighs.]

Al is a good man, incapable of anything remotely evil. Al is a friend to everyone.

Poison becomes the mode of killing for Al's men in his later life. They get very good at creating untraceable concoctions. It saves bullets and creates less of a mess.

[Forced to exist without thighs, half his hips disintegrated, Ned continues to end.]

On the third Tuesday of every month, Al googles his name. He used to do this every day, but the news got stale. Every other day didn't work to get him excited either. It had to be reduced to once a month.

Al has never watched porn.

For dessert, every last Friday of the month, Al will eat one gulab jamun.

[His genitals take as little time as his toes to go; after that, Ned is without belly button, and still further upwards moves the force of Disintegration.]

A hundred thousand women write to Al every year, asking him to take their virginity.

Al prays five times a day; sometimes six times; he hears God's reply to each of his prayers.

Al has been offered knighthood by the Queen every year since 1990 and he has refused every single time.

[His chest, his beating heart now neither stopped nor still beating – just gone, along with his nipples – Ned's remains include his arms, hands, his neck and face.]

Al is not an enemy of his friends' enemies. He knows things are more complicated and non-linear. Suppose X loves Al, and Y loves Al, but X and Y hate each other. How is Al to de-algebrize the equation and make it fit the vagaries of human beings living their lives?

Customs matter. In exile, Al celebrates Eid, Christmas, Hanukkah, Holi, Cinco de Mayo, Halloween, the Chinese New Year, Thanksgiving, the Queen's birthday, and matches each of these with their corollary cuisine. When in doubt, the roti canai at Mandalay on Edgware Road works. Order after order, one hot meal replacing another. Becoming part of Al, becoming more of Al. The more Al, the merrier.

At any one stage, Al can reconcile X and Y. He can dissolve their issues in acid or alkali, admonition or cajoling, depending on the pH required.

X and Y sometimes fight only to have Al personally reconcile their differences.

[Ned's fingers go into non-existence. His forearms, his thick and hard arms, his shoulders, all the muscles of his neck – these disappear from the utter transparence of The Belly.]

9

The Threshold of Return

You know you're in political exile from Pakistan when the First World morning air is so pure that you start crying because it's the smoke and the smog that you miss.

I. George Gary Gregory Jaffar

[Floating in the transparence, George Gary Gregory Jaffar speaks to the white dot.]

ANGEL OF ADMITTANCE: There is just one more thing…

GGGJ: There always is just one more thing, isn't there?

ANGEL: This is the last thing you need to know before your ascension. And you are ready for it.

GGGJ: I sense that this will not be a light thing.

ANGEL: In a way, it is the lightest revelation for you yet. Remember the bullet that ended your life?

GGGJ: Yes. Quite vividly.

ANGEL: You know that the Divine One could have effortlessly swerved it out of the way, so it would have completely missed you. You would have lived, and you would have had a chance to kill Altamaash.

GGGJ: Right, of course.

ANGEL: What you do not know is that the bullet, as Altamaash fired it, was only going to graze the side of your head. But it was ordered to change direction to hit the centre of your forehead. The Divine One changed the direction of that bullet, so that you would die, and your pure intention of removing evil would be preserved across the threshold of your life coming to an end.

GGGJ: Oh. So, God, the Divine One, He changed the bullet's direction so it would end me – my life? Huh. That's … well okay. At this point, it's strange but it doesn't really matter, nor does it bother me. Funny, that. So … is that all?

ANGEL: That is all you need to know, George. But would you like to see how the bullet left the chamber of the gun that Al was holding, and how its original trajectory was altered by bending time and space? It's quite a vision; a tiny miracle.

GGGJ: Not particularly. I'm sure it's fascinating, but I'm quite done with visions of the past. It all seems like someone else's life at this point, to be honest. I don't even remember being bitter about being killed. Why is it that I'm not angry? Is this the process? This letting go of grudges?

ANGEL: It is indeed the process, and you are definitely ready.

GGGJ: And now we ascend?

ANGEL: And now we ascend.

[The white dot begins to unfurl all five hundred wings of itself. George Gary Gregory Jaffar begins to turn from puffs of smoke into a being of light.]

II. Altamaash

The General calls again exactly five minutes after his first missed call. I pick up after the third ring. In this country-rescuing phase of emergencies, a third ring picking-up shows promptness without displaying excessive eagerness.

'Hello,' I say.

'My friend,' the General says on the other end, 'it's such a pleasure to hear your voice.'

'Yes, likewise,' I say. When they expect exuberance, give them the opposite. 'Thank you. We are secure, I hope?'

'As secure as possible. Triple encryption,' he says. *Even the army can't beat PIP Lahore*, sniggers my inner heart. 'Although,' he continues, 'has the threshold been crossed? I wasn't sure—'

'You must have seen the footage of The Fat One's brother being hounded down and then rescued by our people. Yes, General. The threshold has indeed been crossed,' I say. And I scan the living room. The TV has been running ever since I came back from the airport, hours and hours ago; all the Pakistani channels have been scoured for news endlessly. I've made the calls, held the meeting, napped, and eaten slice after slice of pizza and guzzled a gallon of iced tea. The Fat One, The Bitch and Mr Charming Bastard are on the run from mobs in Pakistan. They've condemned the riots without knowing the architect. My own party members are keeping mum other than opening up the sanctuaries, just as they were ordered. *Let the others fill the vacuum.* A short while back, even

Phil and Jordan came in and asked, almost in unison, 'What's the plan, boss?' in their deep bass voices. They offered to give me company. I told them to return to their posts and turn any more grovellers away from the gate. They've been doing just that.

On the phone, the General says: 'What's the exact plan? The Instructions are vague at this point. I know my role, but what are *you* planning?' Of course, like everyone, the General thinks he has got a complete version of the document. And, like the others, he's groping in the dark, just like I want him to. But I must give him something to reach and touch.

'All in good time, General,' I say. Stoic to the core, is Al. The General has known me since I was a third of this weighty substance – back when he was still a colonel. He's the one who, under orders from his boss, escorted my to-be-wife from Karachi to Manchester, so she could join me in exile. It's been over twenty years since that first day of expulsion to London. I change the track of the conversation: 'The country's needs come before our own, of course. Please tell me how my family is. Nothing unfortunate has happened, I hope.' *Yet.*

'Your family is fine,' he says down the line. I wait him out, thinking about the meaning of family. Pinky, Ammi and I will need him right until the end.

Fatima, I mean. It's disturbing that I can't think of my daughter as anything but a little finger. The most vulnerable little finger. I should call her before she suffers the trauma of Mrs Al's imminent departure. But Pinky's grandmother is there and the tragedy has not yet ensued. And if I'm going back … well … tears can wait until I'm there. Soon enough.

'Are *you* okay, my friend?' the General asks, after I've been quiet too long. It's genuine man to man stuff. This is what his tone says: *You can lean on me, compadre; let your feelings out; I'm your shoulder; let yourself loose; you deserve catharsis*. Right. As if. I'm not a nostalgic ninny.

'General,' I say. 'We must do whatever it takes to get the country back into functional order. All of us must play our roles. Tell me, what is the situation on the ground?' They love that phrase, '*situation on the ground*' in the army. It puts them back into the theoretical battlefields in their classrooms, where they can apply their strategies and tactics. Not to say that our common homeland is *not* a battlefield.

'Well, Alta— my friend,' a rare slip-up by the General. To be excused under the circumstances, of course, especially given that the call is so-called encrypted; it's his empathy that's trying to break the wall of impersonal business between us. He can hardly believe the day has come. 'A lot is happening,' he says. 'The armed forces have taken to the streets in all the bigger cities to separate the factions of protesters. All that the army is trying right now is to keep the groups of rioters separated, so damage can be minimized. That's proving difficult with the limited manpower we have, but there's some kind of tenuous stay on the violence. Beyond that, we have other issues of long-term importance; infrastructure destruction being the least of it. You may have heard that the news channels have been ordered not to report the urgency of the situation. It's not being shared on the networks yet, but your Mr Charming Bastard and The Bitch have left for Dubai, and we speculate that they might go on further – maybe Canada, perhaps the United States. My hunch is Canada. They're not looking to return for the foreseeable future.'

Splendid. The Bitch and the Bastard can join Allllie Immigrant in London, Ontario. I hear exile is wonderful for the complexion there. 'Great,' I say. 'Good riddance.'

'Quite,' says the General. 'And the other one, The Fat One, he's getting antsy. We think he's testing the waters in Saudi. You know how that's his favourite hiding place. He wants to spend a few medical-leave months there getting his heart valves repaired, while his underlings suffer through this storm and we in the armed forces tamp down on the riots. He wants to weather out the turbulence, then return once we've sorted it all for him. But I'll be honest, we don't want him back after the royal mess he's created of all the institutions and the economy. So, he'll also be out of the picture soon.'

'Fantastic,' I say, 'So far, that is.'

'Yes,' the General says. 'Perfect for…'

Silence hangs. I guess he will have to be prompted.

'And *your* people, General?' I lay the words out for him so he can find out in which direction he must talk the talk.

There's a cough on the other end.

In the background, on the Impress News channel, the ticker stutters with a 'BREAKING NEWS' bulletin. '*…family of Altamaash the political exile returns to their Karachi residence after twenty-three years…*' I can't read the ticker and listen to the General at the same time. News will break all day. Can always come back to that.

The coughing on the other end of the line turns into words. 'The army and the agencies don't want to take over,' says the General. 'We really want to avoid that scenario, given responses in the past to martial law regimes. But we've got two very greedy people near the top. They are seeking the support of all the generals and brigadiers—' another cough. '*—but,* we are adamant about letting the system of democracy stay intact. And we think – some of us – I mean… Okay, let's be candid, shall we? You've got charisma and leadership potential, my friend. Many among the army generals want you to come and start getting groomed for a role in the future running of the country. Are you interested in something like that? The Instructions say nothing on this.' *Your* instructions, General, I don't say.

As *if*. I called their bluff; timed it perfectly. The men in uniform don't think they have enough support from the judiciary or the other civilian institutions. And even though the people are utterly sick of marching out in favour of democracy against military dictatorships, they'll still do it. They're compelled by the pageant of western democracy that entrances them. If the army takes over, the *bloody civilians* will rave and chant that they want civil representation, not martial law. They won't know what's better. Like donkeys, they'll bray the army into submitting to another election – another few rounds of The Bitch, Mr Charming Bastard and The Fat One returning from exile to split up and share the country's governance in five-yearly chunks ... and even then, the cycle won't end. Their bitch-bastard and fatso kids are being initiated with minor political roles at the provincial level; they are the next-gen leeches. Horrendous image, that. Can't wait to put all that legacy work to the sword. Blood will flow.

'My friend,' says the General, interrupting the procession of drama-laced symbols in my head, 'we can guarantee a few things if you should choose to come back.'

'Oh,' I say. 'You think I should come back? To do what? Provide your uniformed bosses with *other* options? Let the army use me as a figurehead while it handles the disastrous dénouement of Pakistan?'

'You know that's not the case,' he says. 'You know my stance: my allegiance is to Pakistan, the army, and to you, all in equal measure. We in the army can help you to power. But you'll have to be strong. You'll have to be ruthless against your Charming

Bastard and Fat One. You can't pardon them … but, well, that's down the line. First, are you coming? We need to know.'

'You need to know…' I repeat after him, not making it a question.

'And one more thing,' says the General. 'Do you remember what you told me – *me*, personally – when we met in London all those years ago?'

'General, you insult my powers of retention.'

'You remember, then. You said—'

'I said I love my country. I said I love it more than my life, and that I would use power, if I ever got it, to fix every single thing that needed fixing in the country.'

'Yes, you do remember,' he says. He's invoked like a magic spell that intention I once had. Maybe I still have it. *Mayyyyyy*be.

Outside, Phil is turning someone away. I hear him saying 'No, I can't' over and over to someone saying 'Please, I need to see him' again and again. This is the loneliest minute of my life, spent a million miles away from the corridors of power. Nobody to cheer me up; nobody for me to regale.

'As you and I know, General,' I say, 'I've been working on my return to Pakistan ever since I was forced to leave, over two decades ago. Things looked more promising in the past month. That's why I was testing the waters by sending my family home first. But if I come, and I am arrested, or worse—'

'I won't let—' he begins.

'Please,' I say.

'I promise that I—' he tries again.

'Just don't,' I say. 'Yours is not the only powerful institution in the country, and we both know it. What I'm saying is, it doesn't matter any more if that happens. I think I know what my duty is now. I wish I had always known, but now I think I know for sure. You've asked me to tell you whether I'm coming home after two decades of being shut out of my home. You're asking me if I'll bring that same old intention of giving whatever is left of my energy and abilities for the progress of the country that has been heading steadily into the pits of failure. Let me be very candid with you too: yes, my *intention* is still the same. My party, the newly renamed Pakistan Integrated Party – we want to see a shining Pakistan that puts every other Third World country to shame. We want it to have a progressive economy, and long-term regional stability, so that all our detractors, and all those who have counted on the country's demise, are left astounded. As for coming home to do all *the work* that is required to fulfil that vision … well, I'll tell you my answer. But you'll have to give me time. I'll need time.'

'My friend,' the General says, 'the country is burning up. The people want you. They *need* someone like you. The way you have opened up the sanctuaries in this hour of the people's need… Also, you are not inordinately corrupt, and whatever harmful things you did were for the good of the Immigrants, even of your party. And if you did that for a large minority, you can— Look, all we are asking you is: Can you do the same for Pakistan, the entire country? Please, hear me loud and clear as I ask you this: How much will it take to get you here? No, let me be cruder, more direct than I've been before: I know you're planning something extreme. I know you, I know how you think. Is it as drastic as – you know how your Charming Bastard created rumours of an attempted murder of The Bitch to gain the people's sympathy votes and become the prime minister himself in the election before the last one … well, are you planning something similar?'

'General—' I begin.

'It's crude, I know,' he says.

'It's—' I try again.

'Is it also close to the truth?' he asks.

He goes quiet after asking that. I can't say anything. But I have to push for the resolution that I want: the arrangement of a flight.

'You're not wrong,' I say. 'I did consider that. I know it's dark, but I've been in darker places in my life. You don't know what being locked out of home does to a person, General.'

'Okay don't tell me,' he says, backtracking. 'I don't think I want to know. But tell me this: you'll come?' he parrots away at his refrain.

I look around my London prison. Can this actually be happening? Is he truly taking the country out of the frying pan and flinging it into the fire? *Oh, Al*, how are things working out so magically for you? Seeds planted long ago … chickens let out eons ago … what goes around…

'Give me a day to think about it,' I say, playing hard to get.

'My friend, you have three hours,' he says. 'We do have a country to save. We can't rely on just you. You need to tell me in three hours either way; otherwise, we have options…'

'Three hours, hmm? Fine. Three hours it is,' I say, and hold back on telling him what my decision will be. In the mirror on the back wall of the living room, I watch my face brimming with a thick and wide grin. *Sly ol' Al…*

I disconnect, still grinning. After that, I pace the room for a few minutes. I feel damp. So much sweat accumulates in the folds of the human body in a day of lying about. Such filth, such stench. I need a shower.

In the bathroom, under the shower, I let water pour down on my head and watch the routes it takes to the drain. *Oh, life.* At my lowest points, I thought I would never get to leave England. Doubts crept in despite all the extensive planning. Emotional weaknesses made me disbelieve that I would ever sleep in a bed far from London the capital; Westminster, the borough; or St Johns Wood, the neighbourhood. Karachi would always be far, far away.

But it's not as if you can leave a city like Karachi in your past. All the roads and people and dust and salt in the air; and the spit of betel nuts on the pavements. The motley wind. It drags around in the festival under my lids when I lie awake with eyes shut all night on the plush £3,949.95 organic orthopedic memory foam mattress.

Water cascades all around me, draining into the underground system. Feels like I've been showering for hours already.

I have lost count of the murders I ordered because the people, before they became corpses, gave me sleepless nights. Now the unlisted, un*list*able, number of deaths I have brought about give me further nights of watching shadows in the dark. It causes the opposite sensation from the one brought about by cloud-watching.

But here it is. I'm being given a new chance at all of it. Again, in a few days, I will walk down to the sea as I knew the sea when I was still a young man. The marginally tense muscles of youth are gone. But the worries of a future to be carved out are still there. There were, back then, no fears of legacy or violence beyond the point of what was necessary. Lines had not been crossed that could not be uncrossed. That pure life, without the ambiguous black void that life is now.

But I'm unclean no matter how many times I lather myself with soap, shampoo and face wash. The dirt is not on top of the skin. Unclean and filthy like Grandpa Pir always was, no matter how recently he had bathed.

It's come to this. My baby girl, now come of age, and just about to lose her Mama. *I'm afraid Mama's got to go, Pinky.*

The reason she needs to be sacrificed is because my father's bones have grown cold. Nothing less than Mrs Al's demise can guarantee nationwide sympathy for the devil. Once she is done though, they'll practically hand over the country to me. To do with as I please. My people, my people – how disappointingly, predictably emotional they are.

To lose a parent at this age – what misery it can be, when you still think your parents are minor gods. And the memories she won't be able to create. What a sad loss for my daughter. Poor Pinky – she won't ever get to race along the beach with her mother. I remember the best times at the beach with my own parents, and they aren't good enough either. Ammi and I would be watching my father with pity. That man was without vision even at the beach; he could never look out at the waves and meditate; always, he kept his eyes at the ground, looking for shells. But he could never find the unscathed, resplendent seashells that I wanted to take home and add to the dust-and-sand-splotched collection on my bedroom's windowsill.

Maybe some fragments of those shells are still on that ledge, even after all these years. I'll go home and find out in less than twenty-four hours.

Would Grandpa Pir have been proud? My hero, Grandpa Pir. His mystic's eyes, his workhand's breath. Did any of his meditations yield a glimpse of the peace he pretended? That matters least of all.

Forget it. Forget the politics, for a second. Think about my human self, my coffers in which I hoard millions of dollars and pounds and Swiss francs, and uncountable rupees; what's it all worth if I can't go back to the one place of which I wish to be king. An exiled king is like a baboon that rules his tribe from a treetop, never being able to be on the ground with his troops.

So … it's justified. She needs to go. And, yes, the others too, Guardian GJ and Ned; they needed to go for a party of viziers and a country of hooligans to submit, in horror of his depravity, to their rightful king. I am their Mr Hyde, jekylling back across oceans.

With two more calls to make before heading to the airport, I step, unclean, uncleanable, out of the shower, and fold two large towels around me.

The first call is to Karachi Central Zone. 'Hello, Bhai,' says the receiver. 'Phase Three,' I say.

'The riots were flagging, Bhai,' he says. 'So, we did what you asked. We used the circumstances when you left – your father—'

'Stop,' I say, cutting him off. Buffoons. Code was invented for intelligent people. 'Careful. I repeat: Phase Three.'

'Oh, I'm so sorry, Bhai,' he says. 'But the people are furious. They want to avenge the persecution of your family. Phase Three is most welcome.'

He tries to sound encouraging. Humpty Dumpty's minion, holding down the fort. Humpty Dumpty's minion, waiting at the airport. What to do? *Should* I? After all this, there's hesitation… How do I cross over again?

Still in towels, freed from domesticity within the domestic space, I roam near-naked in the house while staying on the line. In the lounge, the television is still on. That breaking news alert, earlier – it's become a constant flashing thing at the bottom. Here's what it says: '*The return of Altamaash's family signals perhaps the return of Altamaash himself*. To hell with 'perhaps'. 'Perhaps' is a half-baked performance; I don't do half-baked. Of course I'm going. I knew this long ago. Even the General did. The party, for sure. But now it's nationwide. It's time to ride the wave … home-time.

Time. It waits for nobody. To *hell* with hesitation. I hang up on my deputy and make the other call.

The only thing I say to the General when he picks up is, 'I'm on board. Get me home.'

III. Edwin 'Ned' Steinberg

[A grey smoky semblance of Ned's face is the only thing that remains.]

Al's people believe Al is fasting on injustice, and waiting to feast on the justice that will come about because of the fast. The physical fast is only symbolic.

[His chin disappears.]

Five people die because they try to form a separate party once Al gets thrown into prison. Nobody leaves Al after signing up to be counted among his people. Al chooses whom he wants. Al refuses whom he wants.

Myths about Al are unlike the myths about Chuck Norris. Al cannot perform a roundhouse kick. He can have Chuck Norris perform it for him.

[His lips turn to nothing.]

Al's mustache is real.

Al has memorized the Arabic Quran's thirtieth chapter. That's the last of the thirty portions, with the shortest, most apocalyptic verses.

[Ned's nose and cheeks disintegrate and disappear.]

When someone donates $5,000 to the cause of Al's political interests, he is asked to sign a document saying he donated $20,000. It's a regular thing. It saves the donor during the tax season.

[His ears and eyes go next.]

Al daydreams of a future in which he parades across Pakistan as a much leaner and physically fit older man, wearing a general's uniform, his torso and head peeking out through the sun-roof, getting salutes and flowers thrown his way wherever his twenty-vehicle cavalcade rolls. Al dreams of saying 'I forgive you', with a loving smile to everyone who has tried to hurt him and survived.

Al is the first man to acknowledge his faults.

Al braves the humour at his expense. Or he doesn't get it.

Much of Al's life has been miserable.

Exiled by his own will, this misery is by choice.

When he sees a work of art he likes, Al does not stare at it for hours. It does not become a source of envy or a hunger for possession inside him. He admires, walks on, and forgets.

In exile, Al likens himself to a broken-winged bird far from its nest.

[His hair and forehead disappear.]

He feels at peace on Edgware Road in the summer, in the few days of sticky heat that London gets, when the Arabs are driving about the city in their temporarily imported Lamborghinis, Maseratis and Ferraris.

Al can bake a perfect lasagna. His mother teaches him an easy recipe: layering sheets of lasagna between sauces, cut vegetables and the minced meat. He bakes lasagna five times after she dies, and it takes him those five attempts to determine that the cooking makes him miserable. He learnt it fifteen years ago and he remembers the recipe still. It's the first thing he will make if he makes anything again.

Al's mother dies in his arms.

Al snores in D minor.

[Of Ned, only his third eye remains.]

10

Master of the Two Worlds

You know you're in political exile from Pakistan when you pull long-distance, tenuous strings to acquire everything you could want from home: mid-summer sindhri mangoes; street nihari and gol gappe tinned and preserved; carpets and rugs from your old home; a play-by-play of the riots you're conducting over the phone; late-summer jaamuns; cute handmade cards saying 'Altamaash Bhai, We love you and miss you' from your party workers' children; sporadic accusations and absolutions by the judiciary, the military, the masses. You wonder at your links. What keeps you tethered at all? These things? Is that all that ever ties you to the Land of the Pure? The soap you use is made and sold on Bond Street. Your cooking oil is extra virgin coconut, pressed in Andalusia. The clothes and materials of your life are motley and sourced from everywhere on the planet. The air you breathe is currented across the world.

What, then, is home?

The last refuge of the scoundrel is not home. Pity yourself all you want. Mourn your loss of a sense of place in life. You know that's all affectation. You took flight as soon as you were ready. You thought: 'If I hold on to my cards too long, they won't come into play; but, if I play my cards too soon, they'll get used up.' Which way does the arrow point? Will you ever get to feel the dusty, baked ground of the Karachi Airport again? Sometimes you find yourself daydreaming about that first step on the tarmac. Will you bend down and kiss the ground? It could feel like a triumph, you imagine. But shake off these delusions. You didn't leave the heat and the salt-laced coastal air to come across oceans and continents to daydream about going back. The river that never remains the same is changed. You are changed. The land, you think, never changes, but it does too. No man ever steps on the same land twice, for it's not the same land and he's not the same person.

I. George Gary Gregory Jaffar

[Trials end. Faces disappear. What George Gary Gregory Jaffar was, he no longer is. Whatever was less than perfect in him is melted away during the process of his ascension. He finds himself embodied again, but not in his old shape. He is now a being of light, resplendent, facing a closed gate also made of light. One more step up, one more step forward, and he will be inside Heaven. But the gate is not open; not yet. The Angel of Admittance has accompanied the spirit of George Gary Gregory Jaffar on his ascension from The Belly. No longer a white dot, the Angel has flown upwards in full glory: five hundred massive wings flapping in the vacuum between realms. Multitudinous splendour in the colours and patterns of each of the Angel's wings has kept George Gary Gregory Jaffar spellbound, but he has also been able to shift his gaze and look around at the vast tracts of universe that exist far beyond what was known to humans during his lifetime; falling stars have shot past them as they have raced light itself; whole galaxies have turned on their axes; empty space itself has resonated with the sound of hordes of choral angels. Now, the two of them are at the gate.]

ANGEL OF ADMITTANCE: This is where I leave you, George. I am not allowed to pass through the gates just yet.

GGGJ: You have been kind to me, Angel. Thank you.

ANGEL: Remember me when you see the Divine One. Mention me to Him.

GGGJ: I will.

ANGEL: And pray for people you knew back on earth. Pray for everyone. Even those who have hurt you.

GGGJ: I understand. Even for my murderer.

ANGEL: He is the reason you're going to enter Heaven; it is only a step away.

GGGJ: Just as I thought. That's when I knew I was ready – when I knew I couldn't hate him for being my reason for earning Heaven. This would not have been possible without him. But tell me, Angel, will there be others in Heaven – his victims?

ANGEL: Yes. Everyone has victims. Even you. But if they reach this door, they've been purified of any grudges, just like you.

GGGJ: Oh. I see. So, this is it, between me and you…? Or will we meet again?

ANGEL: At the end of time, we'll have the best of all possible meetings next time, when the Divine One will be watching us looking at His Face.

GGGJ: In that case, I hope the apocalypse comes as soon as possible.

ANGEL: I've been praying for Judgement Day to arrive since the first moment I knew about it. I can wait for all of eternity if needed. The face of God is worth all of it. Farewell, George Gary Gregory Jaffar. Here, let me...

[The Angel of Admittance pulls open the gate of Heaven and a beam shines on George Gary Gregory Jaffar, light meeting light. Angel and human look at each other, and then at the light's source. Both are struck with near-infinite wonder at the beauty of what they see. George Gary Gregory Jaffar walks one step forward and is embraced in God's clasp. The Angel of Admittance closes the gate slowly, taking one lasting look at that for which he must wait. Having been here countless times, having admitted soul after soul, he has retreated to his domain, looking longingly at the light that shines from inside the gate. Time passes differently for angels, and he knows that it will not take eons for Judgement Day to arrive; for the angels, all time is simultaneous. But what must happen after the end of time is something outside of time. So, he must return to The Belly and continue to admit to the final rewarding place more and more humans – until the final human bound for Heaven has been sent there and, at last, the Angel's job is done. He flaps his five hundred wings and descends through myriad realms to the transparent emptiness of The Belly, where there is waiting for him the next spirit, ready to be processed.

Meanwhile, George Gary Gregory Jaffar sits on a plush seat inside Heaven, watching God and being watched by Him. George Gary Gregory Jaffar trembles with the pleasure of being with his Creator. His soul is purified from other thoughts than those of his desire to be with God for all eternity. This is what he feels: absolute love and awe.]

ANGEL OF ADMITTANCE: Your Will is done. All praise is due to God.

II. Altamaash

This is it. The climax of homecoming. Fifteen more minutes and I'll be on the tarmac in Karachi. Our jet swerves through and around air currents to position itself to meet the runway. Six people on board. Two pilots, two stewardesses – neither one my type – a bodybuilding bodyguard and freshly diplomatically passported Al. What a wonderful thing, to be *wanted*. Even better to be wanted as a ruler of a country than by its police as a person of interest. God bless Pakistan and the winds of change.

One moment, I was persona non grata, living in enforced refuge. The next instance (more than twenty years later, that is) limousined to the airport, taxied to a private jet, cradled in a luxury seat, and flying high, spewing exhaust fumes at the place of exile, which will undergo its own existential crisis.

That's what it's come to. Wherever I flee from, that place begins to die. In the past eight hours of the flight, I've only been able to sleep intermittently. Before departing, there were phone calls from the General and his underlings. Arrangements have been made for a motorcade in Karachi. But my thoughts have lingered mostly on the home away from home.

That call as I was being limousined to Heathrow, the one from the *Guardian* news desk editor. When I thought they'd come arrest me at the airport for Guardian Gary's murder. In my mind's eye, the investigation had yielded swifter justice than possible with the bureaucratic copping I'd assumed would bungle the suicide-murder into a hodge-podge – somehow they'd caught me. Looked at the CCTV footage from street cameras and found my bulky self in the footage. The breathlessness I felt as the editor flipped pages on the other end of the line. And then the pressure valve being released once he said he was calling about Guardian Greg's article – whether he should go ahead and publish it without my reading the draft. He was asking because it was a 'pretty damning piece'. The taste of those words I said, it lingers on my lips: 'Feel free to publish it. And you might require a follow-up. The story isn't quite done yet.'

On the news, I've heard that the investigation into the murder-suicide in Ladbroke Grove has yielded little in terms of evidence. None of the CCTV cameras were working along the routes I took to and from Ned's hovel. They did catch a glimpse of GGJ's face from a camera underground, on the Tube. He's grinning in the image. Scotland Yard is thinking about turning the whole thing into a murder investigation, but they have no suspects just yet. What a farce England's empire is. What a failing illusion of pomp. They can't even create an effective big brotherhood.

This is the reason London's going to collapse without even any of its bridges falling. It's already set in motion. Europe no longer wants to be ruled by British imperialism. What the imperialists wrecked in the world is uncountable; all the wealth trickled over to England and Wales. In its wake, it left postcolonial chaos and garbage across the globe. Now the wake is following the wealth. Europe and its Atlantic cousin, the United States – they will decline.

Colonialism, imperialism, proxy wars, drone bombings, terror attacks, displacement – all those will combine into one mega-shitstorm and come home to roost. It's in the laws of physics, as discovered by inventors across the world, and branded under Newton's name.

All empires turn to dust. I've thought this through, morbidly accepting my role in the passage of power from one generation to the next. It's made me admit that Fatima, Pinky – my daughter

– she will never rule. I will not let her suffer the consequences of generational transference of expectations. She will be a Euro-Pakistani. A resident of Asia's ascent … or … will the whole world collapse once the businessmen politicians take over governments? Fat bastards, all of them. All of *us*.

I'll make it work. Pakistan will resurge. I'll wipe out all zealots except the fanatic supporters of progress.

There it is, under us: Karachi, rolled out like a carpet. The grids of it; roads and buildings choking each other. The slow traffic of human commerce. Blah, blah, blah. Dead and brown, this city. The place I love for some reason.

No matter who gets left behind, this country must progress and catch up to the twenty-first-century world. A culling of its old guard that keeps it stagnant is in order. I can taste it already. The first woman sacrificed will be my own wife. A bullet's already been used up for that, while I've been flying. Poor Mrs Al. A solace though - at least this time I'll be there, on the ground, to make the most of it. I couldn't be there when my father passed away. Poor father.

There's something else to be gained from Mrs Al's passing. A bullet-riding freedom. I – Al – am once more an eligible bachelor. Gives one such a soaring feeling, to be brideless again, does it not?

Progress. Hard work. Nonsense like this. Ghosts of ideas live inside my head, making me want *so* much better for my people – and yet, other ideologies make me want to rip the people apart.

Touch and go. In God's name, we reach the paved runway. Touch and go. I never unfastened my seatbelt even once in the eight hours of the flight. Never looked away from the window, did imperial Al.

The plane whines and decelerates, and my heartbeat speeds up. Home. Sweet blessed homeland. *I'm with you now, Pakistan. You don't need to worry any more.* All the dust in the air. I can actually see the thickness of it; nothing like London's clean and crisp – but never mind.

Home is home. Home away from home away from home. And yet, London is also home. Jordan is still there, living in the annex, guarding a house that will never see my permanent return.

A rush of jet wind is flapping at the air traffic controller's clothes. Mirages simmer on the road. The Karachi heat – am I ready for it?

Phil passes by my seat in the aisle, nodding at the stewardesses. He stands next to the exit door as the plane rolls into its designated spot and rests. Whines of the engine wind down. The stewardesses are professional, courteous. They step aside when Phil asks them to. He opens the door to the exit like he's well-travelled on private jets.

I should get a couple of these. Phils and jets. Of course, the country's airlines and armed forces are all mine now. So why bother? But still... It's good to have a few extra things.

Unbuckled, I stand and stretch. Once the stairs are folded out, Phil leads the way bulkily down, and we all descend after him like mortals after Apollo. Surely he'll catch any sniper bullets just by the sheer size of him. He blocks any wind that may be blowing. Bah! It's wretchedly hot. Sweat instantly pools inside my shirt. Same old sticky Karachi.

But anything else would have been unfamiliar. This is as things should be.

A dark black Mercedes with tinted black windows rolls up, followed by a line of three police cars, a few police motorcycles, and two open-backed army jeeps with two men each in the back; in either of those vehicles, one of the soldiers holds a largish machine gun ready to be triggered into streams of *rat-a-tat*, and the other brandishes on his shoulder what looks like a rocket launcher. Nice! This will most certainly do.

Another Mercedes, one with an army flag, wheels over with its own automobile entourage of five vehicles. I wait up on the steps behind Phil, my shirt getting stickier by the second.

A man exits from one of the black, regal vehicles. It's the General. No red carpets yet – that can wait. But here's the man himself. He walks half the way over. The other half I must cover myself. Phil and I go down the stairs.

'Hello, General,' I say.

'Altamaash,' the General says, nodding, but not saluting. That can wait until more official settings, I guess. He comes closer and shakes my hand. Then he leans further in. An uncomfortable hug ensues. The sweat in the fabric of my clothes and his wet uniform presses into the sponges of our bodies. But it's not exactly a hug he's forcing between us. No. He leans further in, his lips at my ears.

'She was so young,' he says. 'I didn't think you would—' He chokes up and leans back.

So, it's done. I've avoided thinking about this too long. Poor motherless Pinky.

'Yes,' I say, as he leans away. 'She was just young enough.' Not a virgin, was Mrs Al, but her youth should count for something. It should rally the fools of this country behind the one who has lost the love of his life.

The General's looking deep into my eyes, concern in his eyes and a grimace on his lips. Making sure I'm all right to continue – or maybe to convey that he needs encouragement to go on with the developments in the plan. Then he almost, *almost*, does it. I have the pleasure of knowing that he almost salutes me as we part – him to his black Mercedes, me to mine.

The armoured car's chauffeur, who's been standing at attention, bends stiffly and opens the back door for me. He seems familiar. Someone from the party, perhaps.

Phil steps to the other side of the car. He'll ride in the front passenger seat.

I walk with a mourner's dignity to the door held open for me by the driver. As I get closer, he leans forward and says, 'Altamaash Bhai—'

'Call me Al,' I tell him. It's a new world. A post-Mrs-Al-world.

'Al Bhai…' he begins again. Okay. I can work with that.

'Yes?' I ask.

'Al Bhai,' he says. 'There was an accident, and we didn't want to cause any more damage—'

Fine, fine. I wave him off. The General's already told me.

But I know. I put one hand on the roof of the car and the other on the top of the door, and I bend down to take a look inside. Did I always know?

In the cavernous back seat are lodged my mother and my wife. There is no Pinky. I knew. Did I *always* know? That's what will trouble me later.

The market. My wife never listened to a word my people said. Never one to follow any instructions, she had to have it her way.

Took Pinky – Fatima – with her.

Ammi, from inside the car, looks at me like I look at cockroaches. Mrs Al doesn't look at me at all.

I nearly close the door and walk back to the airplane and order it be filled up with enough fuel to fly back to London so I can live out the rest of my wretched life gorging down stale pizza and other poisons that will burn me as much as I'm scalding already, but something stops me.

I look up hoping to see some shade of pink in the celestial canopy, some sign of her; but it's a deep blue sky and I wish myself dead. I close my eyes and feel the wind in my hair and know that I still live. It will pass, this revulsion I feel. This too shall pass.

Instead of kneeling down to kiss the soil of my motherland, as I always thought I would at this point, I turn my head to one side, gather a frothing gob of phlegm in my throat, and spit it out. It slaps the ground and sizzles.

I get in the car without looking at the women again. Their faces are turned away as well. Here it is, the day of my return, triumphant through and through. Except these two women, the whole country will love me like it's never loved anyone before.

It's windy outside, and some of the spit I shot out may have got into my eyes. My lids are closing around liquid that doesn't belong in them. It feels like I'm still descending on that plane, that I haven't touched tarmac at all. Maybe this descent will never end.

III. Edwin 'Ned' Steinberg

[Edwin 'Ned' Steinberg's third eye begins to disintegrate.]

Al lives inside the gates of Heaven.
Al thrives in the deepest pit of Hell.

[There is nothing of Edwin 'Ned' Steinberg remaining. It's as though he never existed.]

ANGEL OF TURNING AWAY: Your Will is done. All praise is due to God.

[Of all the places in all the realms He has created, in a dust-filled country where it would be least expected, a new kind of music begins to play. In its early chords, still, there is no way to tell if it will be a symphony or a cacophony. Or both.]

Acknowledgements

I owe immense gratitude to the ones who enabled my adventures in exile, including my parents, siblings, and Amma and Baba, but especially Guggal Bhai and the Raazis of Saskatoon, under whose roof Al came to life.

Thank you also to my teachers, starting with Saeed Zameer, Amir Hussain and Naila Burney at Aitchison; James Hoch and Patricia O'Hara at F&M; Valerie Sayers and Steve Tomasula at Notre Dame; Ann Martin, Lindsey Banco and others at the University of Saskatchewan; and others who have taught me by example or caution.

I try to follow the footsteps of great artists who create narratives that enflame a desire to devote life to literature; writers who blaze new trails and envision better ways of living in the world. For enabling this journey, I wish to thank all first readers, who help co-create stories out of fleeting forms, as my wife Sheema did. This work and I owe as much to her as we do to my force-of-nature agent, Kanishka Gupta, and my editor, the inimitably thorough Rinita Banerjee. Kudos to her and the team at HarperCollins India that transformed my manuscript into this novel.

I am thankful for the existence of those among us who do enlivening work in countries and homes lost to wars and politics; the ones who rebuild out of ashes, debris, and broken plastic what was once organic but taken for granted; the ones who lead a brigade of dreaming, struggling, creators of 'the good' out of the muck; the teachers and entrepreneurs who are battling primarily by spirit and principles, despite the world telling them to abandon all long-term hope; who strive heroically, and resist, with all their might, the dark forces that threaten to take over our world. Their work mirrors Divine light, and I find constant guidance from it.

About the Author

Sheheryar B. Sheikh has an MFA from the University of Notre Dame, where he won Steve Tomasula's La Vie de Bohème Award and a Nicholas Sparks Scholarship. His first novel, *The Still Point of the Turning World* (HarperCollins India, 2017), was nominated for the all-Pakistan Getz Pharma Prize. He lives with his wife and son in Saskatoon, Canada, where he researches classical and contemporary apocalyptic narratives for his PhD.